WITH THESE FOUR RINGS: WEDDING BONUS

BILLIONAIRE BRIDES OF GRANITE FALLS

ANA E ROSS

CEDAR TREES PUBLISHERS

WITH THESE FOUR RINGS: WEDDING BONUS

Copyright © 2015 by Ana E Ross
ISBN: 9780986339905
Cedar Trees Publishers

Edited by Crazy Diamond Editing
Cover Design by Najla Qamber Designs

paperback ISBN: 9780986339905
ebook ISBN: 9780988367999

ALSO BY ANA E ROSS

Billionaire Brides of Granite Falls Series

The Doctor's Secret Bride

The Mogul's Reluctant Bride

The Playboy's Fugitive Bride

The Tycoon's Temporary Bride

With These Four Rings: Wedding Bonus

Beyond Granite Falls Series

Loving Yasmine

Desire's Chase

Pleasing Mindy

Billionaire Island Brides Series

Seduced by Passion (2022)

To the members of the Ana E Ross Fan Club, and to Mary Pettis, one of my very first, and loyal fans, who nicknamed the billionaires "The Fabulous Four".

CHAPTER ONE

Ristorante Andreas. July – Monday...

"So we've decided on the orchids, right?" Kaya asked, as the four brides-to-be sat around a table at a private dining room at Ristorante Andreas.

"Just because your husband has an orchid delivered to you every single morning, it doesn't mean they should be the dominant flower in our wedding." Michelle took a bite of her broiled eggplant package—a flavorful bundle of plum tomatoes, mozzarella cheese and fresh basil wrapped in thin slices of eggplant.

"You seem to forget that I donate those orchids to your Children of the Future Foundation, so perhaps I'm due a favor," Kaya stated smugly, as she cut a portion from her medium rare Kobe steak.

"And I appreciate your generosity, Kaya, along with the sick, and the shut-in, and the destitute whose lives your orchids brighten on a daily basis, but it has nothing to do with our wedding. I vote for lilies."

"No." Shaina took a sip of ice tea and shook her head emphatically. "Tulips. Red, pink, and purple. Definitely." Purple tulips were her mother's favorite flowers, and every Sunday morning on their way from church, her father used to stop at a roadside vendor. Shaina remembered the smile on her mother's face each time her father presented her with a bouquet of purple tulips. It was always as if she was receiving one for the first time. After her mother died, her father couldn't bear to look at tulips, but with that sentimental flower as decoration, Shaina could imagine her parents watching her walk down the aisle.

"My husband cuts me fresh peonies from his garden. They were my mother's favorite, so I think it should be peonies." Tashi, the newest and youngest member of the Granite Falls Billionaire Brides Club, added her two cents as she dipped a chunk of *ciabatta* into a bowl of *fontina* cheese dip.

"Mine delivers babies, so maybe we should have little baby booties and crib mobiles lining the aisle of the church, and oh wait, a giant stethoscope suspended from the ceiling."

"Well then," Shaina chimed in, "since we're ditching flowers, my man loves pussycats—leopards to be exact. We can sit Jabari and some of his friends next to each pew. Anybody they don't like gets gobbled up. No questions asked." She dusted off her hands.

The women roared as Shaina put the absurdity of their bickering to rest with sudden good humor.

"How is Jabari?" Tashi asked.

"He's much better than when we got there, and he seems to be growing stronger every day, but he's an old cat, you know."

"Has Mass thought about putting him down?" Michelle probed her.

"No way." Shaina quivered at the question. "He couldn't. He'd still be in Kenya if Aria hadn't come down with that virus. He had to choose between his cat and his daughter."

"I can identify." Kaya patted Shaina's hand. "When Webster developed chronic renal failure last year, Bryce spent tens of thousands of dollars on a kidney transplant. Webster was part of his and Pilar's family. He's like the unborn child that died with Pilar, the child they never got to raise together. Okay," she added, when the room grew deathly silent. "We're supposed to be planning a wedding, not a funeral, so let's get back to the flowers and try to make a decision before Fae gets here. We have a little over three weeks before this wedding happens, and we're all leaving on our individual family vacations next week."

Michelle cleared her throat. "Yeah, about Fae. There's a slight change in wedding planners. We had to hire Desire."

Kaya's back went ramrod straight. "You can't mean Desire Summers of Weddings by Desire?" She looked anxiously from one woman to the next.

"Yes, that Desire." Tashi reached across the table and rested her hand on Kaya's. She understood Kaya's reaction to the news that Desire Summers would be planning her wedding—their wedding. The Summerses and the Fontaines had some bad blood between them.

"Bryce will not go for this. You guys know that, right?" Kaya was a bit disappointed that her friends would even consider the option, much less decide on it behind her back.

"I imagine he'll have objections, but like you mentioned earlier, we don't have the time to look around," Shaina replied in a soothing voice. "It's not like we have a long list of planners to choose from. Fae and Desire are the only two in Granite Falls, and Fae has already turned over our account to Desire. She's all caught up and ready to move forward with our plans—Desire style."

"We agreed to hire a local planner for this wedding and we chose Elegant Brides together. Nobody consulted me about this change." Kaya made no attempt to disguise her disapproval.

"In all fairness, you weren't here when we had to make the decision," Michelle said. "You and Bryce were off on your private island in the South Pacific."

"And Mass and Shaina were visiting Jabari in Kenya," Tashi added. "So Michelle and I had to make the decision." Tashi knew that even though she was the newest member of the Billionaire Brides Club—now the Billionaire Wives Club —her opinions and suggestions carried just as much weight as everyone else's.

Shaina swallowed a mouthful of bruschetta topped with tomatoes, then glanced briefly at Michelle and Tashi before catching and holding Kaya's gaze. "To be honest, we initially wanted to hire Desire, simply because she *is* better than Fae. But out of sensitivity for you and Bryce, we opted not to. We have no choice, now. Maybe the cosmos is trying to tell us something."

"Like maybe it's time to forgive and move on," Michelle said, gently.

Kaya crossed her arms and shifted uneasily in her chair. "That is strictly up to Bryce. He has as much say in this as any of us."

"Well, not technically. It was agreed that we, the wives,

would take care of the wedding and our husbands would take care of the honeymoon."

"It's not that simple anymore, Tashi. Bryce needs to approve, and if he doesn't we'll just have to go fishing again." Kaya frowned at her friends. "Have you told your husbands about the change? How do they feel about it?"

Michelle spoke up. "Mass and Shaina returned from Kenya only three days ago, and Erik is still in South America on a humanitarian mission, so, *no*. We wanted to wait to tell you first. And," she added, glancing at Kaya through lowered lashes, "we were hoping you'd be the one to break it to Bryce."

Kaya threw her hands in the air. "Oh sure, take me deep into the thick dark forest and leave me alone with the giant grumpy bear."

"Well, he's kinda big and intimidating. And since he's *your* bear, we figured he wouldn't hurt you." Shaina gave Kaya a hopeful smile.

Kaya glanced out the window at the blue waters of Crystal Lake as she thought of the weeklong break from which she and Bryce had recently returned. It was more of a break for Bryce since he and Massimo had been working double time running Fontaine Enterprises and Andretti Industries, respectively, and also Fonandt Energy—the wind energy company they'd founded together a few years ago.

Kaya's ire dissipated, and a smile played at the corners of her mouth as she remembered the intimate, bonding moments she and Bryce had spent walking and playing naked along the sandy white shores of *Kaya*, and the countless hours of passionate lovemaking every single day and night. Oh, yes, he'd bought her an island in the South Pacific as a first wedding anniversary present, and named it *Kaya*—to make up for the unceremonious way they'd gotten married, he'd told her.

He'd learned well from Erik, who'd bought Michelle her own private island—*Michelle*—in the Seychelles as an apology for hurting her during the months they'd spent apart when she was pregnant with Little Erik. To avoid jealousy and harassment, Mass had followed suit with *Shaina* in the Mediterranean. And for Christmas last year, Adam had purchased *Tashi* off the Amalfi Coast of Italy, where all four couples had celebrated last New Year's Eve.

"So can we count on you to tell Bryce about Desire?"

Kaya started as Tashi's questions cut into her reveries. "Sure," she said, bringing her attention back to her friends. She took a sip of her Bloody Mary. "I'll try to break it to him gently." She would just have to remind Bryce that there were many more passionate moments to come once they left on their honeymoon, the location of which was still a secret to her, as it was for the other women. They knew their husbands were planning something big, but none of them had been able to squeeze any information out of any of them. "What happened to Fae? Why can't she finish the wedding?" she asked grasping at straws.

"She slipped on a blanket one of her kids left at the top of the stairs, and went flying down them. She suffered a concussion, broke both arms, and twisted an ankle." Michelle said.

"Oh my God, that's awful. I hope she'll be okay."

"As long as she follows her doctor's orders and stays off her feet," Shaina said. "So how do you feel about Desire?" she added. "You think you can work with her?"

"It's not like I have a choice at this late hour. Bryce will just have to deal with it."

"I'm sure you know how to help him deal with it," Tashi said with a grin.

"Well, listen to Miss Cloistered and Innocent," Michelle murmured over the rim of her lemonade glass.

Kaya stared Tashi full in the eyes. "This chick may have been cloistered, but she hasn't been innocent since the day she walked up on Adam naked in his garden. Played any games lately, Tashi?"

"Lost any panties lately, Kaya?" Tashi threw a piece of focaccia at her and squealed when Kaya caught it and popped it into her mouth with aplomb.

"Go, Tashi. You're learning the art of backlash, girl." Shaina high-fived her.

"Actually, I seldom wear panties anymore since Bryce is always taking them off and never giving them back," Kaya said with a dreamy look in her eyes. "It just makes more sense to go commando. Easy access, entrance, and withdrawal, especially when he corners me at odd places in the house for a hot and raunchy quickie, if you know what I mean."

"Oh, we know." The women's undiluted amusement echoed throughout the room.

"Well, I'm glad to find you all in good spirits."

"Desire's here," Tashi whispered.

The ladies turned their heads toward the door and, immediately—as if on cue—they sobered up as a young woman with long black hair walked in.

"Please, don't stop on my account." Desire advanced farther into the room. "What's so amusing?" she asked, setting an oversized tote on the floor.

"We're just messing around." Michelle tossed clandestine smiles at her soul sisters. It was one thing to share their secrets with each other, but nobody from outside their circle had knowledge of their relations and daily interactions with their husbands, especially not about their bedroom activities.

She knew it was the same for the men. She and her friends were always wondering how much their husbands shared with each other. There were tacit codes of ethics and protocol within and among the male and female clubs. One thing the women were certain of was that their husbands were always extremely amorous after spending time with each other— which indicated that they shared intimate marriage details. Not that the ladies were objecting. This was *Sex and the Country*, the rustic equivalent to New York's *Sex and the City*.

"Yeah, just inside jokes. You wouldn't get it." Shaina smiled up at Desire. "Welcome aboard," she added, to move the conversation away from their personal lives and on to the business they'd gathered for.

"Thanks. It's really an honor to be working with you ladies. Planning the wedding of four of the most powerful couples in the country will definitely look good on my resume." She gave Kaya a fleeting glance before peering out the window, clearly to avoid her gaze.

Deciding to confront the elephant that had appeared in the room, Kaya turned to Desire. "I'm fine with you taking over for Fae, Desire, and I—" She paused and made an all-inclusive motion with her hands. "*We* appreciate you taking us on at such short notice. We know you're the best, and for obvious reasons we didn't hire you initially, but now that we have, I'm sure you're aware that it will probably cause some tension where my husband is concerned."

"*Probably*? You haven't told him yet?" Desire asked, a disparaging tilt to her voice.

"I was just told about this a few minutes ago. And once we're done here, I will head over to Fontaine Enterprises to speak with Bryce."

"My decision to take over from Fae was contingent upon you informing Mr. Fontaine, immediately. What if he says no? I don't want to waste any more time on a project that I might not be able to follow through to the end. I have two more weddings I'm working on, and—"

"We understand," Shaina assured her. "And we promise that you'll have an answer by the end of the day." She caught Kaya's gaze, silently pleading with her to convince her husband to make it a positive one.

"I'll call you after I talk with him," Kaya promised Desire.

"Perfect." Michelle indicated the vacant chair at the round table. "Should we get down to business?"

Desire's face broke out into a grin as she scooted into the chair between Kaya and Tashi. "Fae told me you're taking pole dancing lessons. Is that for your individual honeymoons?"

"Actually, we're planning to crash our husbands' bachelor party on Saturday." Tashi's eyes lit up with excitement.

"That should get a big rise out of them," Desire said.

"Massive rises that we'll all be eager to relieve."

"No wonder you're always pregnant," Shaina said, eyeballing Michelle.

"Right. Like you and Mass don't get your groove on every chance you get. All you all. I know all your dirty little secrets. So don't you sit there acting all prim and proper, chastising me, just because I once lived on the wrong side of the tracks."

Michelle's fitting retort made everyone laugh, even Desire.

"I wish I had a circle of friends like you," Desire said of their innocuous sparring. "But it's hard to make friends in a town when your family's name has been tainted."

The wives looked at each other, having no idea how to respond.

"At least I have my cousin, Lisa. We're as tight as sisters," Desire added with a faint smile.

"Well, blood is thicker than water." Kaya immediately gave herself a mental kick in the behind. *Oh, this was going to be difficult,* she thought, as she watched Desire pull her laptop, two white binders, and an assortment of fabrics from her tote and place them on the table. "Would you like something to eat, Desire?" she asked to redeem herself. "We still have a ton of food—some we haven't even touched yet," she said pointing at a side table laden with appetizers, lunch dishes, pitchers of ice tea and lemonade, and virgin specialties from the bar. "The Kobe fillet is to die for."

"And so is the Wagyu rib eye," Shaina added. "It was imported from Tokyo."

Michelle snickered. "Not everyone is into the kind of steak rich people eat to remind themselves of their wealth and elevated social status." Ignoring the gasps from her friends, she continued, "From someone who doesn't eat beef, I vouch for the broiled eggplant and the stuffed red peppers."

Desire gave the buffet table a fleeting glance. "It smells and looks delicious, and I'm tempted, but I'm meeting Chad for lunch when I'm done here. It would be rude if I arrived with a full stomach. I hope you understand."

"No problem. Maybe next time." Tashi gave Desire a tight smile. She was the first person Tashi had ever known to pass up the chance to eat at Ristorante Andreas. It was hard not to take it personally, seeing that her husband owned the restaurant.

"You're meeting Chad Hunter?" Kaya asked. He was the only Chad she knew.

Desire's eyes narrowed. "You know him?"

"I've never met him, but I know he's an attorney. Steven Lynd, Bryce's friend, has mentioned him in conversation. They've butted heads a few times in court."

"I know his mom," Michelle added. "She works at Granite Falls General. She's one of the best nurses there. Are you and Chad dating?"

"No. We grew up next door to each other, so we touch base once in a while."

"Doesn't he have an older brother?" Michelle snapped her fingers. "Chase! I've heard his mother talk about him. He left town some years ago and never came back. Where is he?"

Desire's mouth pulled into a tight line and she trembled slightly. "I have no idea. I'll take a glass of water in lieu of the food." She opened her laptop, indicating to the women that her personal life, like theirs, was not open to discussion.

Touché. Kaya grabbed a clean glass from a mobile cart behind her and filled it with water from a crystal pitcher while her friends scrambled to clear the table, taking the half-eaten plates of food over to one end of the buffet table. She refilled everyone's water glasses, and soon they all settled down in their seats again.

Desire pushed the binders toward the middle of the table, and motioned for them to lean in. For the next couple of hours, they discussed the checklist, eliminating, modifying, and adding to their choices of the menu, napkins, seating, cake— flavor and decoration— photographers and videographers, the orchestra and music selections, transportation and reservations at Hotel Andreas for out-of-town guests, and a host of other wedding preparations that none of the brides had foreseen.

Desire finally closed her binders, returned them to her tote, and leaned back into the cushioned chair. "Fae told me you've been having trouble deciding on the flowers for the church," she said. "Have you been able to resolve it?"

"Not yet," Michelle stretched out her legs under the table. "As close as we are, we have different tastes and preferences, and we do want some things to be unique."

"Like your dresses, bouquets, and the four cakes. But your rings are all the same," Desire pointed out. "Designing one set of rings for four couples is a unique idea, unheard of, really. Can I ask why you decided to do it?"

The women smiled and automatically joined hands. "We love each other like sisters," Michelle spoke for all. "The one set of rings is a way of sealing our friendship, just like our husbands sealed theirs in high school in a blood oath. Our rings symbolize our commitment and promise to always be there for each other."

"Not just for each other." Shaina squeezed the hands in hers. "If anything happens to me, I know all these ladies will be there for my kid, or kids if I have more."

"And our husbands, too," both Kaya and Tashi said simultaneously, and then gave each other bizarre stares.

"You even have the same thoughts," Desire said. "Your devotion to each other is positively exemplary. Every couple should have friends like you." She smiled in obvious admiration as the women untangled their hands and sat back in their chairs.

"Friendship aside," Michelle said, "every bride wants the church aisle to be lined with the flowers of her choice—flowers that have a significant meaning to her."

"What do you each want?" Desire opened up an app on her laptop and began typing.

"I want red and white peonies," Tashi provided. "Shaina wants purple, red and pink tulips. Kaya insists on pink, white, and yellow orchids, and Michelle—"

"I want lilies—Peruvian, calla, and those of the valley."

"We thought of using a little of each since the purpose of this group wedding is to symbolize the bond of friendship and sisterhood we've created over the years, but it seems too crazy, like overkill, to have so many varieties of flowers in one place," Kaya stated.

"Then why not have four aisles?" Desire opened another app, and began sketching away rapidly.

"Four aisles?" Shaina strained her neck to peek at Desire's sketches.

"Why not? The church is big enough." Desire motioned them close again. "Instead of walking down one aisle in single file as you'd previously planned," she began, pointing to a rough blueprint of the church divided into eight seating sections and four aisles, "you'll each simultaneously walk down your own aisle lined with your favorite flower. You'll have your own spotlight, and your individual husbands—standing at the head of each aisle under an arched trellis fashioned from the flower of your choice—can focus on you, and you alone, while you walk toward him."

Michelle took a closer look at the drawing. "I like that."

"The great thing about the trellises," Desire continued, "is that they can be remotely controlled, so that once the person who gives you away delivers you—"

Shaina cleared her throat. "We're delivering ourselves. We're giving ourselves to them."

Tashi raised her hand. "About that, my dad insists on walking me down the aisle. Sorry, guys, but he's missed so much of my life, he doesn't want to pass up on this sacred opportunity. You don't have to follow suit, but—"

"Yes, we do," Shaina interjected. "I can have Cameron walk me. He'd love that."

"Robert gave me away once. He'd be delighted to do it again," Michelle said.

Kaya smiled. "Jason wasn't too thrilled about being an usher. He thought it would be cool to walk me down the aisle. It'll make his day when I tell him he can have his wish."

"Wonderful," Desire declared, enthusiastically. "Once you're given away, your husbands will escort you—under your individual trellis—to the center of the church where Pastor Kelly will be waiting to officiate. I've never done anything like this before," she cautioned, "but I'm sure with some adept maneuvering and lots of practice, we can pull it off without a hitch."

"Oh my gosh! Wow! This is awesome! Brilliant!" the women exclaimed in turn as they grinned at each other.

"I like that we each get our individual bride and groom section," Michelle said.

"Exactly," Desire responded. "That way, there's no bickering over which family members get to sit in the front row."

Shaina laughed. "Yeah, we were actually going to toss coins."

"Now you don't have to." Desire closed her laptop and placed it in her tote.

Tashi shrugged. "Didn't make any difference to me since the only family I have is my father, and besides you guys, Mindy is my closest friend. My bride section is gonna be practically empty."

"That's true for all of us," Shaina remarked.

"If there's one thing I've learned in this line of work," Desire offered, "it's that quality is more important than quantity. I know of many brides who've regretted inviting people they hardly know to their weddings, just because they didn't want to offend them. In the end, your wedding day is all about you, and nobody else. Since none of you have much family and since you're all already married, my suggestion is that you don't divide the bride and groom sections. Just quarter off a few rows in the front for your family, closest friends, and VIPs, and have the ushers seat the other guests from front to back. The early guests get the better seats."

"See, this is why we wanted you in the first place." Shaina gave Desire an animated smile. "You have vision."

"You're really giving us the wedding of our desire, Desire." Michelle turned to Kaya. "You have to convince Bryce to let her do our wedding."

"I know. I will." She'd just have to take off her panties before she arrived at his office, Kaya thought, or maybe she'd keep them on and leave them as a scented gift, a reminder of how obliging she could be when he saw things her way.

Desire stood up, picked up her tote, and swung it over her shoulder. "Well, ladies, it will be exciting putting the finishing touches on the planning of your unprecedented wedding." She shook each of their hands. "I'll start my team working on these changes when I get the confirmation call later today." She spoke to everyone, but kept her eyes on Kaya. "If it's positive, we'll set up another meeting for later this week. See you around."

"Anyone for dessert?" Michelle asked, after Desire left. She eyed a piece of German chocolate cake with walnuts nestling in the frosting.

"I have to go home and feed my baby. These things are bursting." Tashi pressed her arms into the sides of her swollen breasts.

Shaina gave Tashi a slanted look. "And by 'baby', are we talking Adam or Alex?"

"Both. Adam is working from home today." She pushed back her chair.

"Didn't I give you a LaCrosse pump at your baby shower?" Michelle watched Tashi walk over to a sofa and retrieve the designer purses they'd all tossed there earlier. "Have you ever even used it?" she asked as Tashi returned and handed the purses to their owners.

Tashi stood behind Michelle's chair and placed her hands on her shoulders. "Adam tossed it. Said he and Alex are the only pumps I need, and there was no way in hell a LaCrosse was pumping his wife's breasts."

The room lit up with laughter.

"Those were Massimo's sentiments. Verbatim. The cousins must have had a discussion about it."

"Anyway, after trying several others and realizing that it really is the best on the market, I had to buy another LaCrosse pump to use during the trial."

"Word," Michelle pinned Tashi with an *I told you so* stare.

"What about you?" Tashi asked Kaya. "Did you ever use the one she gave you?"

"No way. With two babies and a husband fighting for nursing sessions, there was no need." Kaya looked at Michelle. "I think you're the only one of us who uses the LaCrosse pump."

Michelle twisted her lips sheepishly. "Since we're being honest, I do have to get home to nurse Fiona."

Shaina tossed her an evil look. "So you don't use your own pump, hypocrite?"

Michelle grimaced. "Just once. Last New Year's Eve when I had to leave Fiona for a day. Don't need a LaCrosse pump when I have the real LaCrosse's tender lips, do I?"

"Case in point." Shaina vacated her chair and tucked her Zagliani clutch under her arm. "We all have babies at home, waiting to be fed. No, no, no," she added when her friends stared at her with questioning eyes. "I don't still nurse Aria. I just like to have her meals with her."

They let out their breaths, then Kaya said, "I have a husband to seduce, so—"

"Wait." Michelle held Kaya's wrist as she attempted to get up from the table. "Before you go, can we chat a little?" She turned to Tashi and Shaina who were sporting curious stares at her. "You two go ahead. We'll catch up later."

"Sure, Mama. Come on nosy." Tashi tugged a reluctant Shaina toward the door.

CHAPTER TWO

Fontaine Enterprises – Same day…

K aya's heart was beating two miles a second as she rode the up elevator at Fontaine Enterprises. It wasn't the exciting kind of acceleration she'd come to enjoy at the anticipation of seeing her husband. Even after three years of marriage, he still took her breath away when he walked into a room, just as he'd done the very first time she'd laid eyes on him.

No, this quickening of her breath was caused by dread— not necessarily about Bryce's reaction to the news she was about to give him, but about what revisiting the most painful period of his life would do to him—to them as a family.

As far as she knew, Bryce's nightmares had ceased altogether, and he had tucked Pilar to the back of his mind. That's where Kaya wanted her to remain. Interacting with any member of the Summers family would only trigger Bryce's feelings of anger and regret and send him back into the dark pit she'd dug him out of three years ago.

Kaya didn't know if she had the strength and will to handle Bryce's ghosts again once they were evoked.

While on the island of *Kaya*, she and Bryce had talked about the significance of pledging themselves to each other again before God, family, and friends, and especially in the church he'd once refused to attend because it brought back too many painful memories, but where they now worshipped regularly together. The wedding was supposed to be a joyful occasion, a way for them to strengthen their commitment to each other and their children, and move forward into a solid future as a family.

She'd been all geared up to use foreplay and even sex-at-the-office to convince Bryce to let Desire plan their wedding, but after Shaina and Tashi left, Michelle had stayed back to give her some sound advice.

"We've joked about you seducing Bryce, and I have faith in your powers of persuasion, but this situation is a lot more serious, Kaya," Michelle said with warmth and concern in her voice.

"I'm not taking it lightly. Bryce's heart was closed to love and life when I met him. It took a lot to bring him back to a place where he could believe in happiness again. He has buried his ghosts, and—"

"That's the thing with ghosts. Most people bury them, but they never deal with the demons associated with them, and because of that the demons have the power to resurface, and subsequently resurrect the ghosts at will—usually when things seem to be going well. Take this upcoming wedding, for instance."

Kaya frowned in confusion. "Aren't ghosts and demons the same thing?"

Michelle cleared her throat. "No. They're two separate entities. Demons are catalysts for ghosts. I didn't even know that until I had to deal with Erik's demons. You see, after he found out how Cassie lied to him, Erik was able to bury her ghost, and move on with me. But when he learned that my father—or the man posing as my father—was the one who'd killed Cassie, his demons of guilt, anger, and regret came back at him full force, and they brought a couple allies with them for ultimate destruction."

"Allies?" Kaya raised an enquiring eyebrow.

"Um-hmm. Our sessions with Samantha brought a lot to light for both Erik and me. From childhood, the most important people in his life had been secretive and less than honest with him. His demons were born from his parents' unorthodox relationship, being taken from his biological mother as a baby and raised by his biological father and her best friend, practically being coerced into marrying Cassie, and then Cassie not trusting him and blatantly lying to him for five years."

"The people who should protect you as a child can really mess you up for life. My own mother and father included." *As did Bryce's by allowing his grandmother to take over the job of raising him,* she thought, recalling the heated conversation she'd overheard between Bryce and his parents three years ago.

"Tell me about it. Erik thought he'd dealt with his demons until he discovered that I, too, had lied to him. With hurt and disappointment added to the mix, he completely lost faith in everything he held dear to his heart. It wasn't so much about the fact that it was my father who'd killed Cassie, but more about the fact that the one woman he'd grown to truly love, the one person he thought he could depend on, had let him down."

"You."

She bobbed her head up and down. "I didn't trust him, or our love enough to be completely honest with him. Instead, I emasculated him by thinking that he couldn't handle the truth, just like every other woman in his life before me had done. Even Precious was lying to him by participating in every extracurricular activity he'd enrolled her into, even though she hated most of them. She went along so as not to upset him."

"Wow. That's heavy."

"Yeah, but the kicker was Bridget Ashley."

"Bridget? How does she figure into the equation?"

Michelle sighed and took a sip of water. "Bridget was the only woman in Erik's life who was open and honest with him. She didn't hide her feelings for him, or about me for that matter. It was during a session with Samantha that I came to understand why he gravitated toward Bridget after we broke up. He didn't love her, but he could depend on her to be honest with him. She gave him the one thing he needed most from the women in his life whom he did love."

"Trust," Kaya said softly.

"Yes. Trust. My withholding vital information caused him to give up on love, and consequently, he might have married Bridget. Out of hurt and desperation, I might have married Ryan." She shuddered as if a blast of cold air had hit her. "Ironically, it was Bridget's honesty that got Erik and me back together. If she hadn't told him that I was pregnant with Little Erik—even though I'd warned her not to—we might all be living Miserably Ever After."

"No wonder you could wish Bridget well in her marriage

and her new practice in D.C. I thought you were crazy when you let Erik attend her wedding alone."

"I didn't have a choice. I was eight and a half weeks pregnant with Tiffany. I wasn't about to travel and put my baby's and my health at risk just to prove a point. Bridget isn't a bad person. She was just in love with a man who was in love with someone else. She found the right man for her, one who can love her the way she deserves to be loved. But we all learned a valuable lesson from that entire fiasco."

"Which is?" Kaya asked.

"You can have trust without love, but you can't have love without trust. And since love is what we all want most, we have to trust those we claim to love."

"Oh my God, you're so right."

Michelle placed her hand over Kaya's. "Bryce and Erik share a similar past when it comes to their late wives, so their demons are comparable in nature. My so-called father was the catalyst for Erik's demons, and the Summerses are Bryce's."

Her fingers curled around her water glass. "Erik was an uptight mess when I met him, but I loved him anyway. I guess my heart saw potential in him, despite his faults. I couldn't control it. He's such a better man now that he has confronted and slayed his demons. He's more relaxed, and he's genuinely happy because he's not holding grudges against anyone." She smiled again. "The wise King Solomon wrote, 'Whoever tends a fig tree will eat its fruit.' Our marriages, our relationships with our spouses, and our children are our fig trees. We have to tend them daily, constantly weed around the roots if we want them to continue bearing sweet fruits for our enjoyment."

"I know what you mean," Kaya said. "I had to deal with

my issues of abandonment and neglect from both my parents so that I could be a better woman, a better wife, and mother." *My demons were shadows compared to Bryce's, though*, she thought.

Michelle pulled Kaya into a sisterly hug. "Exactly. And I had to slay mine of physical and mental abuse from Timmy Gleason. Both Erik and I had to see him for the unstable monster that he was, and forgive him." Michelle paused for a moment as if she needed affirmation that her demons were indeed slayed.

"Like I said earlier," she continued, "I believe that Bryce has buried Pilar's ghost, but he hasn't dealt with the demons associated with them. He has to journey backward into his past to eliminate them once and for all. He has to deal with the Summers family. He has to forgive them, just like you forgave your parents. I know you're scared about what that would do to him, but you have to trust him, trust your love to see him through it and bring him back a better man. Before you two can enjoy ultimate bliss, not only in your marriage, but in every area of your lives as well, Bryce needs to let it all go, Kaya."

Kaya knew Michelle was right-on, because every time Bryce ran into a member of the Summers family, he would tense up, and his demon of anger would resurface and keep him in a somber mood, sometimes for days. Granite Falls was a small town, so he tensed up a lot. And those were only the times she witnessed. The situation was complex, and seducing Bryce was not the appropriate way to solve it. It would be demeaning to even try.

The chime of the elevator brought Kaya's awareness back to her surroundings and the change in her day's schedule. Henry and Lillian had taken the twins to the petting zoo for grandparents bonding time. Jason wasn't expected back from a two-week-long martial arts summer camp until tomorrow, and since Haley, the nanny, had the afternoon off, Kaya had planned to take Alyssa and Anastasia to the LaCrosse estate to play with Little Erik and Tiffany. To avoid disappointing the kids, Michelle had picked up the girls on her way home, leaving Kaya free to perform her daunting task.

"Good day, Mrs. Fontaine," the armed guard near the elevator said as she stepped off onto the tenth floor.

Kaya nodded on a forced smile and made her way along a sky blue hallway with doors that led to numerous empty conference and training rooms on both sides. She'd taken the elevator farthest away from Bryce's office to give herself time to rehearse the speech she planned to deliver to him. The place was deserted, since apart from Bryce's, only two other offices occupied this floor—Elaine's, his personal assistant, and...

"Libby," she called out as she turned a corner and spotted a young woman in a dark business suit and high heels hurrying ahead of her. Libby was the manager of the accounting division of Fontaine Enterprises.

Libby stopped and turned, a big smile on her freckled face as she shifted a pile of folders from one hand to the other. "Kaya, what are you doing here?"

"I came to see Bryce." Kaya caught up and gave Libby a big hug. "I like your hair," she added, inspecting Libby's red hair that was fashioned into a French braid.

Libby patted her braid. "Thanks. Your mother-in-law has been teaching me to braid so I can do Jenna's hair," she said as they resumed walking.

Kaya smiled at the mention of Libby's two-year-old

daughter—also a redhead—whom she shared with her husband, Steven Lynd, the attorney who'd called her with tragic news that had changed her life, almost four years ago.

Libby was the first friend Kaya had made when she moved to Granite Falls. She'd met her even before she met Bryce and his buddies, *and* before Michelle who was the only other wife at the time. Libby and Steven were two of the few people Bryce trusted.

Libby sometimes joined Kaya and the other wives on shopping sprees and lunch and dinner dates, and she and Jenna were often invited for playtime with all the kids. Steven hung out with the husbands at the country club a lot, and they both attended many of the monthly get-togethers, but understandably, the four couples didn't share the same closeness with the Lynds as they shared with each other.

"Is Bryce expecting you, or is this a *surprise*?" Libby gave Kaya a knowing wink.

Kaya blushed, remembering the time Libby had walked in on her and Bryce about to make love on his desk, during the early months of their marriage. It was embarrassing for all of them, and they never spoke about it, but after that near mishap Bryce began locking his office door whenever she visited, and both Libby and Elaine usually disappeared from the floor when she and Bryce were in session. "No, he's not expecting me. Is he busy?"

"He's in a meeting with Marcus Spencer. You know him."

"Yeah. How long do you think they'll be?"

Libby glanced at her watch. "Maybe another half hour or so, but he has another one after lunch, and then he leaves for that two-day conference in Philadelphia."

"I know. We cut our vacation by one day so he could mentally prepare for that conference."

Libby grinned. "How was it?"

Kaya was powerless to conceal the dreamy smile that parted her lips. "Fantastic. He got a lot of rest." *From work,* she thought with warm memories.

"Good. He's been working too hard. And with the wedding coming up, he's trying to wrap up a few more projects in the making before you leave for your honeymoon. He asked me to fetch these files from the marketing department downstairs so he can work on them right through lunch. I'm dropping them off before I break for lunch. I'm meeting Steven at the Thai restaurant on Oak Street, if he gets out of court on time. With both of us working fulltime, it's hard to…"

Kaya's throat ached at the thought of turning Bryce's world upside down and sending him back into a place from where he might not be able to escape the second time around. Three years ago when she'd told him to choose between her and Pilar, he'd disappeared for four days. Those four days were the most unbearable of Kaya's life—far worse than when her father had walked out on her at five, and when her mother had abandoned her at twelve years old.

She and Bryce were barely a month into their marriage at that time, and she hadn't known him well enough to even imagine he'd choose her, especially since the only reason they'd gotten married was to provide a home for Jason, Alyssa, and Anastasia as they grieved the deaths of both their parents.

While Bryce had been away contemplating, Kaya had begun to believe her mother's words that she was unlovable. If it weren't for Michelle, who'd assured her that Bryce loved her and would come back to her, and the fact that she'd just found out she was pregnant, Kaya would have packed up the kids and moved back to Florida. That was then, before she knew Bryce.

She knew him inside out now, and she knew that he would never abandon her and their children, but she felt as if she was abandoning him by forcing him out of his happy present, back into his dark past that could affect their future for a long, long time.

"Kaya?"

Kaya glanced up to find Libby frowning at her.

"What?" She hadn't heard a word Libby said.

"Hello, Kaya."

Kaya stopped and turned her head into the direction of the voice. "Hi, Elaine." She smiled at the kind-face middle-aged woman sitting behind an alabaster circular desk. The only other furniture in Elaine's open receptionist space were a couple of black club chairs and a marble table that were fixed to the floor, between them. The glass walls gave her an excellent view of the mountains in the background. It was not a place to loiter, but merely a place to state your business and move on. "How are you?" she asked.

"Your husband's keeping me busy, which I like. You look beautiful, as usual. That dress is stunning."

"It definitely is," Libby agreed.

"Thanks." Kaya ran her palms down the soft batik material of her light purple dress with island native flowers printed all over it. The deep V-neck and halter top showed off the nice tan she'd gotten from her recent days in the sun. Bryce had bought the dress for her last year while he was on a business trip in the Dominican Republic. It was simple, but elegant.

"Well, Bryce appreciates your effort. Comes in here with a big smile on his face every morning." Elaine tapped her earpiece. "Oops, back to work. Nice seeing you, Kaya."

"You kind of zoned out a minute ago." Libby resumed their conversation as they continued walking toward Bryce's office. "What's wrong?"

Kaya let out an audible sigh, and moved her white Fendi handbag from one shoulder to the next. "I just found out about Fae's accident, and that Desire will be planning our wedding."

"Oh boy."

"So you knew."

Libby shrugged. "Michelle ran it by me while you were away. You guys want to stay local so—"

"What do you think Bryce's reaction will be when I tell him?" Libby was there when Bryce's world came crashing down around him almost ten years ago, long before he knew Kaya. Libby was one of the first people Bryce had called immediately following Pilar's murder, so the panicky look she gave Kaya was understandable.

"I don't know, Kaya. I mean he's clearly put Pilar to rest in his heart. If he hadn't, he wouldn't be able to love you the way he does. And I know he loves you unconditionally."

Libby was preaching to the choir, Kaya thought as they came to a stop outside Bryce's office. The door was closed, but Kaya could hear voices coming from inside. It reminded her of the day, just months after their marriage when she'd visited him, unannounced, to find him wearing Pilar's wedding band instead of hers. That scenario had brought them to the crossroads where she'd forced him to choose. He'd chosen her and they'd been happy ever since. But according to Michelle, that happiness would remain precariously unstable until Bryce faced his demons head-on.

Libby placed her hand on the doorknob. "You want me to tell him you're here?"

"No. I'll catch him between meetings." She would have loved to deliver the news at the end of his day, preferably after they'd made love and he was still trembling inside her. But he would be gone for two days, and she couldn't keep Desire in limbo any longer. Business was business.

CHAPTER THREE

K aya backtracked to Elaine's desk, hoping to engage in small talk to keep her mind off the impending conversation with her husband. But Elaine was busy on the phone scheduling meetings and arranging travel plans for Bryce—both domestic and foreign—for the next few months.

She strolled back to the commodious waiting area outside Bryce's office. It was classically decorated with black and white leather sofas and chairs, arranged around glass and marble coffee tables that were topped with the latest issues of the leading newspapers and business-related magazines in the country.

A variety of life size trees in terracotta pots were scattered strategically about, blending nicely with the sky-blue interior and the natural landscapes of the White Mountains and Crystal Lake made visible through the walls of glass.

Since it was erected fifteen years ago, Fontaine Enterprises had been voted the most architecturally aesthetic building in Granite Falls. Yet no one but Bryce knew the identity of the young architect, who preferred to remain anonymous. Bryce hadn't even confided in her, not because he didn't trust her, but because he'd signed a contract of confidentiality. Business was business.

Kaya began sorting idly through a stack of magazines on one of the tables, and her eyes popped when she saw the heading of an article sprawled across the top of the latest issue of *Granite Falls People News*. "Love and Marriage – Granite Falls Billionaire Husbands Tell All." An elegant photo of the four couples embracing and staring into each other's eyes took up the entire cover. Kaya remembered the husbands insisting on posing for that photo last July during the private family party at Mountainview Café—the party where the wives had made their husbands kneel and propose to them properly. Philippe had taken several photos of them.

Kaya immediately called the other wives—conference style. Like her, they weren't aware that their husbands had done the interview with Lester Cobbs.

After hanging up, she flopped down on a sofa that gave her full view of Bryce's office door, and flipped open the magazine to page four. They'd gone public with the news of their renewal of vows midway between Thanksgiving and Christmas, hoping that people would be too busy with holiday planning to pay them much attention. They couldn't have been more wrong.

Just hours after the news broke, Granite Falls had become a beehive of activity with paparazzi from every corner of the globe buzzing around. Their phones had been ringing nonstop and the streets close to their individual estates had been lined with photographers and news reporters, trying to snap pictures and procure interviews. It wouldn't have been so bad if they didn't have children to protect. Michelle, who'd just given birth to Fiona, and Tashi, who was six months pregnant with Alex, were in greater danger than the rest of them.

Escaping Granite Falls was the only solution. Since they had an in-house OB/GYN, they'd all given their household staff and nannies a long paid vacation, packed up their immediate and extended families, and jetted off to *Michelle* in the Seychelles for Christmas. They'd enjoyed the peace and quiet so much that they'd decided to make it an annual ritual, spending the holidays on each private island in turn. After Christmas, the parents had left their ten children in the capable care of seven grandparents and two uncles in the Seychelles, and flown to the newly acquired island of *Tashi* off the Amalfi Coast to ring in the New Year in naughty, grownup style.

By the time they all returned home to Granite Falls, the buzz had died down.

Kaya smiled as she began reading the men's versions of how they met their wives, how they knew right away that each woman was *the one* and when they first knew without a shadow of a doubt that they were hopelessly in love.

Erik spoke about his instant attraction for Michelle when she came sashaying up his driveway hauling a suitcase behind her to interview for a nanny position, and that he fell in love with her when she made the most horrible pig face that made Precious laugh. He also talked about his mistakes and how he almost lost her forever. "When I found out that the man who raised her—the man she thought was her father—was the one who'd killed my first wife, like a blind idiot, I took out my hurt on Michelle. That was the biggest mistake of my life." He attributed the reason they made it back to each other to

Michelle's big heart and forgiving spirit. "She proved to me that even idiots deserve to be loved. Even after five years of marriage, every single day I wake up thinking of ways to make it up to her." *Grins widely.* "I'm the happiest idiot in the universe. I love Michelle more than life itself."

Kaya's heart trembled as she read Bryce's story. "When I first saw Kaya, my heart stopped beating for countless seconds. She was the most gorgeous woman I'd ever seen. I just wanted to wrap her up and take her home, unwrap her and gaze at her loveliness for hours on end. Boy, was I smitten. Then my jets cooled when she showed her strong, stubborn-to-a-fault personality." *Looks away dreamily.* "I knew she was *the one* when I tried to pay her to give me custody of my godchildren who'd just lost both their parents. Kaya practically told me to take my money and shove it." *Chuckles.* "I knew I loved her when I walked into the nursery and found her at her wits end trying to comfort a cranky baby. She had no idea what she was doing, but I saw my future with her and our children. At that moment, I knew I would do anything to make, and keep her happy. *Anything.* But as men are wont to do, I hurt her. Thankfully, she forgave me and has given me a reason to live again. I'm nothing, nobody without Kaya. I love her like I've loved no other woman. Ever."

That public declaration included Pilar, Kaya thought on a sob. "I love her like I've loved no other woman. Ever." Kaya said the words out loud.

Tears blinded her as she moved on to Massimo's partially invented story. He couldn't tell the world that he'd met his wife when she offered to sell him her virginity for four million dollars. That was a story best kept in-house. He'd instead reported that he'd fallen in love with Shaina's eyes when she was only seventeen years old—which was actually true—but that he had to wait seven years for their paths to cross again when she fell on the slopes in front of him while skiing. That was their public story and they were sticking with it.

"Many people don't know, but shortly after my father died, I almost followed him into eternity." He talked about his run-in with the injured rhino and about Jabari who dragged him back to the Masai village. "For months I lingered between life and death, and each time I fell into the blackness, Shaina's eyes led me back to the light." *Heavy sigh.* "Here's something else I've kept from the public: in his will, my father stipulated that in order to gain my inheritance, I had to marry before my thirty-fourth birthday, stay faithfully married for three years, and produce an heir within one." *Shakes his head.* "Talk about pressure. When I met Shaina, I was two weeks shy of my birthday." *Chuckles. Waves hands in the air.* "My announcing our engagement that day at the country club made her mad as hell, and she did everything in her power to run. Who could blame her? I was a notorious playboy who wanted to marry her for money—a fact that she was unaware of at the time." Massimo went on to explain about drawing up a prenup for a three-year marriage, and having Shaina arrested, then giving her the options of either staying in jail or marrying him. "Not very heroic, but by then I was deeply in love with her and would have done anything to keep her in my life. I threw out the prenup, of course." *Chuckles again.* "Shaina saved me from a life of emptiness and loneliness. She has changed me in ways I never imagined I could be changed. She provides everything I need and want in a woman. Since the day I met her, I've never given another woman a second glance or a thought. Shaina is the only woman I've ever loved. Will ever love."

Adam recaptured the moment he and Tashi collided with each other in Mountainview Café. "My world stopped spinning that very moment. One glance into her emerald eyes and I felt as if I knew her, like we'd been together in a previous life." *Chuckles and combs fingers through hair.* "I'm a man who'd been hurt, twice, and so *skeptical me* brushed it off as the hormonal reaction of a boy to a girl. But the universe was working against me, or perhaps for me, and two more times, it brought Tashi and me together." *Chuckles again.* "The third time, as they say, is really a charm, although there was nothing charming about that meeting." He went on to explain how he had to crawl through Tashi's bedroom window to rescue her from dying of food poisoning, and that when he saw her lying weak and helpless on her bed was the moment he knew he loved her. "Tashi and I were born to love each other. My life is complete. There's nothing else in this world that I want or need. I loved Tashi before life and I love her beyond death."

As expected, there was no mention of Tashi's New York troubles. Like Massimo and Shaina, there were portions of Adam and Tashi's story that needed to remain private.

"Kaya, darling."

Kaya started at the sound of her husband's voice. She glanced up to see him standing at his office door, his face shrouded in surprise at seeing her. She turned her head in the direction of the receptionist area and realized that she'd been so preoccupied with the article that she hadn't even noticed Elaine had left for lunch. That she could understand, but how the heck had she missed Marcus Spencer leaving Bryce's office and taking the elevator next to it? Had she dozed off?

Bryce strode toward her, his surprise turning into open exhilaration.

Kaya smiled as he drew closer, looking scrumptiously sexy in a pair of gray trousers, white shirt, and gray and white striped tie. He'd removed his jacket, and even from a distance of a few yards, she could see his powerful muscles rippling under the silky material of his shirt. Overcome with affection, Kaya dropped the magazine on the sofa and raced toward her husband. "I love you, Bryce. I love you so much," she panted throwing her arms about his waist.

"Sweet, Kaya. I love you, too, baby." He picked her up and hugged her close as his lips opened over hers.

Kaya wrapped her arms around his neck and hugged him tighter as his tongue worked its way into her mouth. He was bold and masculine, and tasted like peppermint, and the familiar fire that blazed to life whenever they touched began to spread heat through her. Bryce's low throaty groan and the bulge of his erection pressing into her belly were evidence that he too felt the electricity between them. Her panties were already wet. Even though he was busy, she knew it would take very little to entice him to carry her to his office and make love to her.

But she hadn't come here to seduce him. She'd come to destroy him. *I'll do anything to make and keep her happy. I love her like I've loved no other woman. Ever.* Kaya hoped Bryce would remember those words when she dropped the bombshell of Desire on his head. She tugged her mouth from his and wriggled out of his arms.

"We said our goodbyes this morning," he said, steadying her on her feet, "but I'm glad you stopped by."

He sported a happy sexy smile that filled Kaya with guilt. The man had to prepare for another meeting in an hour and then a conference tonight. She was a terrible wife to mess with his head at such an inopportune time.

"How long have you been waiting?" he asked.

"Since Libby brought you those files."

"She didn't tell me you were here."

"I asked her not to. I didn't want to bother you."

He pulled her into his arms, and tangled his fingers into her hair. "Sweetie, you're never a bother. I would excuse myself from an audience with President Obama to see you."

His last statement brought Kaya a mixture of joy and pain. "Oh, Bryce." She sighed into his chest.

He eased her away and gazed lovingly down at her. "What's the matter, baby?"

"Have you eaten lunch, yet?" she asked, stalling for time.

"I grabbed a sandwich from the cafeteria earlier. I ate it during my last meeting."

"Where's Mr. Spencer? I didn't see him leave."

His eyes narrowed and he dropped his hands from her shoulders. "How do you know I was meeting with Marcus?"

"Libby told me."

"Did she tell you why?" He crossed his arms and stared at her.

"No, Bryce. Why are you acting so suspiciously?"

He passed his hands down his face. "I'm sorry. I'm just tired."

Kaya swallowed another mouthful of guilt. "Is he still in your office?" *Say yes. Say yes.*

"Um—no. We took the back stairs from my office down to the garage, and I took it back up. You know that's how I stretch my legs between meetings. If I hadn't come out to grab something from Elaine's desk, I would have missed you."

I wish you had. Maybe she should just go home, and tell the girls that Desire was out. She cared more about her husband's sanity than about throwing the perfect wedding. They were already married anyway, so who cared…

"Is something wrong at home, Kaya? Is one of the kids hurt?" Panic dulled his eyes and voice.

"No. No. It's nothing like that, but you might want to sit down for what I'm about to tell you." Since they were alone on the floor, Kaya led him over to the corner of the sofa she'd occupied earlier. It was probably psychologically better for him if she kept this conversation away from his office where he'd have to concentrate on business shortly.

He glanced down at the magazine she'd dropped on the sofa. "Oh, it's out. Captivating picture." He picked up the magazine and his face broke into a handsome grin. "Is this it? Did I say something in here that upset you?"

She pulled him down beside her on the sofa and clasped his face in her hands. He felt smooth and strong under her palms. "I love every word, every letter, and every comma. What an amazing surprise. I called the girls and none of them knew about it either. You guys can really keep secrets." She gave him a quick peck on the lips.

"I meant every single word. I'm nothing without you." He twirled a lock of her curly hair around his finger, and leaned his forehead against hers. "You make me happy, Kaya," he said, his hot breath fanning her face.

"I know, and I'm sorry, Bryce."

He drew back and frowned at her. "Sorry about what?"

Kaya dropped her hands and her gaze to her lap. "That what I'm about to tell you might put a crinkle in your happiness."

She felt the muscles in his thigh tensing as his hands came down over hers. "Just tell me," he said in a quiet voice.

The proverbial quiet before the storm, she thought, raising her gaze to find him staring at her, his mouth drawn into a firm line. Kaya licked her lips and swallowed. "You know I was meeting the girls and our wedding planner this morning."

"Mm hmm."

"Well. I don't know if you heard that Fae had an accident last week."

"I hadn't heard. What happened to her?"

"She fell down the stairs and broke both arms and a leg, I think."

"Aw! Is she going to be okay?"

"Yes, but she can't do our wedding. She can't finish."

He shrugged. "Well, just hire someone else."

"They did. We did hire someone else," she added after a pause since she'd already bought into the idea of Weddings by Desire.

"Then what's the problem?"

"It's Desire. Desire Summers."

His black eyes blazed and dazzled with fury. Just the thought of the anguish she'd caused him ripped at Kaya's heart. The only other time she'd ever seen Bryce this furious was when he'd found out that Michael and Lauren had left their children to her instead of him.

His best friends had betrayed him then.

His wife was betraying him now.

CHAPTER FOUR

Bryce shot off the sofa with lightning speed, his hands fisted at his sides as he glared at her. "No way in hell is that going to happen, Kaya."

There was a sourness in the pit of Kaya's stomach. "Bryce, I—"

He threw his hands up, cutting her off. "I can't believe you agreed to this, that you'd consider having Desire Summers plan our wedding after what her sister did to Pilar. To me." He pressed his hands against the sides of his head, groaned aloud, and began pacing agitatedly back and forth.

His pain twisted inside Kaya's gut as he relived the nightmare of watching his wife being murdered in front of him. In the space of a few seconds, he'd been transformed from a happy husband, indulging in pleasantries with his present wife, to one plagued by the tragedy of the one from his past. And she was to blame.

"Michelle and Tashi and Shaina had already hired her," Kaya said. She knew it was low to pin the blame on her friends, but in all actuality, it was the truth. "I didn't know anything about it until a short while ago, Bryce, and when they told me, I—"

"And when they told you, you should have said, *No!*" He came to a sudden halt in front of her. "You should have said, *No! No! No!*" He repeatedly slammed his right fist into his left palm as he spoke.

Kaya closed her eyes and cringed every time he said the word *No*—the word he used to scream out in his sleep. It seemed like eons ago that she'd last awakened him from his nightmare.

"You are my wife, Kaya. You are supposed to advocate *for* me, not collaborate with your friends *against* me. How can you ask me to allow Desire Summers to plan our wedding?"

Kaya's stomach knotted with guilt at his accusations, and the emotional and psychological upheaval she was causing him. She opened her eyes, and avoiding his gaze, she glanced at the variety of bamboo, palm, and ficus trees decorating the waiting area, their leaves and branches reaching toward the rays of sun streaming through the glass wall. They were flourishing, abundantly and uninhibitedly, in weedless soil inside the terracotta pots.

You've got to pull the choking weeds from around the roots of your fig tree.

Swallowing the sob that rose to her throat, Kaya met Bryce's furious gaze that was laced with his disappointment in her. *God, give me strength,* she prayed as she pushed to her feet, forcing him to take a backward step. Feeling like a grasshopper in his towering presence, she was overwhelmed with the urge to just hug him and tell him that he was right and she was wrong.

Bryce must confront his demons before he can achieve ultimate happiness within himself, and with you. Well, Kaya thought, his demons were awakened, so he might as well tackle them, slay them once and for all so they never have the chance to torment him, ever again.

She cleared her throat. "It's not just your wedding, Bryce," she said, deciding to take a roundabout approach. "It's mine too, and our family's. Our children and your parents are looking forward to this event. It also involves the LaCrosses, the Andrettis, and the Andreases—"

"Well, if they're all set on having Desire Summers plan this wedding, they can count the Fontaines out."

"You would disappoint your friends? Your brothers?"

His eyes flashed imperiously. "If they agree to this travesty of my memories and my pain, they don't deserve to be my brothers, much less my friends. True friends don't hurt each other."

Sometimes they do, and wives, too, if they think it would make you whole. Kaya swallowed, and like a surgeon digging deep into raw flesh for a bullet, she forged on. "I just finished reading an article where you said you would do anything to make me happy. You just told me you meant every single word. Were you lying in the article, or just now, or both times?"

"Oh, come on, Kaya. I can't believe you're twisting my words and using them against me. That's way below the belt."

"I'm not twisting anything. You said you'd do anything for me. I'm asking you to do this for me. It will make me happy." *And you too, once all this is over.*

"Anything but this." He began pacing again, his back straight, his shoulders stiff and raised, and his hands clenching and unclenching at his sides.

Kaya stomped her foot on the floor. "Bryce! Stop pacing!"

He halted in his tracks, and she could see the muscles in his shoulders and back contracting with tension.

"Look at me, Bryce," she said with gentleness.

After a few moments, he turned and glared at her from across the room like a perturbed little boy who was fighting for what he believed in despite the odds against him. "I can't do this, Kaya. I won't."

With love in her heart, Kaya admired the towering, powerful physique of her husband. He was known in the corporate world as a fearsome lion who went after and took what he wanted. She'd been introduced to that formidable side of him when she first met him, but she'd also come to know and love the gentler side of him—the side where a little boy filled with inhibitions, fear, and pain lived. That was the side that she needed to appeal to now.

She pursed her lips and beckoned him with her finger. "Come here, Bryce."

He remained rooted to the floor as if he had no intention of obeying her command. But Kaya held his gaze and kept beckoning until his shoulders hunched in submission, and perhaps defeat. They'd been together long enough for him to know that a happy Kaya meant a happy Bryce, and vice versa. He wasn't unhappy at the moment, just angry.

A while back when they'd been bickering over something so insignificant that she couldn't even remember the source, Bryce had told her that he could work when he was angry but not when he was unhappy. He had a meeting coming up in less than an hour, and then he was leaving on a two-day conference. He needed to be happy.

When he sauntered over to her, she pushed him back down on the sofa and dropped down beside him. She took his large hands in hers—the hands that loved her and caressed her in the thick of darkness, and soothed each of their five children in the light of day. She began to massage his inner wrists, his palms, the backs of his hands, and gently pulled at the stiffness in his long beautiful fingers. This was his calming mechanism, and Kaya continued working at him until his muscles were relaxed and he slumped back against the sofa with a deep sigh and a satisfied moan.

"There, isn't that better?"

He caught and held her gaze. "Kaya—"

Kaya placed a finger on his lips. "Bryce, just hear me out, please."

He vacillated a moment, then said, "Okay."

"Thanks." Kaya brought his hands to her chest and held them there. "I met you five years after Pilar's death, and at the time, you were still trapped in your valley of sorrow. You were so buried in your grief, you couldn't be the kind of husband I needed during the first weeks of our marriage. But you finally shared your pain with me. I cried with you. I helped you through it. My love helped you heal. I brought you back to a place where you could be happy again, Bryce." Her voice broke with emotions and tears stung her eyes. "The last thing I want to do is reopen your wounds and make you bleed again, baby."

"Then why, Kaya? Why are you asking this impossible and cruel request of me?" His voice was a hoarse whisper.

"Because you're not fully over your pain, your anger, or your hurt. This wedding is supposed to be an opportunity for us to renew our vows, our love, and commitment for and to each other. It's supposed to make us whole, stronger, individually and collectively as a couple and as a family. But you're not whole. The sight of a Summers, the mere mention of the name kicks you off balance."

He shrugged indifferently. "I can't control that. I can't control how I feel about them."

She squeezed his fingers that had begun to stiffen again. "Yes, you can. If you try."

"Why should I? It won't change anything." He gazed at the scene outside the building.

"You remember when I was carrying Eli and Elyse and I told you that I wanted to find my mother?"

"I thought you were nuts, hormonal."

"Maybe I was. But I just felt like I needed to know why she couldn't love me. I was scared that I would be like her, that abandonment and neglect were hereditary traits, and that one day I would just up and walk out on my children."

He gave her a gentle smile. "You're nothing like your mother, Kaya."

"I didn't know that for sure until I met with her face to face and found out about her childhood, how she was molested and neglected. She never had anything beautiful in her life. She felt unworthy of kindness and love, so when my father came along and gave her everything she'd been lacking in her life, she clung to him. Then when she found out that she wasn't the only woman in his life, she took out her anger, and hurt, and disappointment on me. She used me, something he loved, to get back at him. She took me away from him and punished me to hurt him. I was furious at him for leaving me with her when he knew she was abusing me."

Kaya hadn't even realized that she'd been crying until she

felt a tear on her hand and Bryce's arms about her. But this wasn't about her. She swiped at her tears and pushed out of his arms. "Up until I sat down with my mother, I was filled with uncertainty and unworthiness about myself as a woman and a mother, and hate and resentment toward Nadine for making me feel that way. Just the thought of her and of what she'd done to me used to cause my blood pressure to skyrocket."

"I know, Kaya. I was there. You were hospitalized for hypertension when you were pregnant. I was so scared for you and for our babies. That was the longest week of my life." His voice trembled with love and concern.

Kaya had never felt more needed and important than when Bryce had taken a leave from Fontaine Enterprises and taken up around-the-clock residence in her private room at Granite Falls General Hospital. He'd proven to her that she was the most important thing in his life. "You also thought I was nuts when on leaving the hospital, I insisted that you take me to Atlanta to see my mother."

His face contorted with apparent unpleasant memories.

"But I was fine after that trip, Bryce. Even though Nadine admitted that she never loved me, and still doesn't, I was fine because I'd faced her. I was able to let go of all that negative energy when I realized that she had no power over me. You see, Nadine was the catalyst for my demons of fear, resentment, and hate. My childhood memories of abandonment and abuse were my ghost, and each time I thought of Nadine, I was haunted by those ghosts. After I faced her, I slayed those demons, and saw her for what she really was: a sad pathetic woman incapable of recognizing, embracing, and enjoying the most beautiful things that ever came into her life—me, you, our amazing kids."

"Her loss, sweetheart." He traced a finger down her cheek, hooked it under her chin and pulled her in for a lingering kiss.

Melting at the tender caress, Kaya yearned to prolong the kiss and toyed with even taking it to the next heated level, but harnessing her desires, she drew back and smiled. "You know I left my number with her and told her to call me if she ever needed anything. I'm not holding my breath that she will, but if she does, I'll be there for her. I pity her. I don't know if she'll ever seek counseling and healing, and reach out to me, or if we'll ever have any type of a mother-daughter relationship, but I'm fine, either way. I have forgiven her."

"You can easily forgive her because she's your mother. The Summerses—"

"The Summerses are the catalysts to your demons, Bryce. Those demons in turn have the power to resurrect your ghosts of the night Pilar was murdered in front of you. I know for a fact that each time you see a Summers, you're filled with rage and hurt and regret all over again."

His lips twisted and he tried to pull his hand from her grasp, but Kaya held on to him. "My demons don't compare to yours. You lost your wife. Someone you loved was brutally taken away from you. I know you're not bound by Pilar's love anymore, but you're bound by your anger and unforgiving spirit. It's been almost ten years and you're still not completely healed. Aren't you tired, Bryce? Wouldn't you love to walk by a Summers and not feel that pinching in your chest, that heaviness in your heart?"

He twitched, but did not respond.

Kaya squeezed his hand. "It wasn't all in vain, you know.

As horrible as your experiences were, they brought us together. We've adopted three awesome children and have created two more beautiful ones from our love. It's time to eliminate your demons once and for all so they never have the chance to wiggle their way into our lives again. Our kids and I want you completely whole, Bryce. We want *a one hundreds-of-percent* of you."

He chuckled softly at her *a one-hundreds-of-percent* imitation of Alyssa. Then just as quickly, he grimaced and glanced through the door of his office as if the work he'd left in there had called his name.

Kaya's gaze followed his, then a thought crept into her mind. "How can you continue working with Marcus Spencer?" she asked.

"What?" He looked at her as if she'd lost her mind.

"You and Massimo made him the chief engineer of Fonandt Energies even after his twin brother tried to destroy Andretti Industries."

"Marcus is a great engineer, one of the best in the area." He shrugged dismissively. "Why should we hold him responsible for his brother's misconduct? He was not an accomplice in Maurice's schemes."

"My point, exactly! Desire is not Victoria, Bryce. She's her sister. She wasn't an accomplice to Victoria's crime."

He cringed each time she spoke the name of the woman who'd murdered his wife. "That's different, Kaya. Maurice Spencer was a greedy, vindictive bastard who tried to steal something he thought belonged to him. He didn't kill anyone."

"Not directly, but his actions started a chain of events that led to Shaina's father's death. You can't deny that."

He spread his hands in compliance. "In a sense you're correct, but still—"

"Still, I agree that Maurice's crime pales in comparison to —" Kaya paused, deciding it was best she not mention Victoria's name again. "Desire's sister's crime," she continued in a soft, yet persistent tone. "Just as you didn't judge a man by the actions of his brother, you can't judge a woman by the actions of her sister, or her mother, for that matter. My mother is a despicable human being, but you don't hold that against me. Give Desire a chance, Bryce. Allowing her to plan our wedding will open the door of communication between you and the Summers family. Communication that is well overdue."

"I don't know if that's possible, Kaya, and I honestly don't have the time or the energy to give it any thought right now." He looked at his watch, pushed to his feet, and pulled her up beside him. "I hate to do this, baby, but I have a meeting that starts in fifteen minutes and I still have to go over some reports before—"

"I understand." She'd done what she came to do, which was to lay down the foundation to the road to emotional freedom. He'd listened to her argument. She hoped that he would at least consider it.

The faint sounds of voices and the clicking of heels in the corridor alerted Kaya that Elaine and Libby had returned from lunch, and that the tenth floor of Fontaine Enterprises was back in business. She picked up her purse from the sofa and led Bryce over to the elevator—away from the line of sight of the corridor and Elaine's desk. "I love you," she said, as she waited for the doors to open. "And I'm sorry to resurrect your ghosts, but it's for the best."

"I love you, sweetie." He drew her into his arms and fastened his hands on her buttocks. He molded her and rocked against her intimately as he captured her mouth for a deep, passionate kiss.

Kaya was breathless when he lifted his head and eased her away. "I miss you already." His black eyes smoldered with fire as they raked down her body. "By the way, you look ravishing in that dress, Mrs. Fontaine. If I didn't have a meeting, you wouldn't still be wearing it." He cocked his head to one side. "Does your husband know how sexy you are?"

The walls of Kaya's sex contracted. "I don't know. Does he?"

He turned his head and cased the area. "Take off your panties," he said in a throaty voice, his eyes flashing like summer lightning cracking a dark cloud.

Kaya flushed all over at the indecent command—a command she'd come to expect and eagerly obey over the past three years. It was the first time he'd made it in public with the possibility of... She swallowed and licked her lips. "Elaine or Libby can come by any minute."

"Then you'd better hurry. If you want me to consider Desire, give me your panties, Kaya. It might work in your favor tonight when I'm—um—considering," he said with a salacious smile.

"Bryce—" Her breath caught in her throat.

"Now, Kaya. I don't have all day." He held out his hand, palm up.

Kaya's knees buckled and she would have collapsed to the floor if his other hand wasn't still on her shoulder. She wanted him to consider Desire, so if giving up her panties would work in her favor, then...

Her heartbeat thundered in her ears as she hung the strap of her purse over his extended arm. She kept her eyes glued to his as she slowly pulled her dress up and hooked her thumbs into the waistline of her thong.

His eyes shifted to her bare thighs and her hands fumbling under the dress. "Yes, baby, take them off for me. Are they wet?"

"Soaking. The way you like them," Kaya whispered in a breathless murmur as she slid the damp material down her thighs, over her knees, and felt them fall around her ankles. Without the barrier to catch the flow of hot juices churning inside her, it ran freely down her thighs.

"Mmmm," Bryce groaned as his gaze landed on the white pool of lace at her angles. Without saying a word, he bent down and, lifting her feet one at a time, he freed her of her feminine garment. "Mmmm," he groaned again, standing and lifting the thong to his nose and inhaling deeply. "Yes, this will definitely help. Thanks, babe." He pushed them into the pocket of his suit pants, and gently nudged her into the elevator. "Now get out of here, you tempting little hussy. I have work to do." He graced her with a wicked, handsome smile before turning on his heels and striding away.

Kaya's heart thundered in her chest as she admired the tightness of her husband's buttocks pressing against his pants. She was licking her lips and fanning her face with her hand when he disappeared into his office and closed the door without even looking back at her.

Her belly tingled from the imprint of his erection against her, and her thighs were wet and sticky from the hot juices flowing copiously and unrestrained from inside her. She was trembling so hard from the memories of Bryce thrusting deep inside her this morning during their long goodbye session that she had to hold on to the railing inside the elevator for support.

When the steel doors came together, Kaya reached into her purse for a tissue. Maybe two.

CHAPTER FIVE

LaCrosse Estate – Same day. Monday, early afternoon...

"It's a touching article, Michelle. My son leaves no doubt in anyone's mind how he truly feels about you." Felicia closed the magazine and placed it on the table near her lounge.

"No, he didn't. Made me fall in love with him all over again."

"I would too, if Philippe wrote something like that about me."

Michelle smiled at her mother-in-law, who occupied the lounge next to hers under a bamboo cabana in one of the many courtyards at the LaCrosse Estate. A few yards away, Little Erik and Tiffany, along with Alyssa and Anastasia, were splashing around in an Olympic-size, in-ground kiddie pool with Philippe, and Catherine—the LaCrosse children's nanny. The lifeguard of the day, perched on his umbrella chair, kept close watch over them. The children's squeals and laughter brought peace and contentment to Michelle's soul. Life was good.

"I actually cried while I was reading it, not just at Erik's story, but all of them," she added, leaning over to straighten the blanket over Fiona, who was fast asleep in a basinet next to her. Members of the household staff were cleaning up the outdoor grill and clearing the buffet tables, but the pleasing aroma of steak, chicken, seafood, and vegetables still lingered in the air.

"It could not have been easy for him to open up to the world, to admit that he was wrong to treat you so poorly," Felicia said. "But I'm proud of him for doing it. That mess about your father had a lot of tongues wagging negatively five years ago. Now let them wag about something positive for a change." She picked up her pina colada from her table and twirled the straw around the white liquid before taking a sip.

"I don't care what people say about me, Mom. I know what Erik and I have, what we had during the rockiest time of our first marriage." Michelle adjusted the straps of her black bikini top—still a little damp from her romp in the pool with the kids—and buttoned the front of her white cover-up.

"I was mad at him, too, for not going after you, bringing you back home where you belonged. Agh! He was so damn stubborn. I wanted to box his ears, whup his behind or something."

Michelle pressed her lips together and took a deep breath. Everybody blamed Erik when her actions had played just as much a role in their eight months of separation. She turned sideways to look at Felicia. "Mom, I'm gonna say something that I should have said a long time ago, and I'll be frank about it, but please don't think I'm being disrespectful."

Felicia unclasped her lips from around her straw and set the glass back down. "Okay," she said slowly, eyeing Michelle with uncertainty.

"I'm tired of people beating up on my husband, calling him a heartless jerk," Michelle said in defense of the man she loved and had almost lost. "Erik wasn't the only one at fault. Yeah, initially he acted poorly when he learned that my father had killed Cassie, but it was a reaction to my misplaced distrust of him."

"You told him you were sorry. You asked him to forgive you."

"Yes, for a week after my lie blew up in my face. He was still in shock. His pain was still too raw for him to see past my deception. I lied to him. But what I did after that was worse."

"What exactly did you do?"

Michelle focused her gaze on the white netting around the cabana flapping in the afternoon breeze as she recalled her insightful revelation during a visit with Samantha a couple years ago. Erik was the only person she'd shared it with and, being the sweet man he was, he'd blamed himself for causing her to react that way. It was time to get out of the shadows and let the rest of the world know that she'd also misbehaved.

She caught Felicia's questioning eyes. "Because of pride, fear, insecurity, and probably revenge, I kept the fact that I was pregnant from Erik for eight months, Felicia. I could have picked up the phone and told him. I could have gone to see him, but I didn't." She waved her hand around in the air. "After his pain lessened, *he* tried to reach out to me in that letter of apology—the one I didn't get because Jessica hijacked it. Consequently, my nonresponse led him to believe that I was through with him. The one thing he asked me never to do was leave him. Yet I did. I left him, like you had left him by giving him up, like Cassie had left him by dying. The moment I walked out of that house in Amherst was the moment he shut the door to his heart. And then thinking that he'd move on, I punished him by denying him the joy of watching his child grow inside me. Don't you think that was mean of me?"

Felicia merely shrugged, obviously not wanting to call her out.

Michelle allowed her gaze to wander toward the pool where her son was splashing water on the girls, and then swimming away when they tried to splash him back. Her heart leaped with a mixture of love and regret. "I plotted to raise Little Erik alone and deny him and Erik a father and son relationship. That amazing, loving bond they now share almost didn't happen." She shuddered at the thought. "Keeping Little Erik's existence from Erik, and you and Philippe, too, was selfish of me, especially when I knew firsthand what having an absentee father could do to a child."

Felicia's eyes softened. "My God. We're always so focused on a man hurting his woman and then not going after her to make it right, we seldom stop to evaluate the woman's part in the breakup."

"Boys are raised to be strong, tough, and not show their feelings, their hurts, not to ask for help, not to admit they're wrong. And when they behave accordingly, they're labeled as jerks." She balked at the hypocrisy. "I'm not going to raise my son like that. I'm going to teach him that it's okay to cry, to ask for help, and to admit that he's wrong way before the situation gets out of control. I didn't see the double standard until I took a good hard look at myself and realized what a selfish bitch I was back then."

"Michelle, darling, you weren't. You were hurting."

"So was Erik," she responded vehemently. "Why should my pain excuse my actions, when you don't allow his pain to excuse his? By keeping him from his father, I would have messed up my son and scarred him psychologically and emotionally for life. That was insensitive. I was not being a good mother. It wasn't Erik's job to be perfect in order for me to love him, no more than it was mine to be perfect for him to love me. Once we made a commitment to each other, our jobs were to love one another, realize that we're perfect for each other in spite of our mistakes and inadequacies. Love is like a two-lane street with two motorists and no guardrail between them. Neither is blameless when a collision occurs. We go up and down and back and forth in separate directions, but always with the hope of meeting somewhere in the middle for a magical, magnetic connection. Then we meld and cruise together blissfully until one of us hits a pothole again. We both messed up. We were both to blame," she said with finality. "So get off my husband's back, please."

"You're an oracle, wise beyond your years," Felicia murmured in wonder and admiration. "You're barely thirty years old, yet you have the wisdom of a ninety-year-old woman."

"Erik and I are learning a lot from our sessions with Samantha, and I listen in when she counsels the women and children at my foundation."

"My son is so lucky to have you in his life. You have done for him what I should have been there to do when he was growing up—teach him how to love, to cherish and hold on to those he loves. By giving him away, I taught him that love wasn't worth fighting for. We should have all chosen better—Philippe, Danielle, and me. We were so caught up in our own wants and needs that none of us stopped to think about how our decisions and actions would affect him. We were selfish. It's clear as day to me now."

"If you could do it again, would you have chosen not to have him?"

"Oh God, no." Felicia pressed her hand to her chest as if it hurt. "I can't imagine my life without him and the four beautiful grandchildren he's given me. But I would have kept him. I would have raised him myself instead of handing him over to my best friend. That's my regret." Her voice broke on a sob.

Michelle reached over and patted her on the arm. "We all have regrets, Felicia. Don't beat yourself up. You did what you thought was right at the time." She settled down into her lounge and studied a butterfly dancing around a bed of flowers near the bottom step of the cabana before she spoke again. "Even though Erik constantly shows me how much he loves and appreciates me, it was still a nice surprise to read his side of the story along with the public."

Felicia gasped. "You didn't know anything about it?"

"None of us ladies did. Kaya stumbled upon a copy at Fontaine Enterprises this morning and called the rest of us." She wondered how her friend was doing with her chat with Bryce. "I don't usually read *Granite Falls People News*. With Erik gone so much, and four kids to raise, not to mention the time I put in at the foundation, I hardly have time to read my basal thermometer."

Felicia shot upright. "Are you and Erik thinking about

having another child already?" She tossed a glance at Fiona. "She's only seven months old."

"No, Mom." Michelle adjusted her sunglasses. "We're using the rhythm method, so I have to keep daily track of my body temperature, among other things."

"Does that really work?"

"It did with Fiona. We conceived her when we were ready for another child. We weren't using birth control with Tiffany which is why she's so close in age to Little Erik."

Felicia expelled a sigh of relief and reclined into the lounge. "Not that I don't love my grandchildren, but you need to give your body a break, girl. Three children in five years is a lot."

Michelle regarded her with amusement in her eyes and voice. "Why, they wear you out on sleepover nights, Grandma?"

"I'd be lying if I say they didn't. Whenever Little Erik leaves, I always feel like I've spent a week in the ring with Muhammad Ali. Tiffany, I can deal with. She's quiet and sweet, and I hope Fiona will be just like her."

"I think you're just partial to girls. Did you wish Erik was a girl?"

"No. I just wished for a healthy baby." Her smile faded a little. "Sometime I wish I had another child, though. Erik was lonely growing up."

"He told me. That's one of the reasons we decided to have seven chil—"

"Seven!" Felicia barked. "You mean you're doing this four more times?"

Michelle laughed at the absurd look on Felicia's face. "That was the plan, but Fiona was such a difficult birth that

Erik and I got to thinking about adopting. The world is overflowing with unwanted and unloved children who need homes. We have more than enough to provide for them. I fell in love with Precious right off the bat, so I know I can love another woman's child as my own."

"Michelle, that is sweet and generous of you, but you have to realize that your unconditional love for Precious stems from the fact that you love her father. It might not be the same with another random child."

"I don't agree with that. I loved Precious long before I knew I loved Erik." She smiled. "He was a bonus, a sexy one. But I feel that God gave me a heart that can love any child who needs love. That is my special gift to the world." She wrapped her arms about her stomach. "I want to give Erik another son of his own, though. Little Erik needs a brother, or two. When his father is away, he's the only male in the house, and he's always surrounded by girls when we get together with the other families. Jason is too old to be bothered with him. Eli is too young to play the games he wants to play, and Alex is still an infant."

"Hmm. I never looked at it that way." Felicia glanced at Philippe wading knee-deep through the water with his eyes closed, his arms outstretched, and making zombie noises, while the children scampered to keep out of his range. "Except for Philippe, he's the only male in the pool. Maybe you need to put other kids on your playtime list, like Ethan's little brothers, Neal and Sean. They're around Little Erik's age."

"The Bennetts spend a lot of time in England. Little Erik needs brothers who're with him all the time. An adopted one, close to his age, and one who is blood related."

"My son is an OB/GYN, so I'm sure he knows of ways to increase the odds of his Y's beating his X's to your eggs."

"Mom! Telephone."

Michelle sat up and turned around to see Precious, a slender twelve-year-old, descending the steps leading from the porch off the first-floor playroom. She was a bubbling beauty in a pair of white shorts and a yellow top, and long curly brown hair tumbling down to her waist—a far cry from the gloomy seven-year-old little girl Michelle had met five years ago. "Who is it?" Michelle asked as Precious stood over her.

"I don't know. She won't give a name. She says she needs to speak to you or Dad." She handed the phone to Michelle and sprinted over to sit on the edge of Felicia's lounge. "What are you reading, Grandma?" She picked up the magazine and gasped. "Sweet!"

At least it wasn't about Erik, or they won't be asking for him, Michelle thought as she watched Precious flip through the magazine to find the article. And it wasn't a staff member from her foundation in Evergreen or they wouldn't be asking for Erik.

Michelle worried every time Erik was on a mission in a third-world country, especially those that were ravaged by war. He and his team from Doctors Abroad, an organization that serviced war-torn countries and those suffering from natural disasters, were currently on location in South America. Even though the country was politically stable as far as factious outbreaks were concerned, there were still a lot of things that could go wrong, like falling victim to insect and waterborne diseases. *Lord, keep them safe.* She raised the phone to her ears. "Hello, this is Mrs. LaCrosse."

"Good afternoon, Mrs. LaCrosse. This is Nancy Beck from Cape Hill."

"Oh, hello. How are you?" She forced a smile at Felicia and Precious who were watching her curiously. Predicting it might be unpleasant news, she slid her feet into her sandals, descended the steps of the cabana, and walked along a cobbled path, lined on both sides with blooming flowerbeds and pruned shrubbery.

"I'm afraid I have some bad news," Mrs. Beck said.

Michelle's steps faltered as she turned a corner and headed for the tennis courts that were out of sight and earshot of the cabana. *I really don't want to deal with Sarah's schizophrenia right now.* The last two times Cape Hill had called, her family had been put on an emotional roller coaster ride for months. It had drained them mentally and physically.

"Are you still there, Mrs. LaCrosse?"

"Yes. I'm here. What's wrong with Sarah? Did she have another relapse?"

"I'm sorry, but it's worse than that. Mrs. Turner passed away this afternoon."

A knot formed in Michelle's chest. She collapsed onto the picnic bench near the wire fence of the court. "We—we saw her two weeks ago, and she was in good health. What—what happened?"

"We won't be certain until a pathologist does an autopsy. I'm guessing she might have suffered a stroke from cardiac arrest or a cerebral aneurysm." She paused. "You were aware of the possible side effects from the antipsychotic drugs she was taking."

"Yes we were, but we didn't expect it to be so quick and

sudden. Weren't there any symptoms that she was in trouble? What about her alarm bracelet?"

"She didn't sound an alarm."

Michelle rushed her fingers through her short black hair. "Why wasn't someone with her? Aren't we paying for around-the-clock supervision?"

"Your questions are valid, Mrs. LaCrosse, but Sarah apparently died in her sleep. She had breakfast and lunch at the usual times today, and after a little socializing, she took her customary afternoon nap. Her nurse found her when she went to administer her medication. We tried to resuscitate her, but —I'm sorry."

Michelle bit into her lower lip. *Poor Sarah, dying alone.*

"You can take some comfort in the fact that she probably didn't suffer," Mrs. Beck said.

"Where—where is she, now?"

"She's still here with us. I'm calling for instructions from you and your husband."

"Only my husband can make decisions concerning Sarah, and he's not here. He's out of the country. I expect him back on Friday."

"We'll keep her here until he returns then."

"Thank you. I'll try to call him, see if he can come home a day early."

"There's no rush, Mrs. LaCrosse. There's nothing more your husband can do for Sarah. Because of him, the last three years of her life were filled with happiness and meaning. We really enjoyed having her here with us. And I must tell you," she added on a choke, "she smiled for days after every visit. She carried Precious' picture everywhere, and took pride in telling everyone that she was her grandbaby."

That bit of information did ease Michelle's sadness. Sarah had been living in Connecticut when Michelle joined the LaCrosse family as Precious' nanny. Erik used to visit his former mother-in-law alone because Precious was too young to cope with the environment of a mental institution. A few years ago, when Precious began asking questions about her grandmother, Erik moved Sarah to a facility in Vermont—just a few hours away. Her mental state had improved significantly after Precious began spending time with her, so much so that they'd been able to bring her to the estate for Christmas and Thanksgiving a couple times. But then early last year...

"Mrs. LaCrosse?"

Michelle started at the voice on the other end. "Yes, I'm sorry."

"Please accept our condolences."

"Thank you. Thank you, Mrs. Beck. We'll be in touch soon." Michelle hung up the phone, took off her sunglasses, and let the tears flow down her cheeks. She wasn't related to Sarah. She hadn't known her that long, but she did know her, and that was enough for the dear woman's death to affect her.

Michelle had no idea how long she'd been sitting there, but when she felt a hand on her shoulder, she didn't need to turn around to know it was Felicia. It was quiet, so quiet, she could hear the leaves rustling in the trees above her. The raucous from the pool had ceased. She whipped her head around as her maternal instinct kicked in. "Where're the kids? Where's Fiona? Is Precious watching her?"

Felicia sat down beside her. "No need to panic, dear. Mrs. Hayes took Fiona into the nursery. Precious took off when Jason called, and Philippe and Catherine took the kids inside to clean up before they all head over to Mountainview Café for ice cream. I'm supposed to meet them there. Everything is being handled." She placed her hand over Michelle's lying on the picnic table. "Why were you sitting all alone out here crying?"

"It's Sarah."

"Hmm. I figured it was something like that when you left the cabana. Did she have another relapse?"

Michelle shook her head in slow motion, wishing that was all it was. "No, not this time. She's gone, Felicia."

"Oh, poor Sarah. What happened?"

"She apparently died in her sleep. Either from cardiac arrest or a brain aneurysm. We won't know for sure until the autopsy."

Felicia pulled her into her arms. "She's in a better place. You know that, don't you? She was having more bad than good days lately, even with the new medication. At least now she's at peace. Her mind is at rest."

Michelle sniffled. "I know. It's just unfair that when Precious was getting to know her grandmother, she ups and dies. Sarah was the last tie to her mother." She pushed out of Felicia's embrace and wiped her hands down her face. "She will miss her a lot."

"She will be devastated, but she has you and her father, Philippe and me, her siblings, and the extended support of the Fontaine, Andretti, and Andreas families. She has a lot more people in her corner than she had when her mother died."

"Precious has experienced more deaths than any little girl should have to. Seven years ago, it was her mother, then five years ago it was Danielle, another grandmother whom she loved, and now Sarah."

Felicia glanced off across the green lawn, her eyes glowing with apparent memories—both good and bad.

Michelle leaned her head on Felicia's shoulder. "You still miss her, don't you? You still miss Danielle," she said of Felicia's best friend who was once married to Philippe, until she lost her battle with cancer.

Felicia snapped out of her daydream and patted Michelle's hand. "I do, but let's not go down that road. Precious should be our only focus at the moment. Are you up to breaking the news to her, or do you want me to?"

Michelle could understand why talking about Danielle's death would be bittersweet for Felicia. If Danielle hadn't died, Felicia and Philippe wouldn't be together. Theirs was a love that had to wait decades to be fulfilled—empathy, sympathy, and loyalty being the main reasons. As far as Michelle could tell, Philippe and Felicia were blissfully happy, but she was also certain that they both missed Danielle and the friendship they all once shared—a friendship much like the one she now shared with Kaya, Shaina, and Tashi, but even more significantly the one she shared with Yasmine, her childhood BFF. She missed Yasmine, every single day.

Michelle sighed at the intricacies of that thing called *love*, and the sacrifices, the joys, and sorrows that came along with it. But Lord, *love* was so worth it in the end.

"Michelle, you want me to tell Precious about her grandmother?" Felicia reiterated.

"No. I'll wait for Erik. I think he should be the one to tell her. I should probably let Mrs. Hayes know, though. She was very fond of Sarah," Michelle said, suddenly feeling the weight of planning a funeral pressing down on her. "She often visited her on her days off."

"Fancy that. Martha and Sarah socializing. The Turners were so damned stuck-up back when the kids began dating. You should have seen the look on Cassie's parents' faces when they met Erik for the first time. Cassie hadn't yet told them that he was biracial. But once they learned he was a LaCrosse, they changed their tunes real fast. I guess money and prestige were more important than color to them. Sarah was the same way with Martha when she started working for Erik and Cassie. But Martha brought her to heel." She uttered a dry laugh. "Don't ask me how. Martha won't say."

With generous affection, Michelle recalled how Mrs. Hayes had pulled strings to get her the job as Precious' nanny —the job that had changed her life forever. She owed that woman her life, her happiness. Mrs. Hayes wasn't keeping house anymore, but she still lived with them as a member of the family, and she insisted on cooking their meals. The children adored her and she fussed over them like a mother hen.

"Michelle."

Michelle saw Kaya coming toward them. She was still wearing the dress she'd worn to their morning meeting with Desire. She must have come straight from Bryce's office, Michelle thought, anxious to know how it went.

Felicia stood up. "I have to get to the café to help Philippe and Catherine with the kids. Yours included," she said, hugging Kaya.

"How long are you planning to be there? I can come by and pick up the girls in a little while. You and Philippe will probably be ready for a break."

Felicia waved dismissively. "Nonsense. We'll call you. If

you're home, we'll drop them off. If you're here, we'll just bring them back with us."

"Thanks, Felicia."

"Don't let the news about Sarah get you down," Felicia said to Michelle.

"Okay, Mom. See you later."

"What did she mean about Sarah?" Kaya asked when Felicia left. "Did something happen to her?"

"She died. We just got the news."

"Oh, that's sad." Kaya sat down beside her.

"It is, but at least she isn't suffering anymore. She's at peace. So how did your talk with Bryce go?" she asked, anxious to change the subject. She knew Kaya well enough to know that any talk of death always took her to when her sister and brother-in-law died in that tragic accident.

Kaya smiled. "He was mad at first, as we expected, but he listened as I presented my case. I talked about my experiences with my mother and how facing her freed me to go on with my life. I didn't tell him that I spoke with you. I wanted to keep you out of it."

"I appreciate that. The last thing I want is Bryce giving me the evil eye."

Kaya elbowed her in the side. "He'll never do that. He thinks very highly of you. He appreciates that you talked me out of leaving Granite Falls when he was on the fence about me and Pilar."

"Is it enough for him to consider giving Desire a chance, though?"

Kaya stared at Michelle, her lips puckering and her eyes aglow with naughtiness.

"Oh my God," Michelle exclaimed. "You lost your

panties, didn't you? You did it right there in his office. So did you lay it on him before, during, or after, you nasty girl?"

Kaya let her laugh fly. "I'm Mrs. Commando," she screamed, waving her hands high above her head, and twisting her body like an ocean wave.

"Hah! I don't believe you. Here I was thinking that seduction was the wrong approach. I guess you know your husband better than I do."

Kaya dropped her hands on her lap. "Well, true to his nature, he did huff and puff at first, but I calmed him down enough to listen to me. And," she added with a touch of regret, "we didn't do it. There was no time, but he made me take my panties off just before I left—in the waiting area outside his office, of all places. He said they would help him consider," she said without a trace of embarrassment.

"Bryce is bad. They're all bad," Michelle murmured, remembering how Erik had brought her to her first orgasm on a moonlit night in the parking lot of Ristorante Andreas, five years ago.

"Hopefully my panties will swing him over to our side. Desire has ideas and vision that are unimaginable. I can already see myself walking down my own aisle lined with orchids, and Bryce standing at the front under a trellis waiting for me."

"I know. I've been picturing my walk toward Erik since we left the restaurant. Between the trial of the men who killed Tashi's mother, the sibling rivalry going on in the Andretti household, and now Sarah's death, we need something glamorous and exciting to look forward to. We need balance. Bryce is our only hope."

Kaya pulled her smart phone from her purse. "I have to

ask Desire for a little more time. I pray she understands that this isn't an easy decision for Bryce."

"She will. It can't be easy for her family, either. They lost a daughter and a sister. As deranged as Victoria was, she was their family. You know, this wedding could turn out to be more than simply the four most powerful couples in town renewing their vows. It could be a symbol for healing throughout Granite Falls."

"From your lips to God's ears, girl."

CHAPTER SIX

Andretti Estate – Tuesday - the next afternoon...

"What's that one, Aria?" Shaina pointed to the floor-to ceiling LCD video wall in Massimo's man cave. She'd returned home from an informative appointment to enjoy a picnic lunch with Aria at one of the fountains on the estate. Afterward, they'd taken a walk around the grounds before coming inside. Shaina had been quizzing Aria for the last ten minutes to build on her already large vocabulary arsenal. "What's that animal called? Do you know?"

"El-elo-elophant, Mommy. That's an elophant. Elophant's big, and he has big, big ears." Aria opened her arms wide and tugged on her ears for emphasis.

"Good girl. That's an el*e*phant," Shaina replied, putting emphasis on the second syllable. At fifteen months, Aria was far more advanced in her oral communication skills than most children her age. She was already stringing sentences together, especially in Italian, probably because her father had read and spoken to her in Italian while Shaina was carrying her.

Shaina, herself, had picked up a lot of the language and its euphonious cadence by listening to her husband's nightly monologues directed at their unborn child. Massimo was adamant that Aria became multilingual, so from the moment she was born, he began speaking to her in several languages, every single day.

With the Andretti curse hanging over them, neither wanted to know the sex of the child. Shaina's throat tightened as she recalled the moment Mass had gazed into his daughter's face for the first time. He'd been too choked to speak, so with tears running down his cheeks, he'd just stared at her for a long time, his blue eyes glowing with amazement and rapture. Once he found his voice, he cradled her close to his heart—the baby still covered in amniotic fluid, and with her umbilical cord still attached—as he murmured over and over again, "*Mio figlia. Mio figlia bella, dolce. Papà ti amo. Papà ti amo, così tanto, Aria.*"

When she was an infant, he would sit with her in his arms when he came home from the office, and tell her about his day, about the legacies of Andretti Industries and *La Banca di Bianchi*, the European chain of banks he'd founded in her grandmother's name. And sometimes he would take her for long walks around the estate. He'd promised her that even though she was a girl, as his firstborn, it was her birthright to inherit the title of CEO for both companies, no matter how many sons he fathered after her.

Aria would stare at him intently with her big brown eyes, and make gurgling sounds and intense facial expressions as if she understood what he was saying. When she finally began to develop her language skills, Massimo's eyes always lit up with pride and love each time Aria responded correctly to his questions. His daily one-sided conversations with her were probably the reason she began talking long before she could walk. He'd actually broken down and cried the first time Aria had reached for him and said, "Dada," the very first word she ever spoke.

Shaina cleared away the lump that had formed in her throat. "*Cosa dice l'elefante*, Aria?" she asked. Italian was the only language Shaina had mastered so far, and with which she felt confident enough to contribute to her daughter's multilingual abilities.

Aria wrinkled her nose and pouted her cute rosy little lips in thought. "*L'elo—L'elefante dice, bbbrrrrr, pppphhhhttt, errrrrrrhhhh…*" she said, with spit flying everywhere.

Shaina laughed at her baby-girl's attempt to mimic one of the most difficult sounds in the world. She was way off, but close enough for her mama. "*Brava! Brava, la mia ragazza!*" She gave her child an affectionate squeeze, and pushed a button on the projector remote.

"*Puttycat*, Mommy. Nice *puttycat*. Bari. Bari." Aria screamed with excitement and sat straight up on Shaina's lap with both arms stretched toward the screen as if she wanted to hug the cat.

"Yes, that's Jabari." Shaina rested her chin on Aria's head as they watched the week-old video of Mass and Aria on a blanket with Jabari outside their private camp, close to the Masai Mara National Reserve where Jabari lived. The camp was situated in the Lamai Triangle along the banks of the Mara River, and a safe distance from the mainstream safari route to allow absolute privacy. It was more like a luxurious outdoor hotel with spectacular views of the Mara River and the breathtaking landscapes of the Kenyan plains beyond it.

Since they'd visited the motherland in April, a family visit to Africa hadn't been on Shaina and Massimo's agenda when they'd planned a short vacation weeks ago. Their plan was to leave Aria at home with Azi and Reese, her nanny, while they spent some quality time together on her private island in the Mediterranean. But the day before they were set to leave, Servio, Jabari's handler called to tell Massimo that his prized leopard had wandered into lion territory, and had been attacked by the king of a pride. They'd immediately boarded the jet to Kenya with Azi in tow.

"Bari's hurt, Mommy."

Shaina watched Jabari struggle to get up only to plump back down in pain. "Yes, sweetie, Bari is hurt." As Jabari attempted to get up again, with Massimo's help this time, Shaina couldn't help but think about the day when she entered Massimo's master suite for the first time and almost died from fright when Jabari leaped at her. Up to this day, Shaina still couldn't believe she hadn't raced out of this mansion and put as much distance as possible between her and Massimo Andretti when he'd left her out in the hallway while he caged his leopard. That seemed like a lifetime ago. Now, she couldn't imagine her life without Massimo, or this darling child they'd created together.

"Daddy cries, Mommy. Daddy cries for Bari. Daddy loves Bari. Aria loves Bari, too. Do you love Bari, Mommy?"

"Yes, baby. I love Bari. I love him a lot." Shaina swallowed as she watched Massimo pick Jabari up in his arms and walk toward a wooded area that bordered the rear of their camp. Aria was toddling along beside him and he made no attempt to hide the river of tears flowing down his face and falling into Jabari's fur. The video ended when her husband and child disappeared into the trees, because at that precise moment, Shaina had put down the camera and let her own tears fall. Jabari was twenty-six years old. Most leopards lived up to twenty-one years in captivity. Jabari was living dangerously on borrowed time. Massimo had spent more time with his beloved cat than he'd spent with her and Aria on that trip. She didn't begrudge that cat for a moment. If it weren't for Jabari, Massimo wouldn't be alive today.

Jabari's condition had improved while they were there, but because he'd wandered away from his territory in the first place, and because of other age-related concerns, Mass had decided to keep him at the camp with Servio and a few other gamekeepers to watch over him. Shaina welled up as she recalled holding Massimo's hand for most of the flight back home. Even though he hadn't said it, his expression portrayed his thoughts that it might be the last time he would see his oldest and dearest friend alive. He'd wanted to stay longer, but Aria had come down with stomach cramps and they had to get her back home. Thank God, it was just a mild case of stomach flu, and she was fine now. Jabari was still on his way to a full recovery.

Since they got home, Mass had been on pins and needles, fearing every day that he'd get the dreaded call. He was prepared, but the news would be difficult for him. Jabari was the last link he had to his past. His grandfather, whom he loved, had given him the cub when they'd gone to Africa to scatter his mother's ashes in the Serengeti. Jabari symbolized family ties for Mass.

Mass loved Shaina and Aria with all his heart, but except for Azi—whose kinship was so distant, it was senseless calling her a cousin—he had no one to carry into the future to remind him of his past. At least Shaina had her brother, and yes, Mass had Galen, but Galen reminded Mass of the most unhappy times of his childhood.

They'd been getting along well in the beginning. Galen had been excited to learn about their father, his paternal roots, and Andretti Industries. He'd seemed elated to have a family, a brother, in-laws, and eventually a niece whom he adored. That was until he returned from a trip to England earlier this year. He'd definitely changed, and one night after dinner, he'd asked Mass why he waited six years after their father's death to reach out to him. Mass had told him that he simply wasn't ready—which was the truth. Galen then accused him of wanting to keep the Andretti fortune for himself. Shaina didn't know what Galen's mother's family had told him about his parents' relationship, but he was angry, confused, and evidently uninformed.

Mass had ordered him off the estate. Galen had refused to leave, stating that he had as much right to the Andretti fortune as Mass did. Shaina had to place herself physically between them to prevent a fistfight from breaking out. After Mass stormed out of the dining room, she'd warned Galen never to broach that topic with her husband again since he had no idea what his mother's affair with their father had done to Massimo. It had almost killed him—literally. She'd also recommended that he move out of the mansion and into Mass' lakeside villa until the tension between them dissipated. Galen had eventually apologized to Mass, but his accusations had put a huge rift in their relationship. They were civil to each other, but the burgeoning sibling camaraderie they once shared was gone. It was anyone's guess if it would ever return.

"I want banana, Mommy? Banana. Banana. Ba..." Aria

slapped her on the thigh while she repeated the word *banana* over and over again as if saying it would make one magically appear.

Shaina glanced at the blank screen and wondered how long they'd been sitting there in silence. She took a deep steadying breath as Aria turned on her lap and wrapped her little arms around her neck, her knees digging deep into Shaina's stomach.

"Banana, Mommy. Banana," Aria said again.

"*Come è chiedere una banana correttamente*, Aria?"

"No. No," Aria whined, tightening her body in defiance and thumping Shaina on the back. "Banana. I want banana."

"Aria, *non hai una banana fino a quando si chiede correttamente*." Getting her to say *please* and *thank you* was more difficult than getting her to speak in multiple languages. But Shaina was insistent, and had instructed Reese and all the servants not to give her anything she asked for until she said *please*, and to take it away if she refused to say *thank you*. Aria's screams and tantrums when she didn't get her way didn't faze Shaina in the least. She was not raising a spoiled child who thought that the rules of etiquette and simple manners didn't apply to her, just because she was born into wealth. Inside, though, she smiled each time her daughter fought against authority.

"Like mother, like daughter," was Massimo's usual response to Aria's stubborn trait.

After a few tense moments, Aria raised her head from Shaina's shoulder and gazed at her with wide sparkling dark brown eyes. "*Per favore, può Aria hanno una banana, Mamma?*"

"*Certamente, la mia bambina.*" Shaina grinned. It was Aria's snack time, and bananas were her favorite treat.

"*Ti amo, Mamma.*" Aria clasped her hands on Shaina's cheeks and kissed her full on the lips.

"Just like your daddy," Shaina said on a chuckle. They both thought they could kiss her into submission. Well, Massimo usually kissed her... Never mind. "*Mamma ama anche tu, Aria. Moltissima.* "Come on. Let's go find you a banana. She hugged her daughter to her chest as she vacated the leather sofa and walked toward the stairs leading to the second floor.

Aria wrapped her arms around Shaina's neck and her legs around her waist. "Aria loves bananas. Mommy loves bananas, *troppo?*"

"Yes, Mommy loves bananas," Shaina lied as she headed for the kitchen. She couldn't stand the smell of the fruit lately. She hadn't fully understood why, until this morning. "Perhaps we can have *Bibi* peel it and cut it up for you." She wasn't about to stick around the kitchen and ruin Aria's favorite snack time indulgence.

"*Bibi* Azi. *Bibi, bibi, bibi...*" Aria crooned the Swahili word for *grandmother* with a new round of excitement.

Shaina smiled at her enthusiasm. From the moment she'd brought her home from the hospital, Aria and Azi had developed a special kind of love for each other, so it was only fitting that Massimo encouraged his daughter to call Azi *Grandma.* The sweet old woman who'd taken care of him since he was ten years old was a beloved and important part of his family. Shaina loved that Aria preferred to spend more time with Azi than she did with her nanny when Shaina wasn't around. Truth be told, Shaina only kept Reese around to give Azi a break from Aria, and so she and Massimo could hide out in their love nest when Azi wasn't available.

For doing practically nothing, the lucky young woman

was cashing a hefty paycheck each month, living in one of the most luxurious mansions in the northeast, and flying in private jets to some of the most exotic places on the planet. Not a bad life for a twenty-year-old girl. Shaina wished her life had been that plush when she was Reese's age. Instead, she'd been struggling to keep a roof over her and her brother Cameron's heads and food in their bellies while hiding out from the law and a vengeful criminal at the same time.

"Oops." Shaina stopped short of a collision with Azi under the archway leading into the kitchen.

"Miz Shaina. I was just on my way to find you. It's Aria's snack time." She ruffled Aria's hair. "Did you have a good time with Mama, my little angel?"

"*Bibi*." Aria lunged into Azi's arms. "Banana, *Bibi*. Please."

"Bibi has your banana all cut up with a side of homemade vanilla gelato, for her baby. But first we have to wash your hands, make sure they're nice and clean."

"Wash hands. Nice and clean." Aria rubbed her palms together, excitedly.

While Azi took Aria over to one of the three sinks in the recently renovated, contemporary kitchen, Shaina glanced at her three young apprentices—one male and two females—who were already busy with dinner preparations.

Tomorrow would mark the twenty-fifth anniversary of Massimo's mother and sister's deaths. As customary, Uncle Alessandro, Aunt Bella, Adam, and now Tashi, Alex, and Paul had been invited to dinner in honor of the two lives that had been cut short. They were having the dinner tonight because the Andreases were leaving for Ohio tomorrow for the verdict at the trial of the three men who'd murdered Tashi's mom, nineteen years ago.

"There you go, *mwana*." Azi set Aria into her high chair at the kitchen table, filled her cup with water, and placed it on her tray.

Shaina swallowed as Aria picked up a slice of banana and placed it into her mouth, and then immediately reached for another as if she'd just come off a long fast. Even the sight of the fruit was making Shaina queasy.

"I noticed you have developed an intolerance for the smell of bananas, lately, Miz Shaina."

Shaina averted Azi's inquisitive eyes by focusing on one of the young women dressing the turkey they would be having tonight. Thanksgiving was Massimo's mother's favorite time of year, so they always had turkey on the anniversary of her death. "Well, I—" Shaina stopped and tilted her head as the notes of *Für Elise* came floating through the air. Anxiety spurted through her. "Is Massimo home?"

"I don't believe he is. I haven't seen him." Azi made the sign of the Cross over her chest.

"Oh my God. Keep Aria with you." Shaina sprinted out of the kitchen. The music room was one place where nobody was allowed to go. It was the room where Massimo had his last happy memory of his mother, and ironically, his worst. Except for Trudy, the maid assigned to maintaining it, only family—Azi included—were allowed in there. Massimo kept it locked, except on days when he wanted it aired and dusted. Today was such a day. After the celebratory dinner, the family usually gathered around the piano while Massimo played *Für Elise*, the only tune he could play—the tune he'd learned just to honor his mother. It brought tears to everyone's eyes every single time.

Nobody in this household would dare sit at that piano and attempt to play a tune, so Shaina knew that it had to be Galen. Apart from Massimo, he was the only other person in the house who played the piano. What the heck was he doing here? He wasn't banned from the mansion, but since he moved into the lakeside villa, he always called before he visited. Why the hell had he not today of all days so she could warn him to stay away? He was the last person Mass should have to deal with today.

Shortly after he'd moved in with them, Shaina had caught him trying the door to the music room. She'd warned him never to go in there. When he'd asked why, she'd told him that he should take it up with his brother. She didn't think it was her place to discuss Massimo's mother with him. She was certain that when he was ready, Massimo would share that part of himself with Galen. *If ever.*

Galen must have been wandering around the mansion, and finding the door opened, seized the opportunity to go inside. Damn it! Why did that boy have to challenge his brother's patience so incessantly? There would be hell to pay if Mass found out that the son of the woman he blamed for his mother and sister's deaths had been in the room where she had received the news that sent her into early labor, and her and her child to an even earlier grave. Mass was certain that it was Galen's mother who'd called his on that fateful day twenty-five years ago, but he couldn't prove it. He'd been too young at the time to even think of performing the kind of investigation that would give him answers, and by the time he was old enough, the evidence was long gone.

As she turned a corner, Shaina's heart sank to the floor when she spotted her husband running from the opposite direction. He was dressed in his suit and tie and must have just walked through the front door when the music started. She quickened her pace as he disappeared into the music room.

It immediately became quiet, then the distinctive sounds of blows being delivered to a body, followed by curses in Italian, Spanish, and she thought, French, erupted.

Shaina jumped back from the door, screaming, when Galen came flying through the air to land on his ass on the floor in the hallway. He was a big man, but evidently not too big for her husband to pick up and toss around like one of Aria's stuffed animals.

In the next breath, Massimo tore past her like a hurricane, the wind in his wake almost knocking her off her feet.

"What is wrong with you?" Galen yelled as Mass went at him. "It's just a damn room. What's so special about it? Have you gone mad?"

Mass collared him, picked him up off the floor, and shook him. "I'll show you mad." He delivered a crushing blow to Galen's jaw that sent him back to the floor. "I will break you." He dropped his knees into Galen's stomach and tightened his hands around his throat.

Shaina flew into action, all thoughts for her own safety vanishing. "Mass, stop!" She grabbed him around the waist and pulled with no success, so she tried to pry his hands from Galen's throat.

"Stay back, Shaina. This is between me and my brother. It's about time I taught this little bastard that he can't just walk into my house and take it over."

At least he'd called him his brother—bastard or not.

82

There was hope yet. Shaina tugged harder as Galen struggled to free himself from Mass's chokehold. "Stop, Massimo! You'll kill him," she screamed as Galen began to gag and his face turned white. "Is that what you want? Let him go."

Mass let go, but not before he'd delivered another punch to Galen's jaw.

As she watched Galen panting on the floor with blood trickling from his mouth, Shaina blinked away the image of Mass curled up on the floor in the New York City penthouse suite after Cameron had taken out his six years of anger on him. What was it with men, always believing they could solve their problems with cockfights?

"You had no business in there!" Massimo trotted around Galen, clenching and unclenching his fists as he glared at him like a lion glared at a beaten challenger who'd tried to usurp him. "After what your mother did to mine, you have no business here! You don't belong here. Not today of all days."

"What my mother did to yours? What about what yours did to mine, and me?" Galen declared, once he could talk again. He dabbed at the blood that had dripped on to his white Polo shirt. "Because of your mother, I never knew my father. My parents were denied a life together because of her jealousy. She—"

"You son-of-a—"

CHAPTER SEVEN

"Massimo, no!" Shaina planted herself in front of Mass to keep him from going after Galen. He would definitely choke the life out of him this time. She didn't want her husband to end up in prison for murder. She glared at her brother-in-law. "What are you talking about, Galen? His mother was married to his father. Your mother got in between them."

"Why are you defending him, Shaina? He only married you to get all this." He waved his hand around indicating the entire estate. "It probably would have fallen to me if he hadn't tricked you. Now I understand why he didn't contact me for six years."

So he'd read the article in *Granite Falls People News*, and like everyone else, he only had half the story. That's why he'd shown up without calling first. He thought he had a right to the Andretti fortune.

"Excuse me, Mr. Andretti. Would you like some assistance?"

Shaina turned to see two security guards from the

gatehouse coming toward them. Somebody must have called them when the fight started. Shaina laced her arm around her husband's waist and walked him away from Galen. He was rigid with rage, his heart beating a mile a second and his chest heaving like he'd just run a marathon. "Escort Mr. Carmichael out of here. And don't let him back on to the property until Mr. Andretti gives the okay."

"Yes, Mrs. Andretti. Right away. Come on, buddy." The one named Kurt pulled Galen to his feet.

"This isn't over, brother," Galen barked at Mass. "I have every right to be here. Andretti blood flows in my veins, too."

Shaina tightened her hold on her husband and watched with mixed emotions as Galen limped away between the two men. He was so freaking clueless, just like Cameron had been when he'd attacked Massimo. For that reason, Shaina felt pity for him.

"The show is over. You can all get back to work now," she said to the servants who'd wandered into the hallway and on to the balconies above to watch the fight. "This blood needs to be cleaned from the floor." She turned to the maid standing nearby and wringing her hands in front of her. "Trudy, the music room must be tidied and ready for our guests."

Trudy snapped out of her daze. "Yes, Mrs. Andretti."

Shaina led Mass to the elevator. On the third floor, she headed into the direction of *Il Nido d'Amore*, one of the two places on the estate Mass felt closest to his mother, since the music room was out at the moment.

She was grateful that Azi had kept Aria away from the cataclysmic mêlée. She never wanted her daughter to see her father in this state. *She* never wanted to see him like this again, and as soon as she returned from her honeymoon, she was going after the Carmichael clan. Judith Carmichael had evidently fed her family a boatload of lies about Massimo's mother, and she was going to set them straight.

They'd all been expecting this showdown. She'd heard the servants whispering among themselves. Those who'd been on staff when Massimo's mother was alive, and had been reinstated after Shaina and Massimo set up house, couldn't understand why he would want his father's bastard son in his life, and most alarmingly in his mother's home. Yet, despite their feelings, like devoted servants, they'd treated Galen like an Andretti while he'd been living under Massimo's roof.

Shaina felt responsible for the trouble Galen's presence was causing Massimo. She was the one who'd encouraged him to invite his brother to the U.S and to the Andretti estate in the first place. Even after their first fight, she'd encouraged Mass to ask Galen to be his Best Man at their wedding. He'd grudgingly done so, just to please her. Maybe she was trying too hard to get the brothers back to the amicable place they were when they first met. Maybe some sleeping dogs were better left undisturbed. She had no idea if they would ever be able to bridge this widening gap between them.

Inside *Il Nido d'Amore*, she eased Mass down onto a red silk sofa in front of a triple row of French doors that overlooked a courtyard surrounded by trimmed shrubs and overhanging trellises. A steep stone staircase with lampposts descended to a green lawn bordered by beds of summer flowers, and a three-tier fountain with bronze statues of angels spewing streams of water from their mouths. A path led to a garden house a short distance away.

Something pleasant for him to look at, she thought as she helped him out of his jacket, took off his tie, and pulled off his shoes. When she stood in front of him, he circled her waist with his hands and gazed up at her, his blue eyes flashing pain and his hands still trembling with rage. "I'm sorry."

"For what?" She smoothed an errant curl from his forehead and pulled his head against her stomach.

"For embarrassing you. I should have kept my emotions in check. One thing my father drilled into my head when I was growing up was never to lose control in front of the household staff, or the employees at A.I. Never show my weakness."

"You're not weak, Mass." She caressed the smooth strong jawline of the man she loved with all her heart and soul. Two years ago, he probably wouldn't have lost control like that. He most certainly would have tossed Galen out of the mansion, but he would have continued with his day without anyone knowing he was bleeding inside. She'd humanized him, taught him that it was okay to show his emotions. "You're the strongest man I know. I love your strength, your passion."

"He had no business in my mother's music room. He sullied my last memories of her. From now on, every time I think of her last moments in this house, I'll see him sitting at her piano, playing her favorite tune. It's just wrong."

"Shh." Shaina hugged him tighter and tried to caress away his fury and his hurt.

When he relaxed against her, she lifted his head from her stomach and sat down beside him. She held his hands. His knuckles were red but not swollen. She kissed each one ever so gently before meeting his gaze. "I shouldn't have pushed you to reach out to Galen before you were ready. Cameron and I are so close. I can't imagine not having a relationship with him. I just wanted you and Galen to have that kind of connection, you know. But maybe that's not possible. You didn't grow up together. You didn't even know he existed until eight years ago, and the fact that he's a product of your father's infidelity is a lot for you to deal with." She laid her palm against his chest. "It's my fault. I'm the one who should be sorry."

He pulled her close to his side and kissed the top of her head. "It's nobody's fault. It's just a bad situation."

"Do you hate him for what he said about your mother?"

"I don't hate him. He's obviously misinformed and angry. I hate what he represents. I can't get past the fact that his mother is the reason mine isn't here, that I don't have my sister, that every year I'm throwing a Thanksgiving dinner in July." He paused on a deep sigh and his fingers tightened around her arm. "Except for Aunt Bella, my entire family is gone, everyone and everything from my past. All I have are my memories, and I don't want to share them with him," he ground out between clenched teeth.

Shaina lifted her head and stared at him. She'd been so focused on keeping him from killing his brother that she hadn't noticed the deep sadness in the blue of his eyes, the hints of redness in the white. Something else was tearing him apart. "Why are you home so early, Mass?"

Expelling a long breath, he sat forward, planted his elbows on his knees, and stared out the door where the sun was barely visible above the tree line.

She rubbed at the tension in his shoulders and back. "Mass, what's wrong?"

"It's Jabari." He pressed his palm into the scar on his right side—the eternal reminder of Jabari's strength, his wisdom, devotion, and love for him.

"Did he take a turn for the worse? He seemed fine this

morning when we watched him by satellite. He seemed stronger. He was actually running about."

When he just shook his head and sniffled, Shaina knew the inevitable had happened. "Oh, Mass," she said in a broken whisper. She wrapped her arms around him, stretched out on her back and pulled him down on top of her.

He cried, his hot tears soaking into her blouse. He cried so hard that the sofa vibrated. Shaina cuddled her husband as if he were a helpless child in her arms. This hurting little boy, the vulnerable side of Massimo Luciano Andretti, was something the world would never see. This was hers. All hers, and she cherished it with every beat of her heart.

"He was my best friend for almost twenty-six years. I loved him so much, so much. I'm going to miss him terribly."

"I know. I know, baby." The juxtaposition of Jabari's and his mother's exit from this world couldn't be weirder. No wonder he'd lost it with Galen. Weirdness was not an anomaly in this family. Like Aria, both Shaina and Massimo's mothers were born in December, and they both died in July. She and Cameron were heading to Maine at the end of the month to visit their mother's grave, and their father's, who lay right next to her. July wasn't a good month for the Andretti/Norwood blended family. December, they loved.

"I came home to share the news with you and Azi because you were both close to him. But then I walked in to that. Him!"

"You shouldn't have had to deal with Galen. Not on the day before the anniversary of your mother's death, and now Jabari's." She had some news to tell him, too. News that would make him happy, but she didn't want to lessen the impact of Jabari's death. He needed to grieve for his beloved cat. "I'm going to miss him, too. I fell in love with him from the day I met him. Jabari was a beautiful cat, and Aria loved him. We were just watching the video of the two of you on the blanket with him at the camp."

"You were?"

"Yes. Aria got real excited when she saw him, and she started yelling, 'Bari, Bari. Nice *puttyca*t.'" She told me that she loves him, and that you were crying because Bari was hurt. She understood, Mass."

"It must have been around the same time I was watching him take his last breath."

"You watched it happen?"

He lifted his head and rested his chin in the valley of her breasts. "Servio called to tell me that he was struggling to breathe. I cut a meeting short to watch him. It was just old age. He died peacefully." Tears glittered in his eyes. "I'm glad we went to see him last week. "I just wish I was there with him at the end, though." He paused. "I should have gone back after Aria was feeling better. I should have been there with him. I should—"

"No, Massimo." Shaina clasped her hands on his cheeks. "I will not let you do that to yourself. You did all you could for him. Jabari knows you were watching him. He did what he was born to do. He saved your life, and I'll be eternally grateful to him. Now he can rest in peace in leopard heaven." She paused, hesitant to asked, but knowing that the issue needed to be addressed, and quickly. "What are you going to do about his remains?"

He waited a long time before responding. "I'll have him cremated and scatter him in the Serengeti, so he will always be part of the jungle."

"That's nice. His spirit will be free to roam the plains of his homeland forever. Maybe he'll run into your mom." To avoid evoking memories of his father's infidelity, and the events associated with the day he almost died in the jungle, she refrained from mentioning his dad, whose remains were also scattered in the Mara Lands.

"I love you, Shaina. I hope you don't think I married you just for the money like Galen said. I loved you long before I knew I had to marry to secure my inheritance."

"We've been through that, Massimo. I know what we have, and that's all that matters. What you wrote in that article was beautiful. It made me proud to be your wife." She leaned forward and kissed his eyes, his nose, the salty tears from his cheeks, and then she placed her lips on his and kissed him deeply, their tongues dancing around each other as passion gave way to sadness.

He groaned, circling her body and pulling her closer, taking the reins of the kiss, delving deeper, seeking the comfort he needed from her.

Shaina moaned when his hands crawled under her blouse and his fingers grazed her hot flesh on their way to the mounds of her swelling breasts. She felt moisture collect in her panties as he shifted his weight and nestled his pulsing hard-on at the apex of her thighs. Fire sped through her veins. They hadn't made love in five days, not since they returned from Africa.

Massimo had been coming home late and leaving early to try to make up for the time away, and to prepare for the upcoming honeymoon they would be taking. And she had been busy with nursing Aria back to health. It was the longest dry stretch they'd had since they'd been married. It was too long.

Shaina needed her man and from the way he was molding her bare breasts in his warm palms and rubbing up against her, she knew he needed her, too. She swiftly unbuttoned his shirt and reached for the buckle of his belt. The first round would be hard and swift, right here on the sofa, but the next would be slow and sweet on the bed.

She was glad they were here, in *il Nido d'Amore*, the place where their lovemaking always seemed to transcend to a higher level than anywhere else in the mansion. Perhaps it was the fact that the room, the décor had remained unchanged since the last time his parents had been together inside it.

The floor-to-ceiling taupe and red satin drapes that completely covered two of the walls, the mirrored third walls, the red silk throw pillows in front of the marble fireplace, the pillar candles strategically placed around the huge bed in the center of the room, all worked together to create an aura of magic, passion, and love. A small dining table sat near the sofa and offered magnificent views of rolling hills in the north, while northwest, just behind downtown Granite Falls, the Aiken River flowed by. At nights, the scenery created a twinkling canvas against the sky. Shaina could understand why Massimo's parents used to sequester themselves in here, and ask not to be disturbed. She and Massimo had done the same many times, until Aria was born. Their daughter was the only person they allowed to interrupt their time in their love nest.

"Baby, I need you. I need your healing love." Massimo's hands were between her thighs, his fingers making their way inside the wet crotch of her panties, skimming across her hot swollen flesh.

"I need you, too, Massimo. So much. Let's get these clothes off," she said as a poignant vision of her and Massimo sprawled on the pillows in front of the fireplace flashed across her mind. His pants and his black silk briefs were halfway down his thighs, and his hard shaft was grazing the insides of her thighs when she heard Reese call her name, followed by Aria yelling for Mommy and Daddy.

They both stilled and looked toward the door leading into the sitting area of the love nest. The staff knew never to enter this room or the master suite unannounced. "Just a second, Reese," she said, swearing inwardly as the inner walls of her sex seemed to scream in frustration.

Mass pushed off of her, his eyes blazing with passion and frustration. "We're pulling an all-nighter after our company leaves tonight," he said, fixing his clothes. "It's been too long."

Shaina eased her aching breasts back into her bra and pulled down her blouse. "Okay, you can come in," she said when Mass smiled and nodded at her.

Seconds later, Aria came toddling into the room and headed straight into Mass' arms. "Papa, Papa," she chanted, winding her little arms about his neck. "*Aria ama Papà.*" With ease, she spoke in the language her father used most when conversing with her.

"*Ehi, dolcezza di là, e papà ama il suo piccolo angela. Papà sei mancato tanto.*" He squeezed her tightly then proceeded to lavish her face and neck with kisses, making her squeal with delight, even as she kissed him back with zest.

Shaina glanced at Reese standing near the door. "We're entertaining family, so Aria doesn't need you for a few hours. Just be on duty around ten tonight, and be prepared to take care of her in the morning." *Since Mass and I will be taking care of each other*, she wanted to add.

"Thank you, Mrs. Andretti. I'll see you later then."

No you won't. Shaina gloried in the tender moments as she watched Massimo play with his daughter on the floor. Aria seemed to be helping him forget his pain, even if only for a short while. She leaned back into the sofa as playful growls and baby laughter swirled around her. She smiled at the thought of a new voice joining their merry chorus.

She'd slipped up a few weeks ago when Aria had been suffering from an ear infection, a cold, and was running a fever. Mass had been away with Bryce on Fonandt Energies business, and she'd been so preoccupied in taking care of a sick child that she'd forgotten to take her pill a couple of days.

As soon as he'd come home, she and Mass had made love every single day, sometimes twice, for a week straight. It was crazy. Neither one of then understood why they couldn't seem to get enough of each other—not that they were complaining, but as a result of her slipup and the undeniable passion between them, her family was growing, as was her love.

Just as she hadn't experienced any symptoms with Aria, Shaina had none now. She'd suspected she was pregnant when her period hadn't shown up last week while they were in Kenya. She hadn't said anything to Mass because she wanted him to have undivided time with his pet cat, and since they returned, she wanted to make sure before sharing her suspicions—which weren't suspicions anymore.

She was blissful at the thought of giving Massimo another child, especially today when he'd lost so much. She cleared the lump from her throat. "Mass!" she yelled above Aria's squeals as he chased her around the room. When he caught her, he tickled her tummy, and then pretended to gobble it up like Cookie Monster gobbles a cookie.

"No, Daddy, no," she screamed at the top of her lungs.

Shaina called him name again.

"You shouldn't interrupt the fun between a man and his girl, Shaina." He said, tossing Aria into the air and catching her.

"I have something to tell you. Something important. You need to hear this."

He halted in mid-throw, frowned at her, then smiled at Aria. *"Di mamma essendo estremamente persistente. Vediamo qui fuori."* He sat down on the sofa and placed Aria on his lap.

Once she realized playtime was over she laid her head on her father's chest and stared at Shaina as if she understood what he'd told her about her mother being persistent and that they should hear her out. Maybe she did. She was a whiz when it came to languages, just like her daddy.

Shaina's gaze wandered above the marble fireplace to a painting of a young African woman dressed in colorful tribal clothing and wearing bright beaded earrings and necklaces. Her head was clean-shaven and her feet were bare, but her ankles were adorned with matching beaded anklets. Itifaki looked happy, innocent, yet wild and knowing—like an exotic princess. Shaina smiled as she studied the young girl who'd been brave enough to defy her family and her culture, and elope with Amadore, the man with whom she'd fallen in love at first sight—kind of like Shaina when she'd disobeyed her father and gone to the factory to see Massimo. If she hadn't defied her father, she wouldn't be sitting here now with her husband and her daughter.

"We're waiting, Mommy," Mass said.

Shaina took a deep breath and caught his gaze. "Remember when you told Aria that no matter how many sons you have, her birthright as your firstborn child was to run A.I.? Well, I hope she and her sibling will have as solid a relationship as Cameron and I have, so they won't be fighting for power."

Mass sat forward, his eyes wide, his mouth opened in awe. "Are you saying what I think you're saying?"

Shaina nodded.

"But you're on the pill. We decided to wait until Aria was at least three-years old before having another baby."

"You don't want it? You want me to send it back?" Shaina splayed her palms over her stomach. "Are you upset?"

He covered her hands with his. "Are you kidding? No, not at all. I'm delightfully surprised. But how is it possible with your birth control? They told us that next to abstinence, the pill was the safest method."

Shaina told him about her slipup a few weeks ago.

His eyes sparkled as he grinned like a kid opening the present from his best pal at his birthday party. "So you must be about four weeks along then?"

Shaina bobbed her head up and down, tickled that he kept track of her cycle. "I went to see Dr. Walsh this morning, just for confirmation. Even though we didn't plan it, this baby is supposed to be here, Mass. It's part of God's plan."

"I love you." He pulled her close, kissed her passionately, then tucked her against his side and enveloped her and Aria in his arms. "I don't care whose plan it is. I needed to hear something positive, something hopeful today. Thank you for this gift of new life, pussycat."

"*Puttycat*," Aria shouted, kicking her bare feet against the edge of the sofa. "Bari. Nice *puttycat*."

Shaina caught Massimo's gaze, and for a moment she thought he would break down again, but he kept his cool and grinned at his daughter. "You hear that, Aria? *Hai intenzione di avere un fratellino*"

"*O una sorella*," Shaina said, happy he hadn't told Aria about Jabari. Why tell her about something she couldn't understand? Jabari would live on in one of their minds for a good while.

"I don't care as long as it's healthy. You've given me so much joy. I'm so blessed to have you and Aria, and now another little Norwood-Andretti to carry our legacies forward."

"We're blessed to have you, Mass. You're the best husband and father any wife and child could ask for. I love you. We love you."

"Love," Aria said, hugging her parents. "Aria loves Mama and Papa."

Warmth glowed in Shaina's heart, and spread throughout her body. The meaning of *love* was something Aria understood in her own small way. Death could wait.

Even in the face of death, life shone brightly through. God took away today, but he'd already given back, abundantly. The child growing in her womb attested to the ever-spinning, ever-continuing circle of life.

CHAPTER EIGHT

The next day - Wednesday morning...

S andwiched between her father and her husband, Tashi
fought her way through the crowd of curious spectators,
zealous reporters shoving microphones into their faces, and
photographers trying to capture them at just the right angles.
The paparazzi were working overtime outside the courthouse
because they were banned from videotaping or recording of
any sort on the inside.

By the time she ascended the steps of the front entrance
of the Cuyahoga County Courthouse in Cleveland, Ohio,
Tashi felt so exhausted, she just wanted to go home.

"Hang on, baby. This is the last time you'll ever have to
deal with this pandemonium," Adam whispered, as they
walked down the aisle and took a seat close to the front.

The courthouse, situated near the Cleveland Mall, was a
magnificent landmark. Bronze statues of Thomas Jefferson
and Alexander Hamilton flanked the front entrance, while the
rear overlooked Lake Erie. Deeply recessed arched windows

and doors, along with fluted columns and colorful murals, graced the interior. It seemed surreal that people would flock to such a beautiful building just to witness the events of the most ghastly criminal activities that took place in their city. But flock, they did.

The courtroom had been packed for the two months the case was in session, and it was packed today as everyone awaited the appearance of the defendants, the jury, and the judge who would deliver the sentence. There had been many delays, sometimes for days, as the defense tried to have the case thrown out. They presented technicalities and requests for suppression of evidence, one after another. But the judge wasn't hearing it.

Her Honorable Rowena Kingsley had no tolerance for suppression of the poor, and crimes in high places. Alessandro, Adam, and her father had worked hard to make sure she was the presiding judge over Tashi's mother's murder trial.

Since he retired from the FBI last year, her father had been spending a lot of time in Ohio, gathering enough evidence to convince the court to bring the men to trial. Tashi had been hesitant about attending. But Paul had argued that since she was the child of the victim who was left motherless at age four at the hands of the defendants, her presence in the courtroom would strengthen the prosecution's case, and hopefully sway the jury to come back with a guilty plea.

Former FBI Special Agent Paul Dawson was the expert in these situations, so Tashi had taken his advice. Adam had rented a penthouse suite in a hotel last year when her father had begun his investigation. He'd kept it throughout the trial, and had encouraged her to stay over on days when court was adjourned late. But Tashi never did. Every day that court was in session, she boarded the Andreas jet with her father, or Adam. Her in-laws occasionally tagged along for added support. She would spend the three-hour flight to Cleveland gazing out the window. When the day was over, she flew back to spend the night with her husband and her infant son.

The first day was the worst as she anticipated staring into the eyes of the three men who'd killed her mother. But once she saw them, took in their arrogance, their disdain, and lack of remorse, her resolve to watch them go down was strengthened.

One of the men came from a family of corrupt politicians; one was the son of a private health insurance mogul, and the other was the nephew of a prominent Ohio physician. They were young and wealthy and thought themselves above the law when they murdered her mother—a nobody in their eyes, a pawn in their sinister game of human chess. They were older now with children and grandchildren, but evidently not too rich, nor too powerful to be brought under the penalty of the law.

It had taken her dad almost two years to investigate her mother's death, find the culprits, and have them indicted and brought to trial. Because of their wealth and power, it had seemed impossible at times, but her father had been unwavering in his determination to make them pay for what they had done to the one true love of his life.

That first day of the trial had been heartbreaking for Tashi. She'd sat between her husband and her father as the prosecution and the defense made their opening statements, and then through the testimony of the prosecution's first witness—a Carol Sweeney, who'd worked at the drug store where her mother had been employed as a pharmacist, twenty years ago.

Carol testified that just hours before her death, Evelyn Holland had told her that three young men had been forcing her to fill prescriptions for some powerful narcotics. She had to comply with their request or else they would have her arrested on phony charges and her child would be placed in foster care. Carol stated that Evelyn told her that the nephew of the doctor had stolen one of his uncle's prescription pads, written out orders for some bogus patients, and then forged his signature. The son of the insurance mogul wrote up policies for the patients, while the son of the politician had several identifications made up in their names.

Carol was the first person Tashi's dad had spoken to when he began the investigation into her mother's death. Carol had also said that she was with Evelyn the day he'd gone to her house asking for a second chance. She'd begged Evelyn to tell him about her pregnancy, but Evelyn didn't want to ruin his life and his career by tying him down with a child he wasn't ready for. She'd promised to tell him once he made it into the FBI. But she'd died before that day came.

The defense had objected to every question from the prosecution, and every statement the witness made, claiming it was hearsay since Evelyn Holland wasn't around to corroborate Carol's story. In cross-examination, the defense asked why she waited almost two decades to come forward with her cockamamie story. She responded that she feared for her own life after Evelyn was found dead in one of the defendant's homes. The defense brought in their own witnesses to try to paint Evelyn as an unfit mother and drug

ANA E ROSS

addict who turned tricks to support her habit and her illegitimate child whose father was unknown at the time.

Several times, Tashi wanted to stand up in the courtroom and scream "Liar," at the witnesses, but her dad on one side of her, and Adam, Alessandro, or Arabella—whoever was seated on the other side—had held her back. She'd felt the tremors running through her father's body as he too was subjected to the lies about the woman he still loved.

But the prosecution had a trump witness in their back pocket that blew the defense's "not guilty" plea out of the water.

Audrey Ferguson, the ex-girlfriend of one of the defendants, was Paul Dawson's biggest challenge. Just before the defense rested, and it seemed that the defendants would get away with murder, Paul had gotten an anonymous tip that a girlfriend of one of the defendants had been present when the murder took place, and that she had videotaped the entire thing—a videotape the defendants had no idea existed until it was entered into evidence.

Paul had worked diligently to track her down in Florida where she'd fled the day after the murder. Audrey was justifiably scared for her current family, as she'd been for her life nineteen years ago. Paul had told her that she could either testify willingly or be subpoenaed.

Audrey validated Carol's story, and added that after the defendants planned out their scheme, they went looking for the perfect pharmacist to execute it. Evelyn Holland was a young single mother with no one to protect her. They pretended to like her, befriended her, and even invited her to their homes and out to clubs to party with them. They took pictures of her drinking, and on one occasion, she was so drunk, she threw up outside a bar. They threatened to use the photos to paint her as an unfit mother and have her daughter taken away and even harmed if she didn't do what they wanted.

Audrey testified that she'd been invited to her ex-boyfriend's home for a private party while his parents were away on vacation. She arrived earlier than the other guests, and reported that as she approached the pool area, she heard the victim tell the defendants that she was going to report them, even if it meant implicating herself. She wanted out. She was told that the only way out was through the grave.

Audrey reported that it was at that point that she began recording the events on her camcorder. She'd wanted to go to the police, but was so afraid she might end up dead like Evelyn had, that she'd instead changed her name and gone into hiding. She'd made copies of the video and kept them in various safe places as insurance, and told one other person about them, just in case the defendants ever came after her. It was that still unidentified person, who'd tipped Paul.

The prosecution presented Exhibit #15. The judge informed the jury that what they were about to see was extremely disturbing, and she demanded that the court maintain order. Then the videotape detailing the horrifying murder of Evelyn Grace Holland was made public.

Chills had rushed up and down Tashi's spine as she'd watched her mother being pinned to the tiles of the pool by one of the defendants. The other held a hand over her mouth to muffle her screams while the third injected her with a dose of the narcotics she'd delivered to them that day. When they were finished, they tossed her into the pool, and stood by laughing while she splashed around in the water begging for help.

At one point, she made it to the side and began to pull herself out of the pool. "Please, I have a daughter. I have a baby," she begged as she struggled to hold on.

"You should have thought of her before you threatened to rat us out. It's your fault the little bastard doesn't have a mommy anymore," one of the defendants said, as he pushed her back under and held her down until she stopped struggling. When her body floated to the top, they fished her out and pretended to resuscitate her before calling 911.

In the police report, they claimed that she was a friend with a drug addiction. They admitted that they'd been having a party and that Evelyn had arrived early and told them that she wanted to go for a swim while they were in the den shooting pool. Since she was a champion swimmer, they thought nothing of it. But when she'd been gone for a long period of time, they went out to the pool and found her lying facedown in the water. Because of their families' power, money, and prestige, the young men were never under suspicion.

Thus, Evelyn Holland's death was ruled as a self-induced drug overdose and suicide. Since Audrey hadn't come forward, no one investigated the bogus patients and the drugs that had been prescribed and filled during the five months leading up to Evelyn's death.

When the video ended, the courtroom was so quiet, if one listened hard enough, one could hear a butterfly's wing flapping in the nearby park. There wasn't a dry face in the courtroom, not even in the jury box. Some of the defendants' friends and family members had walked out in apparent disgrace and disgust.

There was no way the defendants could deny what they'd done to her mother anymore. They'd changed their plea to "guilty" in exchange for the death penalty to be taken off the table. Tashi wanted to see them fry, or more accurately, be injected with same drugs they'd given her mother, and left to die in the way she was. But it wasn't up to her.

Part of her was glad that her mother's killers had been caught and brought to justice, but another part of her wished she'd been spared the details of her final moments on this earth. It was so cruel, so evil, and senseless. It was then she fully understood her uncle's distrust and dislike for the wealthy. Tashi shuddered, opened her mouth, and sighed aloud as she felt the anger, rage, pain, and hate explode inside her.

Her father squeezed her hand that was covered with her tears. "As soon as you're finished with your statement, we can leave."

"I don't think I can talk. I don't think I can do it."

"You'll do fine, baby. Your dad and I will be right beside you." Adam pulled her against his side and rubbed her shoulders and arm, sending comfort flowing through her like only he could do. "I know the trial was hard, but once they're put away, you'll have peace and closure. I promise." He dabbed at her tears with a white handkerchief. After the first day, he'd made it a habit to bring one along. "You can do it for your mom. Be her voice, just this last time."

"Bastards!"

Tashi lifted her head from Adam's shoulder at her father's under-breath exclamation. The three defendants, dressed in orange jumpsuits with their hands and ankles shackled, shuffled into the courthouse, their chains jangling as they walked. They'd been free on bail during the first half of the trial, and subsequently dressed in suits, looking all innocent, prestigious, and invincible, but after the judge saw the video, she'd revoked their bail and placed them behind bars. She wasn't giving them the chance to flee to a country that didn't comply with America's extradition laws, especially when the death penalty was an option, as in this case.

Tashi didn't think the restraints were necessary, but someone obviously wanted to send a message to wealthy folks who thought they could get away with murder, and to the corrupt politicians who helped them cover up their crimes.

The defendants didn't look so arrogant now that their freedom, their power, and pride had been stripped from them. The heads that had been held high when the trial began were now bowed low, and the contemptuous eyes that had stared at her then, now stared at the floor as they jiggled their way to their seats. Tashi wished she had the courage to run to the front of the room and trip them, watch them fall flat on their faces on the terrazzo floor, and then laugh as they struggled to get back on their feet.

Not one of them looked in Tashi's direction, which suited her fine. After today, she would leave this courtroom and never think of them again.

"All rise."

Everyone stood as the bailiff declared the judge's entry into the courtroom. Once they were seated again, court was called into session and the sentencing procedures began.

Tashi sat very still and erect as the defense and then the prosecution made their pre-sentencing statements. The defense asked for leniency, arguing that the defendants were young and stupid when they committed the crime, but that they have since changed, matured into upstanding citizens who have contributed positively to their communities. The prosecution demanded that the full extent of the law be implemented because of the premeditated planning to commit multiple crimes, and the malicious, merciless manner in which Evelyn Grace Holland was killed, leaving her young child motherless.

When the judge asked if the defendants had anything to say on their own behalf, they declined.

They refused to even say they were sorry. *Bastards!*

"It's time, sweetheart."

Tashi trembled as Adam and her father escorted her to the front where she would be making her victim impact statement. She glanced briefly at the judge, then at the faces in the crowd. Some had been attending the trial out of curiosity, some out of sympathy, some to see justice done, some to sell stories, and some—like the defendants' few remaining loyal friends and family members—had come to wish Tashi away, back into obscurity.

And then there were those, like Carol Sweeney, her mother's former best friend, and her band of supporters who once loved her mother and who missed her presence on this earth. Courage welled up inside Tashi as those compassionate eyes smiled at her. She opened the sheet of paper her dad placed in her hand and stared at it. She'd been working on this statement ever since the court had accepted the guilty pleas of the three defendants. While she was writing it, she'd spent a lot of time in the room where she'd laid out her mother's personal possessions that her uncle had kept in storage for her, and that her husband had flown to Granite

Falls in the Andreas' private jet as if they were precious cargo. They were precious to her. They had helped her fill in some of the blank pages of her life and understand exactly what she'd been missing from not having her mother.

"They're waiting, darling," Adam whispered.

Tashi cleared her throat and began reading. "I never knew my mother. I have no memories of her because I was only four years old when she was viciously and maliciously taken away from me. The only family I had then, my Uncle Victor, sacrificed his life to raise me. He was the only person who was in a position to keep her alive in my heart, but he couldn't."

She swallowed as her uncle's sorrow and the reasons he'd sheltered her from the public came full circle for her. "My Uncle Victor never spoke about my mother, his beautiful, vibrant, younger sister, Evelyn Holland, whom he loved. He never spoke about her because it was too painful for him. Uncle Victor died four years ago, and with him he took any chance I had to learn about my Mom. But thankfully before he died, he gave me the gift of finding my father—or more accurately, helping my father find me—a child he never knew existed until three years ago."

Sighs and murmurs circulated, and the judge had to remind everyone to keep order.

Tashi drew strength from her father's and husband's hands on her shoulders. "My mother had her reasons for not revealing the identity of my father to anyone. But I know if she hadn't been ripped from my life, I would have met my father years ago. Every little girl needs her daddy. I'm no different, and I would have pestered my mother until she told me who he was. My parents were very much in love when they conceived me, but misunderstandings kept them apart. If my dad had known that I existed, they might have had a second chance to build a life together, and raise me, their daughter, together. I'll never know." She swallowed.

"All I know is that my uncle was so scared after my mom died, that he packed me up and took me far away from Cleveland and everyone who knew me, everyone *I* knew. He was so paranoid of something bad happening to me that he kept me in isolation. Instead of growing up in a loving family, I grew up with a huge hole in my heart where precious memories of both my parents should have been. I have a hole where my mother's love should have been."

She paused to catch her breath and blink back the tears stinging her eyes. "I cried out for my mother in the middle of the night, not understanding why she wouldn't come. I had tears she didn't dry, hurts and pain that she couldn't soothe away. I have questions that she will never answer, that no one else can answer. My son, my children will never know their grandmother—a woman who many of her friends now tell me was sweet, kind, loving, and trusting."

Tashi folded the paper, raised her head and stared at the three men. "It was my mother's trusting spirit that made her vulnerable to you. You pretended to be her friends. You threatened my life and made her commit crimes for you. Then when she wanted out, you killed her. While she struggled for life, you laughed and you made bets on how long it would take her to die. You are evil, despicable, soulless, and you deserve to rot in prison for the rest of your miserable lives. You don't deserve to walk among decent people, and I'm asking the court to make sure that you don't."

Tashi was shattered inside, but she would be damned if she let her mother's killers see her cry. Recalling how they'd laughed at her mother when she begged for help, Tashi took in a deep breath. "My mother is gone. But she will never be forgotten. You will remember Evelyn Grace Holland every single day for the rest of your wretched lives. You will be haunted by her cries for help. But the moment I step out of this courtroom, I will forget you, and so will most of the people present here today. Your families will carry your ugliness, your shame for generations to come while mine will carry my mother's beauty and her honor."

Tashi turned to her father. "Get me out of here. I want to go home and hold my son."

She felt like a zombie as Paul and Adam led her out of the courtroom through a side door and to the back of the building where a car was waiting to take them to the airport and the Andreas' jet. As she sat in the limo, cradled between the men in her lives, it dawned on Tashi that she'd never grieved for her mother.

Like all children, she'd cried when she was scared and called out for her during the night. She'd cried when she was hurt, and then cried some more when her mother never came to her rescue. So like all children, she'd simply stopped crying and moved on with her life.

When she was older, she still never grieved. She didn't know how or even why she should cry for someone she never knew, someone who'd faded from her memory, slipped out of her mind. The prosecution had brought in character witnesses —her mother's former friends, coworkers, and even mild acquaintances to discredit the defense's portrayal of her as an irresponsible, drug-addicted party-girl.

Evelyn's friends spoke kindly of her as a responsible employee, loyal friend, and devoted mother. One day when court had adjourned early, Tashi had invited all twenty-four of them, both men and women, to lunch. They'd related stories of her mother's first crush, her science experiment that burned down a table in the science lab, how at age ten, she started a small library in her parents' garage to encourage her friends to read more, of her being the head cheerleader for their high school football team, the trophies she'd won in swim competitions, and the times she climbed out of her bedroom window to meet her friends so they could sneak into the theater to watch R-rated movies. Those amazing people had known Tashi from the moment she was born. They would have kept her mother alive in her heart and mind if her uncle hadn't taken her away.

Carol told her how Evelyn had started a single mothers support group when she was pregnant with her, and that's how many of them had first met. Carol had been her mother's Lamaze partner, and she's the one who'd nicknamed Tashi "Little Eve." Tashi had also learned that Carol was her godmother.

"We used to meet twice a month at the library," Carol had said. "I kept the group going after Eve's death. It has grown over the years. Many single mothers with needs come to us, some without even a place to live. We managed to raise enough money to rent a small space in downtown Cleveland. People donate clothes, furniture, food, and other baby essentials."

"Your mom loved to have fun," Charlie, a former neighbor said. "She wasn't a bad person. She didn't run around and she never did drugs like those people said. She knew how to make people laugh."

As they jumped from one story to the next, images of a

young Evelyn began to materialize in Tashi's mind. She imagined her doing all the fun things they'd described. Her mother was spirited, independent, friendly, and outgoing—all the qualities her uncle had spent his life crushing inside her because he didn't want her to end up like her mother. Those qualities had forced their way to the surface of Tashi's soul the day she'd walked into Adam's garden, and found him naked. Adam had brought her to life.

When she left the restaurant that day, Tashi had begun to identify with her mother. She felt her in her heart and soul. She missed her, needed her, wanted her. Her mother was no longer an entity, a faded memory, or someone imagined. Evelyn Holland, "Mommy," as she used to call her, was a real person with aspirations, dreams, hopes, wishes, and love, lots and lots of love for the little girl she'd left behind. Tashi knew without a doubt that *she* was the last thought in her mother's heart at the moment she drew her last breath.

As the Andreas jet taxied down the runway in preparation for takeoff from Cleveland Hopkins International Airport, Tashi felt the pressure of nineteen years of suppressed grief detonate inside her. She turned to her father and began to cry hysterically. She was faintly aware of Adam closing in from the other side, and then the sobs of the two men in her life mingling with hers.

Three hours later, Tashi walked into the foyer of her grandiose home, took her son from his nanny, and headed for the room where she stored her mother's possessions. Only now did she feel confident and passionate enough to begin to educate him about his other grandmother, Evelyn Grace Holland.

CHAPTER NINE

Andreas Estate - Wednesday evening...

Adam eased the door open and peeked inside. The drapes were drawn, shrouding the room in darkness. Leaving the door open a crack to let in some light from the gallery, he tiptoed across the hardwood floor toward the bed.

He felt a tightening in his chest as he gazed down on his sleeping wife and child. Tashi was still wearing the gray pencil skirt she'd worn to the sentencing, but she'd taken off the matching jacket. The buttons of her white silk blouse were undone and her white lacy bra was unclasped. She lay on her side with their son clutched in her arms, his little rosy mouth nestled between her breasts, indicating that he'd fallen asleep while nursing.

Adam swallowed back the sob of emotion that welled up inside him. He'd been worried about Tashi since they got home and she'd locked herself inside this room with Alex. He didn't think she would do anything foolish; he just wanted to be there for her, to absorb some more of the pain she was experiencing.

She'd cried so hard and so long on the flight back home, Adam had been afraid she would literally break apart in his arms. The only other time he'd seen someone display such hysterical grief was the day his mother received the news of her beloved sister's death. Adam was eight years old when his Aunt Giuliana died, and he remembered fearing that his mother would die from a broken heart. Just as he was incapable of doing anything for his mother then, he could do nothing for his wife today. Nothing, but hold her close and weep along with her.

Adam's concern for Tashi had led him to call Samantha. She was unavailable, so he'd called Michelle who had been providing counsel and comfort for Tashi since the trial began, but she, too, was unavailable. Adam had no idea what it was like to grieve the loss of a parent, so he'd called his cousin, who only last night had celebrated the twenty-fifth anniversary of his mother's death, and sadly, the recent death of his cherished leopard, Jabari.

Mass had told him that all he could do was give Tashi space when she wanted it, not to bombard her with questions about her feelings, but to be there to hold her, and to listen when she was ready to talk. So while his parents and Paul had gathered in the solarium to await the details of the sentencing, Adam had planted himself on a sofa in the gallery outside the block of second-floor guestrooms so he would be there when Tashi needed him. He'd been waiting so long that he'd fallen asleep. Paul had awakened him a few minutes ago with the judge's final decision.

Tashi would be pleased, he thought. It could not bring her

mother back, but it would give her complete closure. Adam sat down on the edge of the bed, ruffled his son's head of curly black hair, and then leaned over to kiss his wife.

As their lips connected, the heavy lashes that shadowed her cheeks flew open. She sprung up in the bed, clutching Alex protectively.

"It's just me," he whispered, turning on the bedside lamp. His stomach clenched when he noticed the swollen pockets beneath, and the sadness buried in her emerald eyes.

Adam gathered his family into his arms, stretched out on his back, and held them tightly. Taking Massimo's advice, he asked no questions. When Tashi relaxed her head against his chest and sighed, he knew she was comforted simply by his presence.

After a while, Tashi eased out of his arms and rested her cheek on a pillow. She smiled at him, and his heart danced at the sliver of light in her eyes.

"What time is it?" she asked.

Adam shifted to his side and placed Alex on the mattress between them. He planted his elbow on the other pillow and cradled his head in his hand. "Late. The sun has set, but it's still light out. You must be starving. You haven't eaten since breakfast." He tried desperately to avoid any talk of the day's courtroom proceedings. "They will be summoning us to dinner soon."

She wet her lips with her tongue. "I am famished. More so because he sucked me dry," she said, smiling down at their sleeping son. She ran her knuckles along his chubby cheeks. "Are we dining alone?"

"Not tonight. It'll be a big Italian family-style dinner, starting with the *aperitivo* in the great room, then moving to the main dining room for the other ten courses from the *Antipasto* to the *digestivo* and everything in between. But if you'd rather—"

"No. I need to be surrounded by my entire family. I need all of you tonight, and just hearing you talk about the elaborate dinner is making my stomach growl." She glanced down at her open shirt. "I should go shower and change into something elegant since we're dining in style." She attempted to cover up her breasts.

"In a moment." Adam brushed her fingers away and cupped one swollen mound in his palm while he teased the smooth nipple between his fingers until it became hard as a pebble. She closed her eyes and sighed aloud, sending a bolt of electricity rushing from his head to his toes.

They'd been making love regularly since the trial began, which also coincided with Dr. Walsh's okay to resume postpartum intercourse. Some days when Tashi got back from Ohio, she would nurse Alex and then call for Adam. If he were downtown at the office, she would request that he come home and meet her in the garden. If he were working from home, she would just walk into his office and close the door. On the days when he accompanied her, they would lock themselves in the bedroom on the jet and make love until they touched down in Granite Falls.

They never talked—well, not with words. Their loving was always intense, hot, and consuming. When it was over, she would come into this room and surround herself with her mother's possessions. It was as if she straddled two worlds— the past and the present—trying to connect to the living and the dead. Today was different. Today, she'd turned to her father for comfort, then when she got home she'd chosen the past and the dead, but she'd brought Alex with her for the very first time. Was their son her bridge across the great divide?

She stilled his hand and, opening her eyes, she stared at him. "I'm not shutting you out," she said as if she'd read his thoughts.

"I know. It's natural for you to turn to your dad in this situation. I'm the outsider here."

"You're not an outsider. He's hurting as much as I am. I'm all he has. I have you and Alex, but I'm the only person with whom he can share his grief."

"You're a great daughter. He's lucky to have you." He caressed her lips with the pad of his thumb.

"I'm lucky to have him. If it weren't for him, this day never would have come, and those poor excuses for men would still be walking around free."

Adam wanted to tell her about Judge Kingsley's sentencing ruling, but decided she should hear it from her father. He followed her gaze as she turned onto her back and focused on the collection of crystal ornaments arranged on a bookshelf. There were bowls, baskets, vases, animals, birds, candleholders, and picture frames—some filled with photos of Evelyn and Tashi from the time she was an infant until she was four years old. That's where the memories ended.

He stilled as her gaze transitioned to two black and white sketches—one of Evelyn and the other of Tashi—hanging side by side on a wall. Adam was still stunned at the striking resemblance between mother and daughter. Anyone looking at them would swear it was the same woman at two different stages of her life. No wonder Tashi was nicknamed "Little Eve."

When her mother's belongings first arrived, Tashi had found the twenty-by-twenty-six inch drawings in a boot box that had been stashed at the bottom of a larger box. Tashi had admitted to having a faint memory of sitting for the portraits during a carnival, a month before her mother disappeared from her life.

Of all Evelyn's possessions, the portraits—along with a China doll tea set with which she used to play tea with her mom—were the only items Tashi had taken to their master bedroom. From time to time, she would lay the tea set out on a table, and take the drawings from the boot box and stare at them—sometimes for hours, as if she were sharing a cup of tea with her mother.

Last Mother's Day, while they were out at dinner, Adam had the drawings framed and presented them to her. He'd been afraid that she'd be upset that he'd infringed on her privacy, but she was thrilled, and said they were the best gift she'd ever received. She'd proved it when she set aside the pink diamond necklace and the two ounces of rare perfume on which he'd spent a fortune, and gave her full attention to the portraits.

"I want to bring her here."

Adam turned his head and recaptured her gaze. "What?"

"I want to bring my mother to Granite Falls. I want her to be close to me, like Erik brought up his first wife to be close to Precious after they moved back here. My dad's living here now, so—"

"Done. I'll make the arrangements as soon as possible. We'll lay her to rest on the hill above our garden. And a thousand years from now when we leave this world, our children will lay us near her." He paused. "We can make a place for your dad next to your mom, if he so desires."

"I think he'd love that. Thank you, Adam." She brushed her fingers through his long hair spread out on the pillow above his head.

He caught her hand and kissed the wrist. "Is there anything I can do to help, sweetheart?"

"You're already doing it by just loving me."

"It will only get better from here. Now we can look forward to renewing our vows without that ominous cloud hanging over our heads."

"Let's skip the wedding and go straight to the honeymoon. Where're we going again?"

"I never said, you sexy temptress."

He swallowed her chuckle when their lips connected above their son's head. As Adam gave himself over to the sweetness of the kiss, he did think about skipping the wedding and heading for the honeymoon haven he and the boys were planning for their wives. He groaned.

"Dada. Dada. Dada."

Both he and Tashi froze, pulled apart, and gazed open mouthed at their four-month-old baby.

"He said, *Dada*. He said, *Dada*." Adam picked up his boy and showered him with kisses. Alex squealed jubilantly and kept saying it when he realized how excited it made his dad.

"You know he's too young to understand what he's saying, right?" Tashi said with a skeptical look on her face. "He's just making sounds."

"I don't care. I heard *Dada* and I'm claiming it as his first word."

"Of course you would. Michelle, Kaya, and Shaina

warned me about this. Mama looks after them, gets up to feed them in the middle of the night, stays up with them when they're sick, and the first thing that comes out of their mouths is *Dada*. What about *Mama*, huh?" she said, getting into Alex's face and kissing his chubby cheeks. "What about *Mama*? Can you say, *Mama*?"

Alex gave her the sweetest smile and blurted, "Mama." His gaze then dropped to her uncovered chest, and drool began to drip from his little baby mouth as he stared at her breasts. "Mama," he said again and reached out to grab one.

"A boy after his daddy's own heart. Daddy drools whenever he sees them, or even thinks about them, too, my boy." Adam hugged Alex to his chest and roared with laughter that quickly turned to enchantment as Tashi leaped off the bed and began dancing around the room, her breasts bounding about, tempting father as they had tempted son, for extremely different reasons.

"He said *Mama*. He said *Mama*. My baby's talking." She rushed back to give Alex a hug, then stopped short and wrinkled her nose.

Adam held his breath and checked Alex's diaper. "Uh-uh, somebody needs a change. Too much excitement huh, buddy?"

"It's amazing how someone so sweet can produce the kind of stink that makes you want to rip your tonsils out." Tashi took another backward step.

Adam held the baby out to her. "Duty calls."

"Pffft!" She threw her hands in the air and smirked at him. "*I* feed him. *You* clean him," she said, buttoning her blouse and walking toward the door. "Duty, my sweet behind."

"*È dolce, e io sarò essere chiamandola al dovere più tardi stasera, probabilmente da dietro.*"

"*Vuoi guardare tua lingua, per favore? C'è un bambino in camera.*"

Adam was astonished at how quickly Tashi had mastered the Italian language. Well, with his parents and Paul as teachers, no wonder she spoke it like a native. And *he* did give her a lot of lessons in the privacy of their bedroom, teaching her dirty words and phrases that he alone would ever hear falling from her honeyed lips. She was a quick study in everything. Visions of his wife on her knees with her sweet tight *cula* pressed into his groin as he took her from behind caused Adam's *cazzo* to tighten painfully.

"*Oddio!*" Adam rose from the bed and held his stinky son close. "My wish for you, my boy, is that you find a wife as beautiful, lovely, enchanting, and irresistible as your mama."

"Mama."

🐚

Three hours later, during *dolce* and *caffè*, Tashi swallowed a bite of her *cassata*, and then downed her espresso. Sounds of satisfaction filled the room as her in-laws on her left, her father on her right, and her husband, sitting at the head of the dining table were engrossed in enjoying the delicious dessert.

Cassata was a sponge cake, moistened with liqueur and layered with ricotta cheese, candied citrus, and a chocolate filling, encased in a pink and green pastel marzipan shell, colored icing, and decorative designs. It was topped off with slices of candied fruit, and in Tashi's eyes, it had looked too good to cut when the servant brought it out.

But she, like everyone else at the table, had been hooked

on the first bite. They were all on their second serving. *I'll work it off tonight*, she thought as she took another bite and smiled at her husband.

Dinner had been delayed because Adam had sneaked up on her in the shower and taken her from behind as he'd promised. It was swift and intense and they'd thought it would hold them over until after dinner, but once they got to the bedroom, the fire started again. They'd taken it nice and slow that time.

When they finally joined the others for *aperitivo* in the great room, long after the appointed time, no one said anything, but she knew they were aware of what she and Adam had been doing in the master suite. Well at least her father and her in-laws knew that their children had a healthy marriage. The fresh hickeys on her neck and shoulders, exposed by her yellow strapless gown, proved it. They also understood that after the turmoil she'd been through that day, she needed the kind of comfort and connection only her husband could provide.

After the first awkward moments had expired, Paul had attempted to inform her of Judge Kingsley's ruling. She'd immediately stopped him, not wishing to have any thoughts of those men in her mind while she dined with her family.

Their conversation had centered around more pleasant subjects, like the upcoming group wedding, the bachelors' party that Paul and Steven Lynd were organizing, Mass and Shaina's news about her pregnancy, and then Tashi and Alex's trip to Santorini next week with Arabella and her girlfriends when Adam and Alessandro left for Tokyo on business.

Arabella had invited Paul along, dangling a carrot named Dafne Bellini under his nose. Dafne was Massimo's childhood friend. Paul had met her several times over the years, and admitted to liking her. Unfortunately, she was involved each time he'd seen her.

"She's been single for about a year," Arabella said, as she stirred her espresso with a silver spoon. "She actually asked about you, Paul."

"You're putting me on, Bella."

"She's not." Alessandro's fingers tightened around his wife's bare arm as he pulled her close to his side. "Bella and I ran into her when we were in Milan last month. We showed her pictures of Tashi and Alex and told her that you were family now."

"She asked how that tower of sweet dark chocolate was doing." Arabella added.

Everyone burst into laughter, and Tashi was tickled to see her father blush.

"She did not," Paul protested and tried to hide his emotion behind his espresso cup.

"I'll ask Massimo to invite her to the wedding, if he hasn't already. You two can reconnect here if you decide not to meet her in Santorini."

"Don't do that, Arabella. She's way too young for me."

"Nothing wrong with a May/December relationship," Adam said, joining the conversation. "As you all know, I was once involved with a woman twenty years my senior. Up until I met Tashi, my relationship with Sadie was the best I've had with any woman. Thanks to my wife, I'm able to keep that relationship going. Sadie and I are still very good friends."

Tashi caught his gaze, and she smiled when his blue eyes glowed with memories of their lovemaking session that afternoon. He'd told her about Sadie and how she was the one who'd told him to open his heart to love again, and to let Tashi in. How could Tashi be jealous of a woman like that? Feeling gratitude, Tashi had given Adam the okay to continue their friendship. There was no reason not to trust him, or her for that matter.

"Since Sadie is closer to my age, maybe I should give her a call." Paul grinned at Adam.

"You, my friend, are too old for her. She likes them young and plump. You're pretty plump, I'll grant you that, but you're not young. Enough."

Adam's statement caused another round of laughter, and as the humor died down, Tashi took a close look at her dad. He was handsome, dashing, and one of the kindest, most caring men she knew. Some lucky woman out there deserved to have him. He'd admitted to having several relationships over the past twenty-three years, but nothing serious or recent. Now that he was retired from the FBI, and had solved her mother's murder, it was time for him to find someone special and settle down. Tashi wanted her father to be as happy as she and Adam, Arabella and Alessandro, and her friends and their husbands.

A couple servants appeared to clear away the dessert dishes and serve the *digestivo*, the final course in a traditional Italian meal. Once the individual choices of *grappa*, *amaro*, and *limoncello* had been poured, and the containers placed on ice on the table within reach, the servants took their leave.

Tashi took a quick glance at the occupants of the table. They all seemed tired, full, and content. Perhaps it was time they all retired for the night. God knows she wanted to have another slice of her husband before they fell asleep.

She took a deep breath and turned to her father. "Okay,

Daddy." To ward off confusion, she called him *Daddy* instead of *Dad* when he and Alessandro—whom she also called *Dad*—were in the same room. "I'm ready to hear Judge Kingsley's final ruling on the sentencing."

Her father laid down his fork and stared at her. "Are you sure?"

"I'm sure. I want it over with. After tonight, I don't ever want to talk about them again."

Tashi could feel all eyes on her.

Paul tugged on the lapels of his suit jacket. "They got life without the possibility of parole in a maximum security prison. They will never, ever walk the earth as free men again."

Tashi closed her eyes and inhaled deeply and harshly as the words registered in her mind. She opened them when her father's hand closed over hers, resting on the white tablecloth.

"That's not all," he continued, squeezing her fingers. "Judge Kingsley ordered each of them to pay restitution to you in the amount of twenty million dollars."

Tashi's mouth dropped open and her eyes widened to the point of pain. "Twenty million dollars for me?"

"Sixty million, my dear." Alessandro corrected her.

"One for each year you had to live without your mother," Arabella said.

"Plus one, just because," Adam added.

"You're wealthy in your own right now." Alessandro refilled Arabella's espresso cup, and then his own. "I already have my financial advisors on call to instruct you on how to invest that money and make it grow into billions."

"Dad." Adam sent his father a silencing stare.

Tashi put her hands up. "Wait up, Dad. That's blood

money. My mother's blood money." She looked at Adam. "I don't want it."

"It's already yours," her father stated. "They agreed to pay it immediately in exchange for not being sent to the toughest maximum security prison in Ohio."

"She should have sent them to the toughest prison," Tashi declared. "I don't want any part of that money."

"Well, you do have the authority to do with it as you please." Adam placed his elbows on the table and made a bridge for his chin. "You can start a charitable foundation in your mother's name. It's a lot of money and it will go a very long way to help other victims of white-collar crimes."

"Or single mothers like my mom." Tashi sat back in her chair and looked at her family. Alessandro looked a bit disappointed that he'd be denied the opportunity to show her his financial expertise. Arabella seemed pleased with her train of thought, and her father had tears of pride and gratitude in his eyes.

"What are you suggesting, Tashi?" her father asked.

"I want to give half of it to Carol Sweeney."

"What?" Alessandro sat up straight. "You want to give all that money to your mother's former friend?"

"Well, not to her directly. You know my mom started a single mothers support group when she was pregnant with me."

They all nodded.

"Well Carol—my godmother," she correct herself with a tender smile, "kept the shelter going. They meet in downtown Cleveland, and collect donations from people. Sometimes those mothers don't even have a place to live. I want them to have a safe place to go, and far more than someone else's hand-me-downs. I want to build the Evelyn Holland Haven for Single Mothers, and start a college scholarship fund for their children."

"And the other half?" Adam asked.

"I'd like to start some kind of foundation for victims of human trafficking. Not many of the young women were as lucky as I was. If I could make even a small difference, then it's worth it."

Paul left his seat and enveloped her in his arms. "Your mother would be so proud of you, my daughter."

"This calls for a toast." Adam stood to his feet and motioned for everyone to do the same.

"Definitely." Paul grabbed his liqueur and retuned to Tashi's side.

She leaned into the comfort of his arms as everyone raised their glasses.

"To Evelyn Grace Holland, and to her College Scholarship Fund, and her Haven for Single Mothers and Victims of Human Trafficking," Adam said. "May she rest in blessed peace!"

"*Salute!*"

§♠

LaCrosse Estate – same day, earlier that evening...

With Fiona on her hip, Michelle watched Precious, Little Erik, Tiffany, and Jason play tag bunny on the lawn below the balcony of the second-floor playroom. Catherine sat in a lounge chair nearby, her eyes darting occasionally from her eReader to the children. Mrs. Hayes was at the library with

Azi and a few other grandmothers for their weekly knitting group, so when Michelle had suggested ordering pizza and a salad for dinner, Precious had asked if she could invite Jason over.

Now Michelle wished she hadn't.

"Aha!" Fiona crooned, kicking her little legs against Michelle's thighs and banging her arms on the screen, as she too watched her siblings having fun.

"Soon," she said to her seven-month-old daughter who'd begun crawling weeks ago. "Soon you'll be running around and playing tag bunny with your sisters and brother." She held her high in the air and pressed kisses on her belly over and over again until Fiona squeaked to her heart's content.

When Fiona began to hiccup from too much laughter, Michelle set her back on her hip and returned her attention to the children on the lawn. She recalled the first time she'd played tag bunny with Precious and her father when they'd stopped at the picnic area by the pond on her first trip to Granite Falls. It was on a sunny summer day, much like today. She'd only been working as Precious' nanny for a few weeks but she'd already fallen in love with the darling little girl, and her father, too. Later that day, just a few yards away from the balcony where she was now standing, Michelle had told Erik that she loved him. Her face burned with the memories.

Despite the insurmountable problems and heartaches that had ensued from that first declaration, her love for him had never waned, but had grown abundantly over the years. Every morning since they reconciled, she woke up happier than the day before, and every night she went to sleep wondering how it was possible that she'd been happier that day than she'd been the previous one. God had truly blessed her. She prayed that God would grant her children the same favor he'd granted her—sooner for Precious who was deep in puppy love with Jason.

Michelle sighed as she sat in a club chair and arranged Fiona on her lap. Erik was due home on Friday, but her excitement at seeing him was tainted by the news of Sarah's death, and the fact that she had to keep a secret from him—Precious' secret.

After dinner, Michelle and Catherine had taken Little Erik, Tiffany, and Fiona into the nursery to wash up, and when she'd returned to the kitchen—obviously too soon—she found Precious and Jason embracing with their lips locked. They'd jumped apart at her gasp. They had assured Michelle that it was the first time they'd kissed and begged her not to tell their parents.

If she were Precious' biological mother, Michelle would have kept her secret, but since she didn't want to actually say those exact words to her, she'd given them a time frame and the option of telling their parents themselves. She'd also assured them that there was nothing wrong with kissing each other, but their parents needed to be aware of the change in their relationship.

It seemed like only yesterday that Michelle was giving Precious a bath and reading her bedtime stories. She was almost thirteen now, taking her own baths, and kissing boys. She'd given her the sex talk years ago when Precious had come to her with questions. Michelle had first cleared it with Erik, who was glad that he didn't have to do it.

To make the milestone more memorable for Precious, Michelle had made it a Mother and Daughter day at the country club where they had lunch and then massages, pedicures, manicures, and facials. Afterward, they'd enjoyed a delicious dinner at Ristorante Andreas and then checked into a penthouse suite at Hotel Andreas for the night. Michelle grinned as she remembered Precious' reaction when she learned what really happened during coitus. Not at all what she'd expected, especially when Michelle took great care to paint a pretty picture about the delicate dance of lovemaking.

"Yuck!" she'd screamed with a convulsive shake of her body. "That's disgusting! My mom and dad did that? You and Daddy…Eww!"

"We do, Precious. Sex is a beautiful act when it's shared between two people who love each other. It's the ultimate expression of love and commitment two people can enjoy."

"Eww…" she'd said again, her face twisted in repulsion. She'd inched away from Michelle as if she had the plague. "I don't care how much he says he loves me, I would never let any boy do that to me. Ugh!" She'd shivered again.

As she'd drifted off to sleep that night, Michelle had the feeling that Precious wished she still believed that babies came from kissing. When Michelle had shared Precious' reaction to their sex talk with Erik, he'd jumped up and down, shouting, "That's my baby girl! That's my Little Muffin!"

Precious had avoided eye contact with both of them for a long time. In fact, she'd gone out of her way not be alone with them together, except during mandated family activities which included meals and the drive to and from church on Sundays.

It seemed that her prepubescent hormones had kicked in overnight and brought along the curiosity about intimacy with them. Michelle had to admit that she was a little hesitant to tell Erik that his Little Muffin was growing up, and that she might no longer think of sex as a gross act. She feared for

Jason, too, and hoped that Erik would remember that he was the fourteen-year-old son of one of his closest and dearest friends.

"Dada. Mama," Fiona chanted as she stretched her hand toward the table.

Michelle smiled down at her baby. "Oh, Fiona. It's your story time, isn't it, darling? And Mommy has been preoccupied. Okay, here we go." She randomly picked a book from the pile of soft cloth interactive storybooks on the table, and began to read to her baby.

She was on her sixth book when a maid appeared in the doorway. Michelle gave her a fleeting glance and continued reading to her daughter. The household staff knew that when Michelle was spending quality time with her children, she was to be disturbed only if the house was on fire, and right now, she didn't smell any smoke.

She gave a lot of attention to other people's kids—those at her foundation in Evergreen, those in Manchester, and elsewhere—and so she had made it a rule that certain hours during the evenings belonged to her own children, especially since Erik was away from home so much. They missed their daddy and asked for him a lot—especially Little Erik. Michelle had grown up with one parent who ignored her, so she tried hard to make up for Erik's absence. She never wanted her children to feel neglected or less important than the ones she helped, and she always turned off her cell phone during quality time with them.

Nettie was young and new to the household, and Michelle was certain that the seasoned maids had passed on the daunting task to the poor girl. Michelle could only imagine the trepidation she must feel. She finished reading the story about the Three Bears to Fiona then looked toward the door. "What is it, Nettie?" she asked, a smile playing at the corners of her mouth.

"I'm sorry to disturb you, Mrs. LaCrosse." Nettie pulled her hand from behind her and held up the receiver to the house phone. "But a Desire Summers keeps calling. She says she's been calling your cell phone unsuccessfully, and it's urgent that she speaks to you."

If it were anyone else, Michelle would refuse the call. She motioned for Nettie to place the receiver on the table.

"Would you like me to take Fiona while you talk to Miss Summers?" Nettie held out her arms.

"No, I'm still on baby time. Thanks. You may go." Michelle tightened one arm around her baby, and coaxed her to hold on to the storybook she'd been reading to her. When Fiona nestled into her arms and began babbling away as she pretended to mimic her mother, Michelle took a deep breath and placed the receiver to her ear. "Hello, Desire. How are you?"

"I'm great, Michelle. And you?"

"Super." Knowing why she'd called, Michelle got right to it. "I don't have an answer for you, Desire. We're not trying to avoid you. We're still waiting."

"I realize that. It's just that we only have a few weeks to implement all the changes and make sure that everything runs smoothly. With the national attention this wedding is receiving, I can't afford for anything to go wrong. My reputation is at stake here. Should we plan on pushing the date back at this point, or maybe you should begin looking around for another planner? Do you have suggestions, alternatives? I was supposed to hear back from you two days ago."

"I understand where you're coming from, Desire, but Bryce was away on business for a couple days. He just returned home this evening. I'm sure Kaya will have an answer for you first thing in the morning."

Michelle knew it wouldn't be tonight. She'd called Kaya's cell phone earlier, but each call had gone straight to voicemail. When she'd called the household line, she'd been informed that Mr. and Mrs. Fontaine weren't available. She knew exactly what that meant, and had hung up, hoping that her friend's seductive persuasions would work in their favor.

"If I don't hear from her tomorrow, I'm afraid that I'll have to back out of this contract and focus on the other two weddings I'm planning," Desire said.

"I'm sure it won't get to that. And even if Bryce doesn't approve, you can keep the deposit. You've spent valuable time with us already, and it won't be your fault. We probably should have consulted with Bryce before we hired you."

"I probably should have waited until after you spoke with him before accepting the job."

"I guess the excitement about the wedding blinded us to the huge elephant in the room."

Desire sighed. "It's an elephant that should have been addressed a long time ago. I spoke with my parents and they want to mend the rift between the Fontaines and us. They just never knew how to approach Bryce."

"Even if Bryce says no, you should still pursue healing for both your families. The door is opened, so you may as well walk through it and take advantage of the opportunity."

"You're right. Seeing that my dad was once the mayor of

Granite Falls and is still active in the city's House of Representatives, and Bryce is one of its most influential citizens, they should get along, or at least be on speaking terms. I want to put this conflict behind us."

After she hung up the phone, Michelle thought of her conversation with Kaya a couple days ago when they'd talked about the far-reaching benefits of the wedding. It wasn't just about the four couples renewing their vows and committing themselves to each other as families and friends. It was about Granite Falls—a town coming together for healing.

She'd heard so many stories of people not speaking to each other for one reason or the other—some as stupid as leaves from a tree falling into the neighboring yard, the noise from a motorcycle waking someone up at midnight, or the honking of pet peacocks at dawn, and countless others. Some of those nuisances happened years ago, but the quarrels had been passed on to the younger generations.

If I could just find a way to bring everyone together, Michelle thought...

CHAPTER TEN

LaCrosse Jet and LaCrosse Estate – Early Thursday morning...

"The morning weather is perfect in Granite Falls, Dr. LaCrosse. Since we are the only aircraft, we've already been cleared for landing. We should be touching down in about an hour, sir."

As he glanced out the window of the jet to the range of mountains and bodies of water below, Erik's heart skipped a beat at the anticipation of seeing his wife. He'd been gone for two weeks and he couldn't wait to hold her in his arms, kiss her, and make timeless love with her. Even five years after he first laid eyes on her, he still got as nervous as a schoolboy when he thought of seeing Michelle. He ached for her. He missed his family, and couldn't wait to tell them that he was taking a break from humanitarian trips for a while.

He was absent for too many "first" milestones in his children's lives. He'd left home one week, and when he'd returned Precious was wearing a training bra. His little girl had become a young woman while his back was turned. He'd missed her first day of Junior High, Little Erik's first T-ball tournament, Tiffany's first steps, and now Michelle had told him that Fiona said "Dada" for the first time two days after he left on this trip.

Erik finished his coffee, folded his arms across his chest, stretched his legs out in front of him, and closed his eyes. He loved the work he was doing, helping those less fortunate and making a difference in the lives of countless children around the globe, but in the meantime, he was sacrificing watching his own children grow and develop. When he was home, he made his family his priority, but it wasn't enough, not for him, and not for them.

He knew Michelle worried sick about him whenever he was gone, but she would never tell him, because she was the most selfless person in the universe. His mission to help the needy mirrored hers. In fact his passion was deepened because of her. True, he was involved in humanitarian work with his free clinic in Manchester long before he met Michelle. But she opened his eyes to the possibilities of global humanitarian services. He wasn't limited to Manchester, anymore. The Erik LaCrosse Doctors Abroad Foundation was global, and Erik attributed much of its success to his wife's caring and loving character.

After he'd relinquished all the hurt pertaining to Cassie, Erik had gotten in touch with his old friend Clayton Monroe. Once they'd managed to put their past behind them, Clayton had gotten on board, and was working in some of the most remote places in Africa with the LaCrosse Foundation's financial support. Michelle had taught Erik so much about forgiving, letting go, and moving on.

She understood his mission and he knew she tried to make up for his absences, but it wasn't fair to her. It wasn't right. It was time he took a break from saving the world, and concentrated on his family before he lost them in the shuffle. This wedding they were planning couldn't happen at a better time. He was recommitting himself, his time, and devotion to Michelle and his children. Videos and pictures weren't enough anymore. He needed to see them grow and develop in real time. He needed to make his own memories.

"Would you like another cup of coffee before we begin making our first approach, Dr. LaCrosse?"

Erik opened his eyes to find the flight attendant standing beside him with a coffeepot in her hand.

"I'm fine, Susanna. Thanks for seeing to all my needs on the trip home." He handed her his empty mug.

"You slept for most of the eight-hour flight, Dr. LaCrosse, as did I," she admitted.

"Yes, and now I'm rested, showered, and hungry." He emitted a hungry bear growl and grinned.

Susanna smiled. "I offered to make you breakfast, but you declined."

"I'm saving my appetite for my family."

"It's always a pleasure, sir." Susanna returned to the galley to shut down for landing.

Erik wasn't expected home until tomorrow, so it would be a nice surprise when he walked into the kitchen to find his family having breakfast. They'd been early risers since Little Erik was a toddler. By the time Tiffany came along, they'd given up on sleeping in and had decided it was best to just get the day going—which meant he had to get up even earlier for his daily run or do it at the end of the day.

He wouldn't be running today. After breakfast, he planned to spend the rest of the day in his bed with his wife beneath him. Warmth spread through his body as the sensational images formed in his mind.

His pleasing thoughts were interrupted by his ringing cell phone. He picked it up from the table beside his chair. It was Bryce. He raised it to his ear. "Hey, Bro."

"Hey, Erik. Are you home yet?"

"Will be shortly." He'd texted Bryce yesterday to let him know he was coming home a day early so he could set up a meeting tomorrow with the architect who was working on their honeymoon haven. "What's up?" he asked detecting concern in Bryce's voice. They'd known each long enough for one to know when something was bothering the other—even through a telephone line.

"Did you hear about the change in wedding planners?"

Erik took a moment to bring his seat back to an upright position and fasten his seatbelt as his pilot announced the first decent into Granite Falls Regional Airport. "No I haven't. I've been in a South American jungle for two weeks. I guess Michelle didn't want to waste time talking about such trivia during our few and far between video chat sessions. What happened to Fae?"

"She had an accident. Fell down her stairs, broke a leg and both arms. She's in slings and a cast."

"My God."

"She'll be fine. She just can't finish planning the wedding."

"Who's the new planner?"

"Desire Summers."

Erik closed his eyes briefly. He opened them as the jet made a turn and began cruising along one side of the Aiken

River. On the other side, and far on a distant hill, the wind turbines on the Fonandt Energy Wind Farm lined the horizon, casting iridescent beams of the mesmerizing sunrise in every direction. It was good to be home. "How do you feel about that?" he finally asked Bryce in a cautious tone.

"How do you think I feel, Erik? I can't have that woman planning my wedding."

"Have you told that to your wife?"

"Not yet. I wanted to talk with you—you know since you had a similar situation with Cassie as I had with Pilar."

Erik raked his fingers through his hair. There was no point tiptoeing around the subject. "You can't punish Desire for Victoria's crimes, Bryce. Don't make the same mistake I made by punishing Michelle for something her father did."

"It's not the same thing. I'm not marrying Desire."

"It's the same concept. By not allowing Desire to plan our wedding, you're punishing Kaya. Kaya had nothing to do with Pilar's death, no more than Michelle had to do with Cassie's. But in order to build a life with Michelle, I had to forgive her father."

"That man was not Michelle's biological father, Erik. You didn't need to forgive him."

"The devil is in the details, my friend. Timmy Gleason raised Michelle. For twenty-four years of her life, she thought he was her father. The hardship she endured at his hands helped mold her into the strong, sweet, forgiving woman she is —a woman who identifies with and advocates for children who're suffering the same neglect and abuse she did. A woman who forgave me the greatest error of my life and showed me that even an imperfect ass like me can be loved. As horrible as it may sound, that awful man was responsible for bringing Michelle and me together. He was part of her life—the only father she ever knew. There comes a time when we just have to let go, and move on."

"That's easy for you to say. Timmy Gleason is dead and you don't have to worry about running into him around the next corner. But every time I see a member of the Summers family, I remember the sound of the gunshot, the sound of Pilar's body hitting the floor, and her dying in my arms, and I get angry all over again."

"I understand, buddy. I used to hyperventilate each time I heard a car tire screech. But you're going to have to decide if your anger is more important than your happiness. Michelle told me that the true test of forgiveness and moving on is when we have no feelings of resentment toward those who've wronged us." Erik paused to send up a silent "thank you" as the jet touched down and began taxiing down the runway. "I never met Gleason, but I had to forgive him, not for his sake, but for mine, and my family. Desire didn't kill Pilar, Bryce. Her sister did. Your anger is misdirected, just as mine was."

"You sound like my wife."

"Maybe you should listen to her." Erik unfastened his seatbelt as the jet came to a stop and the pilot announced that it was safe to disembark. "I'm sure if our wives didn't have their hearts set on Desire planning this wedding, they wouldn't have begun this discourse. We are blessed to have these remarkable women with whom to share our lives and create beautiful families."

"Yeah, I know. Our lives would be pathetic without them, especially where you and I are concerned. Neither one of us thought we'd ever be this happy again."

"Exactly. So if we want to maintain the level of bliss we've had so far, we need to keep our wives happy. They say a mother is only as happy as her saddest child. I say a husband is only a fraction as happy as his wife. I don't know about you, brother, but I like the fraction of happiness I have. My advice, Bryce, is that you find it in your heart to forgive, and let Desire plan our wedding, because if your wife isn't happy, none of ours will be. I like my wife happy."

"I guess I should have a talk with the Summerses, then."

"You should. Not just because of the wedding, but for your emotional, mental, and physical health, as well. You'll never experience ultimate joy in life until you eliminate your demons. Take it from someone who existed in a fool's happy paradise for years until I found the real thing with Michelle."

Bryce's sigh of resolve echoed in Erik's ear. "Look," Erik said, vacating his seat and pointing out some bags to the skycaps who'd come aboard, "my jet has landed. We can chat some more about it when we get together with Adam and Mass tomorrow. I'll be reuniting with my wife until then."

Bryce laughed. "I hear you. I had my reunion last night, and this morning. Have fun."

"I plan to. See you around." Erik slipped his cell phone into his pocket, descended the steps of his jet, and hopped into a waiting limo.

Thirty-three minutes later, Erik stepped into the foyer of his home and instructed his surprised staff to keep his presence a secret. He was floating on a cloud as he strolled through the east wing hallway and headed for the kitchen where the delicious smell of blueberry pancakes hot maple syrup, bacon, and fried eggs whetted his palate.

As he got closer, voices and laughter drifted toward him—his parents among them. It was Thursday, and he supposed his parents had come to take Little Erik and Tiffany on their weekly grandparents/grandchildren excursion with Lillian and Henry, and since they were in town, Alessandro and Arabella, who'd adopted Aria as their granddaughter and included her in the excursions since she had no biological grandparents of her own.

It brought back memories of Erik's fishing, hiking, and golfing trips with his paternal grandfather, along with Mass and Adam and their *noni* when they were kids. There weren't any girls when he was growing up, but since this younger generation had more females than males, Lillian had started a traditional grandma/granddaughter day. It was nice to carry on old traditions and begin new ones, and it was the perfect day to come home since he and Michelle would be toddler-free for most of the day. Precious was old enough to take care of herself, and Fiona had her nanny and Grandma Hayes to see to her needs for a couple hours.

Erik ran into Mrs. Hayes around the corner from the kitchen. He silenced her with a finger to his lips, and after greeting her, he sent her on her way back to the kitchen. He grinned with anxiety and mischief as he watched and listened to his family.

"Why don't you want to be called Little Erik, anymore?" Michelle asked their son.

"Because girls make fun of me. They say I'm small and tiny."

"What girls?" Philippe placed his coffee mug out of Fiona's reach, as she sat on his lap eating boiled egg yolks from a plate.

"Alyssa."

"Well that's just one girl." Michelle ruffled his head of curly brown hair. "Other girls might not think you're small and tiny. They might think you're the biggest boy they've ever seen, and the handsomest, too."

Erik was touched by his wife's response.

"And Precious." Little Erik pointed his fork at his sister who was sitting across the table from him.

"Precious, you make fun of your brother?" Felicia tossed Precious a mock look of disapproval. "Shame on you," she said as she refilled Tiffany's cup with orange juice.

Precious rolled her eyes. "I—I don't make fun of him. I—"

"And Jason." Little Erik was having a field day pointing out his accusers, even if they weren't around to defend themselves.

"Jason's not a girl," Precious said pouring syrup over her pancakes and reaching for another helping of scrambled eggs.

Erik frowned at the "you should know" look Michelle tossed his daughter. A look that made her drop her gaze. *What had happened while he was away this time? What new milestone was he about to learn of?*

"Jason says I'm little," Little Erik continued. "He won't play with me. I'm not little. I'm big." He dropped his fork, fisted his hand, and made a muscle. "I'm strong. I have muscles like Daddy."

"Yes you do, ba—my big man." Ignoring Precious' chortle, Michelle leaned over and tested his puny little bicep. "Mm hmm. You're almost as strong as your daddy."

"Is he now?" Unable to resist any longer, Erik stepped into the kitchen and made his presence known. Michelle's gasp of surprise was swallowed up in his children's shouts of joy.

"Daddy! Daddy! Daddy!" They jumped from their chairs and ran into his arms.

He picked all three of them up from the floor and bear hugged them at once, reveling in the enjoyment they displayed at seeing him.

He trembled as he kissed and squeezed them tight. He'd hugged a lot of children in the past two weeks, but nothing compared to having his own in his arms. Their individual scents overpowered the breakfast aroma that had greeted him when he first approached the kitchen. Precious smelled like a summer rose garden. Little Erik carried the green apple scent of his organic shampoo, and Tiffany was just drenched in innocence and sunshine.

Erik inhaled deeply as if he could breathe them into his pores. He never wanted to let them go. "Oh, I missed you guys so much."

"We missed you too, Daddy," Precious said. "I'm glad you're home."

"Daddy. I love you, Daddy." Tiffany clasped her syrupy hands on his cheeks and kissed him on his lips.

"Daddy loves you, too, my little princess."

"Me too. I love you, Daddy." Little Erik wrapped his arms around his neck.

"So much love," he heard his mother say with a catch in her voice.

Erik set his children on the floor and marched over to his wife, who'd risen from her seat, and had been looking on lovingly as their children welcomed him home.

"My sweet, sweet Michelle," he whispered in a choked voice.

"Erik." She trailed her fingers along his freshly shaven cheeks.

The happy tears pooling in her mesmerizing black eyes, her soft touch, and the sexy sound of his name on her lips thrilled Erik to the bone. He picked her slender frame off the floor, wrapped his arms around her, and covered her mouth with his. He groaned and kissed her deeply and hungrily, right there in his kitchen with his entire world looking on. She smelled like *Moonlight*—the most intoxicating scent in the world to him—and tasted like French roast coffee and blueberry pancakes. His heart trembled with love, his loins stirred with need. In spite of his hunger for food, he was tempted to skip breakfast and take her upstairs.

"There's enough food here, son. You don't have to suck your wife's from her belly."

"Don't mind your father, Erik. You keep showing your wife just how much you missed her in whatever manner you choose, son."

"Oh boy. Here comes another Baby LaCrosse," Precious stated in a comical voice.

Erik reluctantly dragged his mouth from Michelle's and slid her down his body until her feet touched the floor. He held her chair, and once she was seated, he walked over to his parents, hugged them in turn, then lifted his youngest child from her grandpa's lap, and held her close to his heart. She smelled like cooked eggs and baby lotion. Sweetness to him.

"Fiona, my darling baby girl." His heart danced with merriment when her tiny hands went around his neck. "Daddy loves you to pieces. Daddy missed you." He held her up and smiled at her. "Can you say *Dada* for your dada? Can you, baby? Daddy wants to hear you say *Dada*."

"Dada." Fiona gave him a big toothless grin.

Erik kissed her egg-yolk covered cheeks and chortled with joy.

"Dada, Dada, Dada," she repeated as she kicked her legs and clapped her hands in excitement.

"This is the best homecoming I've ever had." Erik surveyed his family. He wasn't leaving them again. He took his seat at the head of the table and sat Fiona on his knee.

"Take that away," he said as a maid pushed a highchair next to his. "My baby is fine in her daddy's arms." For the first time in a long time, Erik felt like the head of his household, not superiorly, because his wife had as much say in all matters as he had—maybe more—but protectively. He'd promised Michelle that he would love and protect her and their kids. He couldn't protect them from halfway around the world. Daddy was home to stay.

"Here you go, Doctor." Mrs. Hayes put a stack of hot pancakes on his plate. "Just the way you love them."

"Thank you, Mrs. Hayes." Erik smiled at the old woman who still refused to retire from his kitchen. "I've dreamt about your meals every single night for two whole weeks." He piled some bacon beside his pancakes and took the fruit bowl his mother passed to him.

"Now you don't have to dream anymore." She patted him on the shoulder and moved over to Little Erik. "And here's to making you stronger," she said, placing a fresh stack of pancakes on his plate. "Soon you'll be so big, your big sister will be straining her neck to look you in the eye."

"Thank you, Grandma Hayes." Little Erik beamed up at her as the chatter started up again.

Erik poured hot maple syrup over his pancakes and dug into his breakfast like he hadn't eaten for weeks. Ready-to-eat meals weren't real food, and he'd been living on them for two weeks. "So what is this I hear about a name change?" he asked his son. "You don't like 'Little Erik', anymore?"

With a mouth full of pancakes and bacon, Little Erik shook his head, negatively.

"What would you like to be called instead?" He wiped his mouth with his napkin and pulled Fiona's bowl closer so she could grab a handful of egg yolks.

"Just my name. Erik."

"When you're with Dad, you won't know which Erik they mean. That's stupid."

"Ha ha, he's *Tupid*." Tiffany was in the habit of repeating everything she heard, whether or not she understood it. "*Tupid*," she said again and giggled as she placed a piece of melon into her mouth.

"Tiffany. That's not nice," Michelle scolded her daughter. "We don't call each other names in this family."

"I'm not stupid." Erik dropped his head on the table and began to cry.

Michelle picked him out of his seat and cradled him on her lap.

"See, that's why we call you 'little'. One minute you're running around like you're crazy and the next, you're crying like a little girl," Precious said.

"Little Erik's crying like a girl." Tiffany reached for her cup.

"Precious, stop it!" Felicia cast her granddaughter a withering stare.

"I'm just kidding." Precious flashed a devilish smile.

"You of all people shouldn't be teasing him," her grandfather said. "Especially—"

Michelle cleared her throat. "Apologize to your brother, Precious."

"I'm sorry."

There was that look between his daughter and his wife again, Erik thought. He would get to the bottom of it later. "What about Erik Junior?" he asked his son, who was back in his chair.

"No."

"EJ?" Michelle asked.

He shook his head again.

Philippe raised his hand to silence everyone. "I know. You're Erik Philippe LaCrosse, The Third. Since you don't like EJ, what about PJ for Philippe Junior?"

"You want to call my son *Pajamas* in lieu of Little Erik, Dad?"

Philippe chuckled. "Ahh, bad idea."

"Let's switch the letters and make it JP," Michelle blurted. "Do you like JP?"

He nodded on a smile. "I like JP, Mommy."

"Then JP it is. From now on you'll be known as JP LaCrosse, until you decide you want to change it again."

With the matter of Little Erik's new name put to bed, Erik thought of another subject he would love to take to bed.

In the middle of answering questions about his trip, Erik glanced at his wife and the look in her eyes told him that her thoughts mirrored his. He downed his grapefruit juice, kissed his infant daughter before handing her over to her grandmother, shot to his feet, walked up to his wife and lifted her from her chair. Without saying a word, he carried her to the elevator and pushed the *up* button.

❦

As soon as her parents left the kitchen, Precious excused herself from the table and went to her bedroom on the second floor. She pulled her cell phone from the pocket of her shorts and texted Jason: My dad's home.

A few seconds later a response came through.

Jason: Crap. How long ago?
Precious sat on the edge of her bed: This morning. He's with my mom in their bedroom.
Jason: U think she'll tell him?
Precious: IDK. She said she won't. I trust her. Is ur dad home?
Jason: Yeah. Last night.
Precious: Did u talk to him?
Jason: I haven't seen him yet. I'm not at home.
Precious: Where r u?
Jason: At Ethan's. I spent the night.

Precious pouted. How come she didn't know that? Oh yeah, Michelle had banned her from talking with Jason until her father got home. It wasn't even a full day yet, but it was already killing her. Her dad was home now so it wasn't like she was breaking any rules.

Jason: U still there?

Precious: I'm scared my dad will ground me till I'm 30. I don't want them to keep us apart.

Jason: I'm scared, too. But I liked kissing you. (Smiley face)

Precious bit into her lower lip: Me, too. (Smiley face and a heart).

Jason: I'll talk to my dad when I get home. When r u going to talk with urs?

Precious: IDK.

Jason: It'll be okay. I promise.

Precious: Okay. Bye, Jason.

Jason: Bye, Precious. (A heart).

Precious plopped down on her back and stared at the ceiling, a sweet smile perched on her face. She was so in love. She hoped her dad and Uncle Bryce would understand how she and Jason felt about each other since they were so much in love with their wives. Especially her dad, seeing that he and her real mom had been together since they were teenagers. She would just have to remind him of that fact.

She'd kissed Jason because she wanted to know what a real kiss felt like, but she was also scared that he would think she was still a little girl. Her friend Teresa had told her that her older sister had told *her* that a lot of girls in high school thought Jason was hot. Precious didn't like girls thinking about him that way, and she didn't want him going to other girls for things he couldn't get from her. She might still be in middle school, but she wasn't stupid. She knew what boys in high school did with the girls who let them. She didn't want Jason doing those things with other girls. She just didn't. Her little heart began to beat real fast.

Forty-five minutes later, in the privacy of their third-floor master suite, Erik dragged his lips up along his wife's damp body as she trembled from the force of her second orgasm. He lay on top of her, his thick hard erection pressing into the hot slickness between her thighs where his mouth had taken up residence for the past fifteen minutes. He kissed her breasts, sucked on her nipples, and her lips while Johnny Gill sang "Behind Closed Doors" in the background. The fact that they were actually behind closed doors heightened his fantasy, sweetened the thrill of Michelle's love. Her passion, her unquenchable desire for him, always set his soul on fire.

Dragging his mouth from her nipple, up along her chest and throat, he gazed into her misty black eyes. "Are we safe?" he asked in a rough voice as he felt her warm hand grasp his shaft, guiding the tip to the entrance of her body.

"We're safe. You can come inside me."

With a deep groan, Erik entered her, and for a few intense moments, his heart stopped beating as he savored the hot, tight sweetness of her. Even after giving birth to three children, she was still as tight as the first time they made love five years ago. *It will always be like the first time with Michelle.* When her legs wrapped around his waist and her arms circled his neck, he buried his face into the valley between her breasts and whispered her name.

"Erik, I missed you so much," she moaned as she raised her hips, squeezing her vaginal muscles around his shaft.

He began thrusting slowly inside her, going deep and sure, until passion and heat and fluid radiated from the soft core of her body, and she cried out his name over and over again. When Ne-Yo began singing "Religious," she got religious, clawing at him, singing *Hallelujah* and begging him to take her higher and deeper. Powerless to resist, Erik gave himself over to the divine pleasure, the erotic madness she evoked in him, and sang *Hallelujah* right along with her.

"Michelle." He groaned out her name in the heat of it.

"Love me, baby, love me. Yes, yes. Don't stop. Don't... Don't. Oh God, I'm coming. I'm coming... Erik..."

"Yes, baby. I'm right with you." Erik snuck his hands under her to clasp her beautiful buttocks and hold her still as the electricity arching along his back warned him that he wouldn't last much longer. When he felt her walls quivering around him, he lifted his head, gazed into her beautiful black eyes, and spilled his seed as the turbulence of their passion whirled around them. *Hallelujah....*

To his delight, Michelle wasn't done with him. "Roll with me," she whispered, locking her legs around him and flipping him over onto his back. She straddled him, entwined their fingers, pushed up on her feet and began to dance on his waning erection until it was standing at full force again as Raheem DeVaughn sang "Temperature's Rising."

Erik's temperature broke its own record. He could say it was because he hadn't made love in over three weeks, but he knew it was more than that. It was because of the woman with whom he was making love.

Two hours and thee sessions later, Erik lay replete on his back with Michelle sprawled on top of him, her cheek against his steady beating heart, their sexes still joined in a hot sticky muddle. "Untie me, wench," he murmured.

She giggled and reached up to release his wrists from the scarves she'd used to restrain him to the bedpost while she loved his brains out.

His wife was the sexiest woman in the universe. She loved

to tie him up and have her way with him and he loved to indulge her fantasies, even more. "I have a present for you," he said, kissing her forehead. He ran his hands up and down her damp warm body, reacquainting his fingers, his palm with the silky feel of her skin.

"You just gave me four." She giggled again, causing the walls of her sex to grip his semi-hard shaft. "What could be better?"

"Not having to wait for this." He groaned and thrust up into her, making her sigh in pleasure. He fought against the desire to take her again. "It would be nice to do this every single day and night, wouldn't it?"

She raised her head and gazed at him, her black eyes full of expectation and hope. "What are you saying, exactly?"

"I'm saying that I'm giving up traveling. I'm staying home." He traced her eyebrows with his thumbs.

"No more missions."

"No more. I don't want to miss any more of my children's childhood milestones. I need to be here for you and them, every day. I spoke with Clayton and he's happy to take over as CEO of the foundation."

"Erik, this is so, so…" At a loss for words, she rained kisses all over his face. "Thank you. It was tough trying to explain your absence to the kids every single day. Especially Little—JP. He needs his dad."

"And his dad needs him. I need all my children."

Her face clouded and she slid off him to the mattress.

"What is it?" He turned sideways and cradled his head in his hand so he could look at her. "What bad news do you have to tell me? Is it about Precious? Something's going on between the two of you."

"No," she said almost too eagerly. "Well, yes. It's about Sarah."

"What about her?"

"She died, Erik."

The news hit him like a big truck. He collapsed on his back, breathing deeply and sharply for a few seconds. "When? What happened?" he asked when he finally caught his breath again.

"Monday."

"Was she ill? I mean apart from the—"

"Mrs. Beck said she was fine for breakfast and lunch. After lunch, she went to her room for her afternoon nap. Her nurse found her when she went to wake her for her medicine. She apparently died in her sleep. I guess her heart just gave out."

Tears stung Erik's eyes. When Michelle's arms closed around him, he turned to her and wept his sorrow into her neck.

"I'm sorry I had to hit you with such bad news as soon as you got home. But it's been three days and we have to make plans for the funeral before we go away next week."

"Where is she?"

"Still at Cape Hill. They were keeping her until you got home. Mrs. Beck wants to know if you'd like to order an autopsy."

"I don't think there's any reason to cut her open. We've known something like this could happen." He eased out of Michelle's embrace and stared at the ceiling, a horde of conflicting emotions racing through him. He'd put Sarah on an experimental drug that came with a lot of side effects. He had consulted with many specialists before he'd made the decision. In the end, everyone had agreed that it was better for

Sarah to have a few quality years with her granddaughter than to spend the rest of her life in a deteriorating state. It must have been the drugs that caused her heart to stop. "As insensitive as it may sound, it was the best way for her to go. Peacefully."

"I agree."

"At least Precious was able to enjoy her for three years. They had the chance to know each other, and she learned a lot about her mother from Sarah. It was worth it." He paused to absorb the pain in his chest—pain for his little girl's loss. "She's taking the news well."

"She doesn't know yet. I thought you should be the one to tell her."

"I'm not looking forward to breaking her heart, but the sooner the better, I suppose."

"I'm here for Precious, Erik. I'll do everything in my power to help her through the grief of losing her grandmother. If it weren't for you, Sarah probably would have died a long time ago, and Precious wouldn't have gotten to know her on such an intimate level. You're a great father. Your love for and devotion to Precious was one of the main reasons I fell in love with you five years ago. I wanted my children to have a father just like you. And now they have you."

As Michelle's arms closed around him again, Erik expelled a deep long groan. "Thanks baby. I hope I never disappoint you. And thanks for being an exceptional mother to my daughter, to all our children. I love you so much, Michelle, my darling."

"I love you, too Erik. More today than I did yesterday, and not nearly as much as I will love you tomorrow."

Erik tightening his arms about her. This was heaven. Just

before he left on this last trip, they'd celebrated their fourth "public" wedding anniversary on their private island of *Michelle* in the Seychelles. The entire family was headed back to the island next week so he and Michelle could spend some quality time with the children before the wedding and honeymoon. The timing was perfect for him to reconnect with his children and let them know that Daddy was home to stay.

CHAPTER ELEVEN

Meanwhile at Fontaine Estate – Thursday morning – same day...

B ryce dropped his smart phone on a table in the sitting room of his third-floor master wing and glanced down when a warm furry ball brushed against his legs.

"Webster," he whispered, picking up the cat and burying his face in his glossy black coat. Webster purred in contentment as Bryce walked over to the glass door, that led to a balcony and gazed out at the sunrise bursting with vigor and color across the sky.

Nothing Erik had said was news to him. He'd come to the same conclusions since Kaya approached him on Monday. He knew that allowing Desire to plan their wedding would please the wives. Trouble was, it came with a price—the torture of revisiting the most painful place in his past.

He'd said goodbye to Pilar when he'd finally admitted to himself that he loved Kaya. He'd moved on and built a life with her and their children. He was happy, and he owed a lot of it to Erik who'd reamed him out three and a half years ago when he'd been hovering between choosing a life with Kaya and staying in the past with Pilar.

Erik had called him in his hotel room in Chicago and told him to get over himself and get his ass home to his wife before he lost her like he'd lost Michelle. Bryce never told Kaya about his conversation with Erik because he didn't ever want her to think that his decision to return to her was influenced by anyone. He never wanted her to doubt his commitment to their vows or his love for her, because deep in his heart, he knew he would have come to that decision without Erik's intervention. It might have taken him longer, but he would have chosen Kaya in the end. Nevertheless, Erik's admonition to him, and Michelle's advice to Kaya to take him back without hesitation, had spared them months of pain and regret—the kind of pain and regret his friends had lived through, and that had afforded them the authority to counsel others.

A husband is only a fraction as happy as his wife. You're going to have to decide if your anger is more important than your happiness.

Bryce sighed as Erik's words echoed in his mind. He was happier now than he'd ever been in his entire life, but was it a fool's happiness like Erik had said? Could he be even happier? Could his fraction be greater if he'd just let go of his anger?

The thought both thrilled and scared him, but he'd promised Kaya that he'd do anything to make her happy. And if that meant raking his soul over hot coals one last time, then that's exactly what he would do. As if reading his mind, and agreeing with him, Webster meowed, jumped out of his arms, and headed toward the bedroom, his bushy tail twirling behind him.

Chuckling softly, Bryce followed the wise old cat. He eased the door open, stepped into the room, and tiptoed over to the bed. Kaya was still fast asleep on her tummy under the covers—in the same position he'd left her when he'd snuck out to call Erik. She didn't even budge when Webster jumped up on the mattress and settled down at her feet.

She was so lovely, so tempting, with her long brown curls spread out above her head on the white pillowcase, and her dainty little mouth parted in sleep. Fire shot through Bryce's body at the recent memory of Kaya's lips clasped around his shaft, and her passion-filled brown eyes gazing seductively into his as she pleasured him with her tongue.

Even though their last lovemaking session had ended a little over an hour ago, Bryce would love nothing more than to crawl back into bed, wake her up with a gentle poke, and make love to her until the town's clock rang out the noonday hour. He would never stop desiring more and more of her.

He leaned over and kissed her warm cheek. She stirred, stretched, and then burrowed deeper into the covers with a deep sigh. Bryce stood erect again, and with an insatiable smile on his lips, and the sweet taste of Kaya still in his mouth, he tiptoed into his bathroom and dropped his robe on the floor.

Ahh, not a cold shower, his burgeoning erection seemed to scream as it twitched restlessly against his thigh.

"I'm sorry, buddy, but I do have a conscience," he said as he entered a series of timed temperatures on a remote control pad on the wall before stepping into the shower stall. He raised his face and gritted his teeth as the cold sprays automatically pelted him from several angles of the marble stall. *Yeah, that will do it*, he thought on a sigh as his mind wandered back to his homecoming yesterday.

He'd returned from Philly to find Kaya and the twins waiting for him at the airport. Alyssa and Anastasia were with his parents, and Jason was spending the night at Ethan's house —Kaya's idea. It was nice to come home and bond with just his wife and his youngest children. After playing with the twins in the playground, and then a picnic dinner in one of the gazebos on the estate, he and Kaya had handed them off to their nanny, and locked themselves in their bedroom.

They'd been making love since, and he knew she was probably as worn out as he was, maybe more so because she'd been taking care of their five kids alone while he was away. Three and a half years ago, when he and Kaya had become full-time parents overnight, he'd quickly come to realize that the profession of parenting was far more physically and emotionally exhausting than any other in the universe.

It was one thing when he was acting as godfather to Jason, Alyssa, and Anastasia, but after he and Kaya assumed the roles of substitute parents, Bryce's respect and appreciation for parenthood had shot up to the top of his profession-rating chart. He'd thought he'd figured out the science of taking care of children until it became a twenty-four/seven job.

Gone were the days when he came home from a rough day at the office to a quiet, orderly home. There'd never been a dull moment with his godchildren at *L'etoile du Nord*, and there were even fewer at his three-hundred-acre estate now that he'd been blessed with his own little bundles of joy—Eli and Elyse, named after Kaya's father, and Bryce's grandmother.

Bryce had begun appreciating his parents more, even

though they'd practically shoved most of the responsibility of raising him on to his grandmother. But his grannie hadn't minded one bit, Bryce thought with a pleasant smile as he held his washcloth under the soap dispense and lathered up his body. His parents were now behaving like his grannie—always dropping by unannounced to see their grandkids, and wanting to take them out and show them off.

He'd thought them overly obsessive with Jason, Alyssa, and Anastasia, but they'd gotten worse after Eli and Elyse were born. It had gotten so bad, he'd had to curtail their visits, and asked them to take the older kids so he and Kaya could have quality time and bond with their infant children. Thus, Grandparents' day was instituted. Every so often, his parents would alternate between taking his godchildren, and the twins, and once in a while, they took all five—well four now that Jason thought he was too old to hang out with his younger siblings. He never passed up spending time alone with his grandpa, though.

Bryce was grateful that they gave his adoptive kids as much attention as they gave his biological children. *His progeny*. Affection welled up into Bryce's throat as he thought of his two-and-a-half year-old-miracle twins. Kaya had been so ill when she was carrying them that the entire family had lived on the edge for six months of her pregnancy. Several times, they'd thought she would lose them, but with lots of prayers, tender loving care, and the skills of the best OB/GYN money could afford, she'd delivered two healthy babies—the most beautiful babies Bryce had ever laid eyes on.

His heart rocked as he recalled the day he and Kaya found out they were having twins—a boy and a girl. It was as if God was blessing him twice for the one he'd lost with Pilar. For nine months, Bryce had talked to them, read to them, sang to them, while they grew inside their mother's womb. And each time he felt them kick against his palms, his stomach, or any other part of his body, his love for them increased. From his experience with his godchildren, he thought he'd been prepared for the swarm of emotions that came with holding them in his arms for the first time. But he was wrong. It was a million times more intense. His expression of joy was so great, Dr. Walsh and Erik had cried along with him.

There's no greater joy than holding your own child in your arms for the first time, Michael had said to him three times over the course of their friendship. Those words had come back to Bryce as he'd stood in that delivery room, cradling his own children in his arms just moments after they were born. He'd also remembered Michael chastising him about his obsession with his godchildren. *I appreciate everything you do for my children, Bryce, and it warms my heart to know that if anything should happen to me, you'd be there for them, and Lauren. Pretending they're yours is good for them, but it's not good for you. You need your own brood to carry on your family name. My children are Rogers. They will never be Fontaines."*

"I have my own brood, Michael," he whispered with a smile. Eli and Elyse were Fontaines, part of him, flesh of his flesh and bone of his bones. His blood was running through their little veins, but it didn't mean that he loved his godchildren any less. He loved all his children, and he would gladly lay down his life for each one of them.

He and Kaya had recently talked about having another child, and Dr. Walsh did promise that it would be different this time since the three factors that had put Kaya's first pregnancy at risk had been removed from the equation—

dealing with Lauren and Michael's sudden and tragic deaths, changing her entire life and becoming a wife and mother overnight, and anxiety about being a despicable mother like Nadine.

In spite of Dr. Walsh's optimism, to say he was concerned was an understatement. Bryce was petrified, for as much as he would love to create more babies with Kaya, losing her wasn't worth the risk. He'd prepared himself to be content with the two they'd created from their love, and the three they'd adopted.

Bryce turned and stopped short when he encountered a mini replica of himself, standing just outside the shower stall, one hand stuck down the front of his blue and white Red Sox pajama pants, the other holding his favorite blanket, and a red fire truck at his feet. Bryce blinked the warm water from his eyes. "Eli."

"Hi, Daddy," his son said with a big grin. "You're taking a shower?"

"Yep." Bryce took a swift glance around, grateful that his daughter hadn't joined her twin in his bathroom. "Where's your sister?"

"With Mommy. They're making breakfast."

"Good." Bryce stepped out of the shower, and the sprays immediately stopped. He reached for an oversize burgundy towel.

"Is that your penis, Daddy?" Eli pulled his hand from inside his pants to point at Bryce's groin.

Bryce froze for an instant, then slowly pulled the towel from its rack and dabbed at the moisture on his face, deliberately not attempting to cover up himself too quickly. Eli had seen him naked several times before, but since he'd recently discovered his own penis, like all little boys his age, he'd been fascinated with it, and had been asking questions about the magnificent appendage that only boys owned.

Samantha had told them not to make a big deal out of his interest, and to answer all his questions as honestly as possible, and then subtly divert his attention to something else. She said the phase would pass. His parents told him that he was around Eli's age when he'd found his.

"Yes, Eli," he said, drying off the rest of his body, before wrapping the towel around his waist. "This is my penis." *Last time I checked.*

"Does Mommy know you have a penis, Daddy?"

"I'm pretty sure she does." Bryce cleared his throat and tried to keep a straight face as he gazed down at his curious son—a prodigy in his own right. Eli was way ahead of his sister who was born a full ten minutes after him, and weighed a pound and a half less than him.

It was as if he couldn't wait to get out and start exploring the vast world around him. Elyse, on the other hand, had been in no hurry to leave the cushiony comfort of her mother's womb, and once she did come out, she was quite content to remain totally dependent on anyone she could con for as long as she could. Eli had begun teething, crawling, walking, and talking months before Elyse, and he was already reading while Elyse was still stuck on recognizing letters and sounding out words. A good four inches taller than his twin sister, Eli seemed to be destined to be a giant like his father, while Elyse would be petite and dainty like her mother.

"Has she seen it?"

"What?" Bryce took a sharp turn off Memory Lane.

"Have you shown Mommy your penis?" Eli asked matter-of-factly.

All the time. "Yep, she's seen it," he said as blasé as he could. He supposed Eli's question stemmed from the fact that they'd spoken about exposing his penis in public—something he'd started doing when he first discovered it. Eli didn't understand why he couldn't show off something he was obviously proud of possessing.

"Does she like it?"

She keeps telling me she does. "Yeah. I think so." He clamped his mouth tightly to muffle the chuckle tickling the back of his throat.

"Why?"

Divert. "Speaking of Mommy, what is she cooking for breakfast?"

Eli shrugged and spread his hands. "I don't know. Eggs and toast?"

"That sounds good. I'm hungry. Are you?"

"I'm starving." Eli rubbed his hand on his little tummy, and followed Bryce over to the counter. "Why is your penis so big, Daddy? It's way bigger than mine."

The boy was like a puppy with a kong filled with peanut butter. "Because I'm a grown man, and you're still a little boy," he said crouching down to his son's level, and staring into eyes that were as black as midnight. He rested his hands on his shoulders. "Don't worry, yours will grow," he added at Eli's look of confusion.

"I don't want my penis to grow, Daddy."

"Why not?"

"Because my hands are too small and I won't be able to hold it, and when I go pee-pee, it'll be everywhere. Like *squushh*," he uttered, waving his arms in the air like a live garden hose out of control. "Like Niagara Falls."

Bryce couldn't hold back his ripple of mirth. He pulled his son into his arms, fell back on the floor and laughed his heart out. Boy, did his baby boy have a lot of growing up to do.

"Is that funny, Daddy?" Eli asked with a little chortle of his own.

"Yes, that's very funny. Probably the funniest thing I've heard in a long while." *One of these days, I will have a field day recounting this conversation with you.* He rearranged the towel on his hips, picked Eli up and sat him on the counter. He inspected his little face judiciously. "Looks like you need a shave, young man," he said, reaching for the tub of shaving gel on the counter. He covered his own chin and cheeks with the gel, and then gave some to Eli.

Bryce's eyes misted as he watched his little replica imitate him.

"I love shaving with you, Daddy."

"Me, too, son." Bryce picked up his monogrammed Zafirro Iridium razor that Kaya had given him for Christmas last year. It was a limited edition, only ninety-nine made by the manufacturer when they first hit the market a few years ago. Kaya had made a special request that they make a replica toy one for Eli. With the name Fontaine Enterprises behind her, they'd scrambled to make her every wish come true. Bryce loved his expensive toy, and he loved his wife for presenting it to him, and for making one for their son. He placed Eli's razor in his hand. "Ready son?" he asked, turning to their reflections in the wall-to-wall mirror.

"Ready, Daddy. Let's do this. Man style."

Twenty minutes later, dressed in a pair of jeans shorts and

a T-shirt, Bryce hoisted his son over his shoulders and headed into the direction of the kitchen on the east side of the third floor, passing a trail of toys scattered about the floor on the way.

They had a full-time gourmet cook and tons of servants at their beck and call, yet when they'd been planning their home, Kaya had taken a page from Adam's book and requested a kitchen on the third floor where she loved to cook breakfast for her family without servants milling about. They always had dinner together, and sometimes lunch in the formal dining room on the second floor. The private kitchen was also great when he and Kaya wanted to be naughty with whipped cream and fruits, warm liquid chocolate, edible panties and briefs, and whatever else their licentious minds could cook up. And like Adam, she'd added a waterbed for convenience. When not in use, it was hidden behind a retractable wall in the kitchen.

"I smell eggs," Eli said, tightening his hands around Bryce's head as they drew near to the kitchen.

"Me, too. And waffles, you think?"

"Yeah, undeniably!"

Bryce missed a step. "Undeniably? Where'd you learn that word?"

"From Jason. He's smart."

Bryce's heart warmed at the mention of his adopted son, whom he loved just as much as he loved his own. Jason was turning into a responsible young man who looked out for his young siblings—all four of them. Michael and Lauren would be so proud of him.

"Do you know what 'undeniably' means, Daddy?"

"I have no idea, Eli," Bryce replied, playing along.

"It means you can't deny it. Like definitely." He sniffed the air. "I definitely, undeniably smell eggs and waffles."

"In that case, I undeniably smell them, too."

"You learned a new word, Daddy. If you study your books really hard, maybe one day you'll be as smart as Jason."

"Maybe." Bryce walked into the kitchen to find Kaya standing at the stove with her back to him and Elyse perched on one of her hips. Webster was lying at her feet next to some crayons and coloring books. His grandmother's coffee maker chugged noisily on the counter.

"Daddy." Elyse held out her arms as soon as she spotted him. "I want my Daddy."

Kaya turned and smiled at him. "Finally. I thought you two might have skipped out on us. Breakfast is almost ready."

Memories sent Bryce's pulse pounding as his eyes feasted on the soft curves of her body under her white satin robe.

"Mommy." Eli struggled off his shoulder and raced over to wrap his arms around his mother's legs. "Daddy learned a new word."

"Oh, yeah? What's it this time?" She handed over Elyse to him then hunched down to gaze into her son's eyes.

"Undeniably," Bryce answered, pressing his daughter close to his heart as a different kind of love welled up inside him. Over the years, Bryce had come to realize that he could love his children with the same degree of depth and passion, yet feel paradoxically different about them. Daughters, he'd learned, had a way of wrapping their little fists around their fathers' hearts, and squeezing, like no one else in the world could do. His love for his daughters was mushy and protective, while that for his sons was firm and robust.

"How's my favorite girl?" he asked, kissing Elyse's cheeks,

and tickling her while she giggled and grabbed on to the front of his shirt.

"I thought I was your favorite girl." Kaya pouted in mock hurt as she stood up, with Eli in her arms. "Seems like I was undeniably misled last night, and this morning."

In response, Bryce kissed her lips, tasting her, feeding on her as the smell of eggs and waffles and ham, and Kaya, wafted up his nostrils.

"Daddy's kissing Mommy," Elyse whispered, clapping her little hands together.

"Daddy's always kissing Mommy because Daddy loves Mommy. I love Mommy too." Eli pushed his face between Bryce and Kaya.

"Kissy. Kissy." Elyse dove in for hers, and soon all the Fontaines were kissing and sharing love and hugs.

Bryce had learned about healthy family living from Michael and Lauren, and even before them, from Alessandro and Arabella Andreas, whose home he used to visit with Adam when they were in high school. From observing those two exemplary couples, Bryce had learned that children who observed their parents showing affection for each other felt a whole lot more secure and were a lot happier than those who didn't.

Neither he nor Kaya had that experience growing up, and so they had agreed to continue the tradition for his godchildren, and eventually for their own. All of his kids cheered whenever they saw him kissing their mother, even Jason who sometimes jokingly told them to get a room.

"Okay, guys, as much as I love these special moments, I have to finish Elyse's oatmeal," Kaya finally said, breaking away. "Make yourself useful and set the table," she ordered

Bryce before putting Eli on the floor and returning to her pot of oatmeal.

"Yes, Ma'am. Eli, can you help Daddy, buddy? Grab the mats." As his son got the mats from a drawer, Bryce smiled into his daughter's big brown eyes—her mother's eyes—and brushed a handful of curly black hair from her face. "Will you try some eggs today, sweetheart?"

"No." She shook her head from side to side. "They're dirty, Daddy."

Elyse used to love eggs until she learned where they came from. One children's educational TV show, one rainy afternoon, one hen laying one egg, and his daughter's perspective about the ultimate super food was changed forever—well, he hoped not forever. Bryce pulled some plates and bowls from a cabinet and handed them one at a time to Eli, who placed them on the mats.

"Just a little bit?" he asked Elyse as he reached into another cabinet for some glasses and mugs. "You can only eat oatmeal one way, but you can have eggs in many different ways—scrambled, boiled, poached, fried—"

"I like my eggs scrambled," his son said.

"No. I don't want eggs, Daddy. I just want oatmeal, and ham and waffles. No eggs," Elyse stated, beating her hand on his chest for emphasis.

"You can actually have oatmeal in a variety of ways," Kaya said as she filled a bowl with oatmeal, garnished with nuts and raisins, and took it over to the table. "You can add walnuts, pecans, raisins, dried cranberry, cinnamon, and a host of other nuts and fruits. I hate to tell you, but you're wrong, baby."

"Yeah, Daddy, you're wrong." Elyse backed up her mother.

"Okay, okay, I'm wrong. It won't be the last time." Bryce grimaced in good humor as he filled the stainless steel coffee carafe and set it on the heat resistant coaster on the table.

As Eli climbed up on his chair, Bryce settled Elyse into hers, and helped Kaya take the covered dishes out of the oven warmer, and bowls of fruits from the fridge and placed them on the table. His mouth watered as she pulled the covers off to reveal a smorgasbord of banana waffles, baked Canadian ham, blueberry muffins, a cheese and bacon soufflé—his favorite breakfast dish.

If Bryce didn't know better, he'd think his wife was buttering him up for something. *Wait*, she was. Bryce seated Kaya before taking his place at the other end of the table. He motioned for the family to hold hands in preparation to say Grace before they began to enjoy their delicious breakfast. "You cooked enough for an army," he said.

"Mom and Dad are coming to pick up the twins for their grandparent outing with the LaCrosses and the Andreases. They weren't sure if they'd make it to the café for breakfast, so I cooked enough just in case."

Excellent! He'd have her to himself for the rest of the day.

They were almost through their meal when the motion sensor flashed. "The rest of the brood is here," Bryce said, wiping his mouth on his napkin.

"Lyssa and Stacia are home." Eli and Elyse jumped down from their chairs and raced into the hall, calling out their sisters' names.

Bryce appreciated the fact that the children got on well with each other. Anastasia was barely a year old when Eli and

Elyse were born, but Kaya and Bryce had been worried that Jason and Alyssa would be jealous of them, especially Alyssa who was head-over-heels in love with Bryce. But their worry was in vain. His godchildren took to his children as if they all shared the same mother and father. Jason was the one who'd asked if they could call him and Kaya "Mom" and "Dad" so the twins wouldn't start calling them "Uncle Bryce" and "Aunt Kaya." They were one big blended happy family.

"When is Jason due home?" he asked over the rim of his coffee mug.

"Later. Duncan is taking him and Ethan to the racetracks, then he'll bring him home this afternoon."

"Thank you for giving us this special time alone with the twins. I needed that," he said as voices and the clambering of feet approaching reached his ears.

"We both needed that." She wrapped her slender fingers around her coffee mug. "Saturday is Alyssa and Anastasia's time with us."

He tilted his head. "Not Jason?"

"He opted out when the girls insisted on teatime at the Princes Palace."

"I love you," Bryce blurted, his heart hammering foolishly against his chest. "You can hire Desire."

Her eyes and mouth opened wide, then she jettisoned from her chair and ran around the table to jump on him like an excited little girl on Santa's lap. "Thank you, Bryce. Thank you."

"I promised to make you happy. Undeniably so," he said.

"I'll go dress Eli and Elyse. We'll talk later. Oh, I'm so happy. I can't wait to tell the girls." She jumped off his lap.

"We'll be doing a lot more than talking, *ma petite biche*."

Bryce slapped her sweet little derriere. "You owe me now. Big time."

"Hey, I made a deposit last night, or perhaps you made several, in which case, I do owe you," she jested, moving out of the way as Alyssa and Anastasia brought their flirting to an end.

As four little arms went around his neck, Bryce enveloped the little girls in one big bear hug. "Hey, Little Ones."

"Daddy. I missed you, this much," Anastasia said, giving him a choking hug as her skinny knees poked into his overstuffed stomach.

"Did you bring me a present, Daddy?" Alyssa asked. "I'll give you two-hundreds kisses if you brought me a present."

"Me, too?" Anastasia bobbed her head on a pixie smile.

"And if I didn't bring you presents?"

"Then you only get one hundred kisses," Alyssa replied.

"Is that fifty, or one hundred kisses from each of you?"

"Stop trying to manipulate us, Daddy," Alyssa said with cool authority.

"Yeah, it's not gonna fly." Anastasia shook her head and glared at him from beneath a pair of long black lashes.

Bryce stared, dumbfounded, at the seven, and three-year-old little girls. When did they start using words like *manipulate*, and phrases like *it's not gonna fly*? And then there was Eli with *undeniably*. His kids were growing up. He only had one baby left—his darling Elyse.

"Still the master of negotiations, aren't you?" Henry slid into the chair next to Bryce and placed a Mountainview Café coffee cup on the table. "Fifty each, girls."

"Stay out of it, Henry. Let the girls think for themselves." Lillian kissed the top of her son's head. "Sorry we had to cut your bonding time short, but we have plans with the other grandparents."

"So I heard."

"Daddy, did you bring us presents?" Alyssa grasped his chin and turned his face back to her.

So bossy, Bryce thought affectionately as he stared down at her. Or perhaps she had exceptional leadership skills. She was one daughter he didn't have to worry about anyone taking advantage of. "Yes, Alyssa. I brought you presents."

"Where is it?"

"Not even a thank you?"

"Thank you, Daddy. Thank you, Daddy."

"Then we owe you two hundred kisses." Alyssa's said.

"I'll take a rain check. Your presents are in your rooms."

They left him, whipped away in the eye of the same whirlwind that had dumped them on his lap. God, he was already tired and the sun had barely made it above the horizon. Maybe he and Kaya *should* stop at five. "Where are you headed?" he asked his parents, grateful for their help with raising the kids. He doubted he and Kaya would manage without them.

"We're hiking up Blue Hill before the sun gets too hot, then we'll head over to the children's theater for lunch and a puppet show. After that, we'll just hang out at *L'etoile du Nord* for the rest of the day. Maybe take a couple canoes out on the lake later," his father said.

"Sounds like a lot of fun. Can I come along?"

"Wouldn't you prefer staying home with your wife?" His mother gave him a secretive wink, as she sat down on the other side of him. "Speaking of which, on her way out the door, Kaya told me that you've decided to let Desire do the wedding."

"Good news travels fast." Bryce emptied the coffee carafe into his mug and took a sip of the dark hot liquid.

"It's the right thing to do, son," his father said. "You've been carrying this burden for far too long. You need to free yourself of everything related to that period of your life."

Out of the corner of his eye, Bryce watched Webster poke his head into the kitchen and when he was certain it was safe, he sneaked over to his bowl under a bay window and began nibbling on his dry food. Webster was getting on in years, and he tried to avoid the children as much as possible, especially since his kidney transplant last year. Webster was his one remaining link to Pilar. Webster had seen him through many sad, lonely nights following Pilar's death.

"I'm not doing it for me. I'm doing it for Kaya. I want her to be happy," he told his father.

His mother laid her hand over his. "You need to do this for yourself, Bryce."

"You can't do it halfway. It's all or nothing," Henry admonished. "You must have a conversation with the Summerses and end this animosity between our families. Think about your children."

"What do my children have to do with anything?"

"Granite Falls is a small town, Bryce. I'm sure that at some point Desire Summers will have children."

Bryce shrugged. "So?"

"Your kids will eventually run into each other on the playground, at school, little league, ballet. The thing is if you don't take care of it now, this feud will continue for generations until neither the Fontaines nor the Summerses will know why or how it started in the first place. All they will know is that they're supposed to hate each other." Henry placed his hand of Bryce's shoulder and leaned closer. "Is this the kind of legacy you want to pass on to your children, son? Do you want to teach them to hold on to grudges and not to forgive those who hurt them?"

"Son, your father is right. It's not just about you. It's about the future of your children, of the Fontaine family."

Bryce closed his eyes at his parents' poignant words. The last thing he wanted to pass down to his children was the burden he carried in his heart. It was his, not theirs. Both Jason and Eli looked up to him. They wanted to be like him. He had to make himself worthy of that honor. What they saw should be what they got.

The thought of sitting in a room with one member of that family was suffocating, but Bryce knew he had to do it for his children, even if it killed him.

CHAPTER TWELVE

Fontaine Estate – Thursday (same day) - late afternoon...

E *ven if it kills me.*
Bryce plunged in and out of Kaya as she laid facedown, on the massage bed in their master spa, their bodies glittering and slippery from sweat and the oils they'd used to give each other full body massages. Massages that had steadily turned into a marathon of hot lovemaking session while Raheem DeVaughn sang, "Temperature's Rising," and scented candles flickered around them. It was a lovers' nest, created by his crafty wife.

"Bryce. Oh yes. Deeper, deeper, baby," she pleaded, arching her back and pushing her hips and derriere into him, as they now danced to the seductive sounds of Teddy Pendergrass and Stephanie Mills singing "Feel the Fire." "Oh, God that feels so good. Oh yeah, baby, give it to me. I feel the fire. Make me come. Make me come, baby..." She reached behind her and curled her arms around his neck, leaving her chest bare and open to him.

Bryce cupped her firm breasts and groaned as her hard nipples grazed his palms. He pulled her closer and leaned into her back, pressing her into the soft mattress, going deeper and harder as she writhed and cried out her pleasure under him. When she began to quiver from her gusts of desires, and the hot wet inner walls of her sex gripped him so hard that he was incapable of moving an inch, Bryce exploded deep inside his wife, flooding her womb with his seed as she vibrated around him. He collapsed on her, trembling as she milked him.

"*Mon chéri*," he whispered, jerking inside her as he felt her walls quivering on another orgasm, the sweet little "thank you" orgasms he'd grown to expect and love over the years. He wrapped her close to his chest as they both quivered in the aftermath. His balls ached.

A long while after, while they were still joined together, he lifted her from the bed, walked over to the whirlpool overlooking a courtyard, a green lawn with a water fountain in the center of it, and lakes and mountain ranges in the background. He carefully climbed in and sat down, straddling Kaya across his lap, facing away from him.

They both sighed in total satisfaction and comfort and sat quietly for some time, wrapped in each other's arms as the warm bubbling water vibrated around their aching limbs, soothing the tired muscles they'd been overusing all morning.

"I like your penis," Kaya finally broke the silence. "Thanks for showing it to me," she added with a chuckle.

Bryce laughed as he cupped water in his hands and let it fall over her shoulders. He'd told her about his conversation with Eli. "At least I didn't lie to our son."

"No, you didn't. Samantha said we should always answer his questions truthfully."

"I can't wait for him to forget he has a penis, except when he has to pee. Maybe then his questions will cease."

"I'm sorry to tell you, Daddy, but he'll always have questions. They'll just change as he gets older."

"Yeah, I can't wait to remind him how he didn't want his penis to grow."

Their laughter was deep and jovial as they reveled in the sweetness of each other and the innocence of their children. Bryce was certain that his fraction of happiness just got a little bigger, and he was determined for it to keep growing, even if it killed him.

Bryce's home office. A few hours later...

"Hey, Dad."

Bryce looked up from his laptop as Jason walked into his home office. Jason had gotten home hours ago, and after Kaya left to meet with Desire in town, he and Jason had gone out to the tennis court to play a few sets. "Hey, Jase."

"You busy?"

Bryce smiled at the handsome, tall-for-his-age teenager he'd been raising as his own for three years. Jason resembled his father so much that each time Bryce looked at him, it was like Michael gazing back at him through those piercing gray eyes. Bryce closed his laptop and set it on the table in front of the sofa. He patted the leather seat next to him. "What's on your mind?"

Jason eased down on the edge of the sofa and placed his hands on his knees. "I don't want you to get mad. You have to promise," he said staring uncertainly at Bryce.

Oh boy. Bryce tried hard not to let his alarm show. How bad could it be? Jason was a straight-A, sensible and responsible teenager who never got into trouble. He was a saint compared to Bryce when he was that age. "Okay. I promise not to get mad."

"How old were you when you had your first kiss?"

Bryce narrowed his eyes. "Umm… Why do you ask?"

"Because I kissed a girl."

"And who's this girl you kissed?" Bryce asked cautiously. *Please don't let it be Precious.* He didn't want to have this conversation with Erik.

"Precious."

Damn! Bryce closed his eyes for a second as a vision of some future fourteen-year-old-boy kissing one of his twelve-year-old-daughters flashed across his mind. He didn't like it. Not one bit. He inhaled a deep breath of composure. "So, when and where did this kiss take place?"

"Yesterday. In her kitchen. Aunt Michelle had invited me for a pizza dinner." He shrugged. "And then after she and Catherine left—that's when it happened."

At least they weren't secluded in her bedroom or in some closet groping each other. "Who initiated the kiss?"

"She did."

"Oh sure, blame her." Bryce threw his hands in the air.

"It's true, Dad. She said she missed me when I was away at camp and it was a welcome home kiss."

"Was it the first time?"

Jason nodded.

Bryce stared him full in the eyes, daring him to lie. "Was there tongue involved?"

"A little."

"There was either tongue, or no tongue. There's never a *little* tongue."

Jason wiggled on the sofa and scratched his head. "Okay, yeah, there was tongue involved."

Bryce swore inwardly as that vision of his own daughters with some horny teenage boy's tongue jammed down one of their throats flashed across his mind again. He hadn't even realized he was balling his fists until the pressure of his nails digging into his palms sent a pain signal to his brain. "And then what happened?"

"Nothing."

"Nothing? Then why are you confessing as if you were caught with your hand in the cookie jar? I don't think I ever discussed my first kiss with either of my parents, and I'm sure the girl I kissed never told hers. Why are you telling me?"

Jason dropped his head and stared at the floor. "Aunt Michelle caught us. She made us promise that I would tell you, and Precious would tell Uncle Erik. She said we couldn't talk to each other until we talked with our dads."

"Ahh! You need a get-me-out-of-jail pass." Bryce shot up from the sofa and strode to the sliding doors overlooking downtown Granite Falls. *Damn it*! With Sarah's passing, Bryce was certain that a conversation with his daughter about her first kiss was not what Erik needed on his return home when he had a funeral to plan.

Jason followed behind him. "You promised you wouldn't get mad, Dad."

"I'm not mad. I'm...I'm concerned. You're becoming a

young man. It's natural for you to want to kiss girls." He was glad his son had told him, even if he was forced into it. "So, how was it?" he asked, to hopefully encourage him to seek his advice in the future.

Jason grinned. "It was cool. I wanted Precious to be the first girl I kissed."

How many girls did he intend to kiss? Bryce wondered. He placed his hands on Jason's shoulders in the same way he'd placed them on Eli's this morning when they were discussing penis sizes. What was this, talk-to-my-sons-about-sex day? Kaya was right. The questions never stopped. They just got different. Bryce had yet to decide which phase he liked less.

"Listen, Jason, I know your mother talked to you about sex before she died, but do you need a refresher course?"

"No. I'm cool. I know everything about sex."

Bryce laughed. "Maybe you can teach me a thing or two. I'm thirty…something, been married twice, and fathered two children, and I still don't know everything about sex."

Jason stared up at him, his brows furrowed in confusion and disbelief. "You don't?"

"Sex is complicated, and the older you get the more complicated it becomes, and the more you learn about it, the more you realize that you don't know much about it."

His frown deepened. "Why? Why is it so complicated? It's just an act."

"Ah, son, sex is much more than an act. It's simple for those who just treat it as physical. But good sex, the best sex is spiritual, physiological, and emotional." *And extremely religious* he thought as he had flashbacks of making love with Kaya to "Religious" last night. The woman had him flat on his back, thrashing about on the mattress, and talking in tongues. "And that's just some of the factors that make sex complicated," he told Jason.

"I don't get it."

"I didn't at your age, either. Boys your age are hung up on the physical aspects of sex. Blame it on your raging hormones."

"It's not just about hormones with Precious. I like her a lot. Ever since we were kids."

"You're still kids. And you better remember that!" Bryce wagged a finger in his face. "You are always to treat her with respect. Treat all girls with respect, for that matter."

"I know, Dad. My mom already talked to me about that."

"Precious is Uncle Erik's daughter, and if you disrespect her, he will come after you. I won't blame him. That's his little girl. No matter how old she gets, she will always be his baby. It's the same way I feel about your sisters. What would you do if some guy hurts one of them?"

"I would punch his face in." Jason slammed a fist into his palm. "I'd break his nose."

"Remember that, because it's exactly what Erik *will* do to you if you compromise his daughter's character in any way. Don't be in a hurry to get into sex with Precious, or any other girl. You're both too young. You both know what sex is and where babies come from, so neither of you can say you didn't know what you were doing. That's not gonna fly. Not with me, and certainly not with Erik."

"I get it." He grinned like the silly, horny teenager he was. "Can I call Precious now since we've talked?"

"Absolutely not. Michelle's order still stands. You are not to contact her until I know for sure that she's spoken with her father, after which, Erik and I will talk, and depending on how he wants to handle it, we'll sit down with you and Precious. We need to establish a set of guidelines for both of you to follow."

"What kind of guidelines?"

"Like no fondling of her breasts," Bryce said, deciding not to be delicate about it. "No touching or rubbing together of each other's private parts, no kissing any parts of her body, except for her forehead and her cheeks. And definitely no tonguing. It'll just lead to situations you won't be able to control."

Jason gave him a *then what's the point* kind of look.

"Those are the same kinds of guidelines I'd set for any boy who becomes interested in your sisters when they get older. And if he broke them, I'd break his arms and legs." Bryce knew damned well that he wouldn't be setting parameters; he'd be enacting prohibitions. "If Erik decides that he doesn't want his daughter dating until she's older, you will stay away from her, or I will ship you off to an all-boys boarding school in Europe. And I swear the only females you'll see for the next four years will be your grandmother, your mother, and your sisters. Got that?"

Jason stared at him, fear, stark and vivid glittering in his eyes. "Yes... yes, Dad," he said in a tremulous voice. "I—I got it."

Bryce pulled him into his arms, a smug smile spreading his lips. Their family vacation to the South Pacific next week couldn't have been planned at a better time. It would give Jason and Precious breathing room that they clearly needed. He was also going to sit him down and give him some serious advice about protection. It was always better to be safe than sorry. "You know I only have your best interest at heart, right?" He stared at him. "I'm saving you from yourself."

Jason laced his hands around Bryce's waist. "I know. It's what my real dad would have done. I love you. Thanks for being my dad."

"I love you, too, son. Undeniably, so."

LaCrosse Estate: Simultaneously...

Erik floated on cloud nine as he lounged on the master suite balcony and took in the sights of mini yachts sailing up and down Crystal Lake in the far distance.

He gave in to the contented smile of happiness bubbling inside him. He and Michelle had spent most of the morning in bed, just reconnecting—body, mind, and spirit. Then in the early afternoon, they'd taken a page from Adam and Tashi's book of love and done some naked couples yoga, after which they'd enjoyed a couples' massage, administered by two of the most highly skilled masseuses from the country club.

Michelle had pre-booked the sessions for tomorrow, the day he was set to come home, and so she had to pull some strings to get their schedules rearranged. Bless her dear heart. This was just the kind of welcome home Erik needed, even though it had been marred with news about Sarah's passing, *and* Jabari's, too.

After their massages, he and Michelle had spent some quality time with Fiona before Michelle headed into town to meet the other wives and Desire. He was glad Bryce had agreed to the change in wedding planners. The pressure was off, at least that pressure. Before she left Michelle had insisted that he speak with Precious before the day was out. He'd instructed the staff to send her to him when she returned from her volleyball practice.

A tender smile settled on Erik's lips as his mind shifted to his oldest daughter. She was blossoming into such a beautiful, cultured, well-mannered young lady, and he couldn't be more proud of her. Her mother would have been pleased at the way she carried herself. She would have been as proud of her as her grandmother had been.

Erik took a sip of his Scotch. Telling Precious about her grandmother wasn't something he was looking forward to. The poor kid had only really known her for three years and she'd been looking forward to spending more time with her in the future, but as fate would have it, that hope was lost. Memories were all Precious now had from her mother's side of her family. Erik hoped that his decision to put Sarah on the drug that ultimately shortened her life was worth it. He trusted that Precious would understand the concept of quality of life versus longevity.

Speak of the angel, Erik thought as he heard Precious calling out to him from the sitting room of his master suite.

"Out here, sweetheart."

She sauntered out onto the balcony, still wearing her red and white volleyball uniform. Her long brown hair was pulled back into a ponytail, and her natural flawless skin glittered in the rays of afternoon sun streaming through the tree branches. He hadn't yet given her the okay to wear makeup, and as far as he knew she wasn't sneaking around behind his back and putting it on like girls her age sometimes did.

"Hi, Dad." She came over and gave him a peck on the

cheek, then stood back and stared down at him. "Grandma Hayes said you wanted to see me."

"You could have showered and changed." Erik frowned at the hint of apprehension in her voice and eyes.

"Do I smell?" She sat down on the edge of the lounge across from him and sniffed her armpits.

Erik chuckled as he sat up and placed his bare feet on the cool tiles. "No, Precious, you don't smell. I just thought you'd want to be more comfortable as we talked."

"Grandma said you wanted to see me right away, so…" She shrugged, pulled her gaze away from his, and focused on the hot tub a few yards away.

Erik watched as she slid her hands under her thighs, then pulled them out and crossed her arms over her stomach, before fidgeting on the seat. Alarm bells went off in his head as he experienced the same uneasiness he'd had that morning at the eye-exchange between Precious and Michelle at the breakfast table.

He'd called Precious to tell her about her grandmother's death, but the way his daughter was behaving, and the fact that Michelle had insisted that they talk today, warned Erik that something else was going on. Precious' restlessness couldn't be about Sarah since she wasn't yet privy to that information.

Oh boy. Erik cleared his throat, drawing his daughter's attention back to him. "Is there something you need to tell me, Precious?"

She turned her head and gazed at him with her big brown eyes. "I guess Mom told you."

He was right. It wasn't about Sarah. "Told me what?" he asked quietly.

She slid her hands under her thighs again. "About me and Jason."

"What about you and Jason?"

She caught her lower lip between her teeth and stared at him as if trying to figure out if he already knew whatever it was she thought he knew and was waiting for her to confess, or if she should just let the whole cat out of the bag since its head was already poking out.

"Mom hasn't told me anything about you and Jason," Erik said as a way to give her the choice to come clean.

"Oh, man." She shook her fist in the air. "I thought that's why you wanted to see me. She said I had to tell you myself, but I thought she'd let it slip."

"It's not. She didn't, but since you brought it up, what's going on?"

She dropped her head. "Mom caught me and Jason kissing."

Erik groaned inwardly. *She's not a little girl anymore, not your Little Muffin*, he told himself. He knew this day was inevitable, but Lord, not at twelve years old. Eighteen perhaps. She'd be legal then and he needn't ever know about it.

"Dad. Did you hear me?"

"I heard you." Erik got off the lounge, stumbled over to the alabaster railing, and looked down into the courtyard below. "I just… I need a moment to process it."

"Am I in trouble?"

Oh yes. I'm locking you up and throwing away the key. Erik wished the days of chastity belts were still prevalent. Michelle had warned him that the day would come when Precious would no longer think that sex was a gross act. He'd been hoping for age twenty-five or so, not twelve. He hadn't even had his first real kiss until he was sixteen.

"Dad?"

At Precious's impatient call, Erik turned and leaned back against the railing. He drank in the uncertain expression on his daughter's face. "I'm surprised— Um, a bit—" He didn't want to say *disappointed*. "I'm taken off guard. I didn't realize that you and Jason were—" He cleared his throat. "I didn't realize your friendship had turned into—" He flared his hands in the air, searching his brain for a word to describe their relationship. "Was that the first time you kissed?"

"Well, it's the first time we kissed on the lips."

I imagine that. If it were just a peck on the cheek we wouldn't be having this conversation. "Was it a—um—just a peck on the lips kind of kiss?"

She dropped her gaze and his heart dropped right along with it. "It was more than a peck, Dad. Our mouths were opened."

Erik dropped his face into his hands. He liked Jason, but the thought of his tongue inside his little girl's mouth made Erik want to throw up. *Okay, time to be practical.* He lifted his head. He didn't want to screw up her curiosity about her sexuality like his had been screwed up. He didn't want her to ever be afraid to talk with him about boys, although he guessed that he would not have been hearing about this incident if Michelle hadn't caught them. Since she was her stepmother, Michelle had probably thought it best that Precious told him herself. He was sure she'd give him the news about Tiffany and Fiona when they came of age. This was just one more good reason, he needed to stop traveling and pay attention to his children, especially Precious, who was obviously growing up way too fast.

Erik went over to sit beside Precious. "Tell me what happened," he said, taking her hands in his. He could better control the situation if he knew what was going on. "I don't need the details of the kiss," he added at the questioning frown on her brow. "Just what triggered it. Obviously you and Jason are developing feelings for each other." Erik was driving over to the Fontaine Estate as soon as this conversation was over. He hoped his jets would be cooled by the time he got there.

"Well, he—Jason came over for dinner yesterday. I'd missed hanging out with him when he was away at camp. Kind of the way you miss Mom when you are away, Daddy. The way you kissed her in the kitchen this morning right there in front of all of us expressed how much you missed her. I missed Jason like that, but I didn't know I missed him like that until I saw him. So when Mom and Catherine left the kitchen with Tiffany and Fiona, I just kissed him."

Whew. Lucky for Jason that he hadn't initiated the kiss. Erik wished for the days when Precious refused to let boys kiss her because she thought that's how babies were made. "Your mom and I are adults, Precious. We're married. We are free to express our feelings in any way mutually pleasing to us. You're still just a kid."

"Dad, I'm twelve— and a half," she added as if the half really mattered. "Just because we're young it doesn't mean our feelings aren't real. Plus, you and my mom were teenagers when you started dating. You were about as old as me and Jason."

For the first time, Erik wished she was not privy to that

information. She was craftily using it against him to build her case. "True, but your mother and I were both virgins when we finally got married."

Precious was taken aback. "Really? I can see Mom, 'cause she was a girl, but, *you*? I thought guys—" She stopped and dropped her gaze.

You thought that guys what? "Yes, *me*."

"Are you saying I have to be a virgin until I get married?"

Absolutely. Erik squeezed her hands and held her gaze, the embarrassment he'd anticipated he'd have when he finally had this talk with her was gone. She needed sound advice, and Michelle obviously thought that he should be the one giving it to her since he had more experiences talking to girls her age about this particular topic. "Look, sweetheart, I understand that a lot of changes are happening in your body, and with those changes come desires. Sexual desires. There's nothing wrong with those feelings. I don't want you to ignore them. You shouldn't ignore them. You should embrace them, but with boundaries. You can't just give in to every urge you get. You're not mature enough to handle the consequences."

"Like getting pregnant?"

"I wish that was the worst of them, but no. I'm talking about sexually transmitted diseases—some curable, some not —but all leave a lasting negative effect, nonetheless. As a gynecologist, I encounter these medical issues on a daily basis. Some of my patients are as young as you, Precious, some even younger."

Her face crinkled. "Really?"

"Yes. And then there is the mental trauma—broken hearts, broken dreams, and regrets, that even many adults still can't handle. Your body will tell you that you're ready for sex with someone you feel strongly about, but you're not emotionally mature at this age. Sex isn't just physical, Precious. It's emotional, psychological, and spiritual. And if those areas of your life aren't fully developed, indulging in sex can leave scars that can haunt you for a very long time, sometimes for the rest of your life. Don't be in a hurry to grow up, baby."

"Believe me, Daddy. I'm not ready to have sex," Precious said, pulling her hands from his. "I just wanted to kiss the boy. That's all."

"Good". He'd scared the thought of having sex out of her. *He hoped.* "Now, the kind of kissing you did yesterday can lead to other things that will eventually lead to sex. And because of that, I have to set some parameters."

Precious grabbed his arm with one hand and placed the other over her heart. "Please don't tell me I can't see Jason anymore, Dad. He's my best friend." Tears glistened in her eyes.

"Of course not, sweetheart. I know how important that relationship is to you. But you have to promise me that there's never going to be another kiss like that one. Not for a long time."

"I promise, Daddy. Can I go call Jason now? Michelle said we couldn't talk to each other until we spoke to you and Uncle Bryce."

"Did you obey her order?"

She shook her head, negatively.

"Precious! You couldn't hold off for twenty-four hours? How can your mother and I trust you when—"

"I just texted him this morning to tell him you were home and to see if he'd spoken with his dad."

"Had he?"

"Not yet. He was at Ethan's and he said he would talk with him when he got home."

Erik held his hand out and Precious pulled her smart phone from her jersey pocket and placed it in his palm.

He entered her security code—something he'd promised never to do except in her presence, and for as long as he knew he could trust her. He scanned through her messages until he found the exchange between her and Jason. *Cute*, he thought, trying not to let his amusement show at the innocent infatuation going on between them. If Precious was going to have a crush on any boy, he was happy it was Jason.

He could forbid her to see him, but that would be foolish. She might decide to take up with some scumbag behind his back. Erik had dealt with many rebellious, vindictive teenagers who'd gotten themselves into trouble just to spite their domineering parents. He didn't want his daughter to become one of them. He wanted to maintain the level of trust he'd built with her over the years. Jason Rogers was the safest boy with whom he could do that for now. He handed her back her phone.

"So can I call him?"

"Not until I have a chat with Uncle Bryce. Then we need to sit down with you and Jason and set some ground rules. The same kinds your grandparents set for your mother and me when we began dating. If you want to keep seeing Jason—as a friend—you will obey those rules."

"I will, Daddy." She grinned and threw her arms around his neck. "Thank you for understanding. I love you. You're the best daddy in the world."

"I love you, too, Muffin, with all my heart." Erik held her

close, his heart racing with love and fear. There were so many bad wolves out there in the big wide world ready to gobble her up. He just prayed that when she did venture out on her own, she would be well equipped to handle all that life threw at her. It was the most any father could wish for his child, especially his baby girl, his Little Muffin.

His smart phone rang. Erik eased Precious away and went over to retrieve it from a table near the lounge he'd been occupying before she arrived. It was Cape Hill. He let it go to voice mail. They were probably calling to finalize some of the funeral arrangements he'd made with them earlier.

He turned to see Precious heading back inside. "Precious," he called out. "We do need to discuss something—the reason I asked you to come see me."

"Oh, yeah. I forgot."

He pulled her down on the lounge beside him and wrapped his arms around her. "Honey, I have to tell you something about your grandma."

She raised her head. "Grandma Felicia? She was just here this morning."

"No." *God no.* "Your Grandma Sarah."

"What about her? Is she sick again?"

"No baby. Your grandmother passed away."

She stiffened against him for a moment, then held him tight as reality sank in. "No, Daddy. No. I hardly got to know her. She's all I have of Mom. No." She beat her fist into Erik's stomach as sobs rocked her slender body. "No. It's not fair. No. Grandma Sarah. No…"

Hot tears ran down Erik's cheeks as he held his daughter, his little broken daughter in his arms. Her pain of loss seared straight to his heart, so painfully, that he could hardly breathe.

It took him back to the place seven years ago when he'd had to tell her about her mother's death.

She'd healed and had come a long way, thanks to Michelle who'd entered their lives at just the right moment and brought them both back to life. He wouldn't have survived without her. Precious wouldn't have survived without her. He owed her everything.

"What happened, Daddy? How did she die?" Precious asked, her cheek against his chest and her hot tears scorching his skin.

Erik rubbed his hand soothingly up and down her back. "She had a cardiac arrest, baby. She went to sleep and her heart stopped beating. She wasn't in any pain. She died peacefully."

She shuddered. "When? When did she die?"

"Three days ago."

She lifted her head from his chest. "On Monday?"

He nodded.

"They called and asked for you or Michelle. I took the phone to her. Why didn't she tell me?"

"She thought I should be the one to tell you. I was married to Sarah's daughter. She was my mother-in-law. It's my job."

"I wish I'd seen her one last time." A fresh batch of tears appeared. "Tell her that I loved her."

"She knew, baby. You told her each time you saw her." His little baby was hurting, and it was tearing him up inside.

"Can I see her?"

"If you want to. Sure. I made arrangements for a small ceremony at the home tomorrow, then we'll lay her to rest in the town's cemetery."

"I'm gonna miss her. All the stories she used to tell me about Mom when she was a little girl, and about my grandpa. I don't have anyone to talk to about my Mom anymore." Her head fell listlessly on his chest as her grief overtook her.

"You have me, Muffin. You have me. You'll always have me." Erik wrapped his hands around his little girl and laid back on the lounge, pulling her down on him. He soothed her as he tried to absorb her grief.

CHAPTER THIRTEEN

A remote single-family house in suburban Evergreen – Thursday night...

The music pumped and the lights were low, creating an aura of enchantment, but Kaya wasn't feeling it. The pole that was supposed to be her friend, her partner for the next hour felt cold and unresponsive, and like an indifferent lover, it had tossed her off a couple times already.

She glanced over at Michelle and Tashi, hanging upside down. They weren't into it either. How could they, when one of their own was missing, and two were hurting? Kaya slid down the pole and motioned for Cookie, their dance instructor, to cut the music. Michelle and Tashi followed her to the floor.

"What's up, Kaya?" Tashi asked.

"Come on. We're not here. You're home with Erik and Precious, and you must be worried about Mass and Shaina." She pointed to them in turn. "And me—even though Bryce has given Desire the go-ahead, I'm still worried about what it's doing to him. He still has to face the Summers family."

"You're right." Michelle pulled her bandana from her head.

"Whew! I was wondering what was going on with you," Cookie said. "I don't care how in love your husbands are with you, they would have been turned off by watching what you were doing tonight."

"Sorry, we made you come out for nothing." Tashi picked up their scarves from the floor. "We probably should have canceled."

"No problem. This was your last class before the bachelors' party, but if you want, I can squeeze you in tomorrow—"

"The party is postponed. Perhaps canceled. My husband's former mother-in-law passed away," Michelle told Cookie. "The funeral is on Saturday. I'll be busy with arrangements tomorrow."

"Oh, I'm so sorry." She gave Michelle a quick hug. "That explains your lack of enthusiasm, then. So all your hard work is going to waste?"

"No way," Kaya said. "We've been practicing for months. Plan B is to surprise our husbands on our honeymoon."

"Sweet! We can totally work that. I know you're all leaving on vacation next week, so call me when you return, and we can get a couple sessions in before your honeymoon. You're going to rock your husbands' worlds. Now, get dressed and get out of here." Cookie shooed them away. "I'll lock up."

"We're already rocking their worlds," Kaya said, as they walked into an adjacent room.

In order to avoid attention and to keep their husbands in

the dark, the women had rented a house in suburban Evergreen and had paid Cookie a whole lot of cash to give them lessons for the past four months. They would have loved more time to perfect their performance, but they had to wait until after Tashi had given birth before they started, and even then, their practice sessions were still limited by Tashi's mom's murder trial.

"Bryce and I rocked to "Temperature's Rising" and "Feel The Fire" this afternoon." Kaya closed her eyes and squeezed her thighs together as the memories washed over her. After reading those articles in *Granite Falls People News*, they'd decided to start making love to the songs they were pole dancing to, just to raise the stakes and their husbands' temperatures when they eventually performed.

Michelle pulled off her stockings and retrieved a blouse and a pair of shorts from her tote bag. "Girl, I danced under and on top of Erik to "Behind Closed Doors," "Religious," and "Temperature's Rising" this morning. Mmm..." She licked her lips. "It was so good. I had him singing *Hallelujah. Lord, have mercy*." She shivered outwardly. "What about you, Tashi?" she asked, turning to Tashi who hadn't said anything yet. "Have you tried any of the songs with Adam?"

Tashi glanced up from lacing her sandals. "Not yet. We've been preoccupied with the sentencing. At least I was."

"So you haven't been making love?" Kaya pulled on a pair of white shorts and an orange top.

"Oh, we've been making love, but I wasn't in the mood to set the mood, if you know what I mean." A quiver raced through her body as she recalled the hot session in the shower and then on the bed before they joined the family for dinner last night. "Maybe I'll try a couple tonight after we put Aria and Alex to bed." She was watching Aria until Shaina and Mass returned from Kenya.

"Get working girl," Michelle said. "You have eight specific songs to get through from our list of twelve. You want Adam to remember making love to you as he watches you make love to your pole while those specific songs play in the background."

"Plus, remember we're starving them after we return from vacation. No sex for them until the wedding," Kaya added. "We have to make them hungry for us that first night of our honeymoon."

"I know." Tashi picked up her gym bag from the floor.

Like high school BFFs, the ladies laced their arms around each other and exited the house through the back door where three luxury sport cars were parked next to each other—Michelle's red Pagani Huayra, Kaya's gold and silver Maybach Exelero, and Tashi's white Bugatti Veyron. Shaina's yellow Lamborghini Veneno was missing.

With all the children between them, it was very seldom that the wives were able to enjoy the luxury of driving their sports cars, instead of the practical, but just as luxurious sedans and SUVs they used for family outings. Tonight was one of those privileged nights, and after meeting with Desire at her place of business, they'd ordered takeout from Mountainview Café, and then driven to a secluded beach on Crystal Lake, spread some blankets on the beach, and watched the sun set as they enjoyed their sandwiches, and time alone from their husbands and children. Their joy was nonetheless marred by Shaina's absence.

"It's such a beautiful night," Tashi said, gazing up at the

stars and the crescent moon. "I think I'll take Adam to the garden for a moonlight romp."

"I thought you were babysitting." Kaya poked her in the side.

"Listen, guys, I have an idea about the wedding." Michelle unlaced her arms from around her friends, and leaned against the hood of her car.

"What now, Michelle?" Kaya asked, glibly.

"You remember we talked about how hiring Desire could be a way of healing for Bryce and the Summers family? Well I was thinking, why not make it a time of healing for the entire town?"

"*What'chu talkin' 'bout*, Michelle?" Tashi asked in her Arnold Drummond voice.

"I mean, there are so many people in this town who don't talk to each other for one reason or the other."

"That's in every town," Kaya stated.

"I know, but there aren't billionaires in every town who go out of their way to mingle with the locals, to show that they care. Our husbands' families practically built this town. Their hard work, their sweat and blood transformed it into the beautiful, almost crime-free, little mountain mecca that it is. Bryce came later, but he has already contributed just as much to Granite Falls' prosperity as the Andreases, the LaCrosses, and the Andrettis."

"Don't forget the Forsythes," Tashi said with a smug chuckle. "They may not be in power anymore, but their ancestors were there with our husbands' forefathers."

"See, that's what I'm talking about." Michelle patted Tashi's knee. "In spite of what Claire did to you and Adam, you can still find it in your heart to speak well of her."

"Pff. I'm not speaking well of her. I'm speaking well of her parents."

"But won't it be nice to put all that behind you?"

Tashi shrugged. "How? I'm not gonna go looking for her, or try to be her friend. For all I know, she might still be scheming to sell me up the river, thinking she still has a chance with Adam. The woman is evil."

"Okay, so we'll cross Claire Forsythe off the list."

"What list?" Kaya asked, almost afraid to hear what new proposal Michelle had in mind. She loved her friend and she appreciated her compassion for the less fortunate, but Lord, she needed to give it a rest sometimes, especially with so much going on in their personal lives.

Michelle clapped her hands. "Glad you asked. I was thinking that we should open up the wedding to the general public. The church is huge, and we don't have enough friends and family to fill up the pews. Let's send out a general invitation to the residents of Granite Falls, and that includes the Forsythes," she said as an aside to Tashi. "Let them come watch us exchange our vows to our husbands and to each other as friends, and then let them enjoy a fairytale night of music, dancing, and the best food on the planet. It might help some of them to mend bridges and bury hatchets. One of these days our sons and daughters will be running the four most powerful corporations in this towns, just as their fathers are doing now. Wouldn't it be nice to pass down an amicable community where most of the people get along? We could start a tradition for other neighborhoods to follow."

"The church is big, but not big enough to hold the entire town," Tashi pointed out.

"I thought of that. We can do a general raffle, or make it a first respond, first attend invitation until all the seats are filled."

Tashi smiled. "I like that, Michelle. That's some altruistic thinking, girl." She bumped her shoulder to Michelle's. "You should be mayor of Granite Falls."

"Thanks, but I'm quite content with my role as Queen of LaCrosse Estates." She chuckled.

Kaya bit her lips thoughtfully. "So who's sending out the invitations and keeping track of RSVPs? My hands are full with my five kids, and I suspect yours are, too, with your four, Michelle. I doubt Shaina wants this responsibility, or you, Tashi. We decided that our only duties for the wedding would be working with the designers for our dresses and the rings, creating our cakes, and choosing our flowers. We're done."

"We can hire people." Tashi pushed off the hood of Michelle's car. "But we don't have a lot of time. The wedding is in three weeks; we're all going away next week, and the following week we'll be busy entertaining our out-of-town guests and family members who're coming for the wedding."

"I know a few people at my foundation who would be happy to take on this project for some extra money."

"Did you run it by Shaina?" Kaya asked Michelle.

"Not yet. She and Mass had already left when I thought about it. But with the sibling rivalry going on between Mass and Galen, I think she would welcome any opportunity to help those two settle their differences."

Not to mention the fact that Shaina is pregnant, Tashi thought. Mass and Shaina had told her and Adam about the impending addition to their family, but had asked them not to spread the word yet. They'd been planning on sharing their news tomorrow night when they were all assembled at Kaya's house for their monthly get-together, but Jabari's and Sarah's deaths had put a wrench in their plans. Tashi was dying to tell her friends, but she had to respect Mass and Shaina's wishes. "I agree. This town needs some healing," she said instead.

"Then it's settled," Michelle said, bringing the discussion to an end. "I'll get my people on it tonight."

They hugged each other before driving off into the cool summer night, back to Granite Falls and their families.

♪

The Masai Mara Lands – Dawn, Friday morning-Kenyan time...

Massimo kept the urn close to his chest as he took the lead up the off-the-beaten-path through a forest of cedar and acacia trees and short grass, over shrubbery and rocks, tree stumps, and fallen branches.

While it was still dark, he and Shaina had started out toward a plateau above the banks of the Mara River that offered magnificent views of Kenya's Mara Lands and Tanzania's Serengeti ecosystem—one of the most important ecosystems in the world.

He and Adam had discovered the secluded escarpment as teenagers when they opted to continue the annual safari that Luciano and Alessandro had started when they were young men. Adam had been hoping to find his one true love like both their fathers had, and Massimo had just been looking for his next piece of tail, back then. He'd gotten plenty while Adam had gotten nothing.

Today, he was hoping that he and Shaina—his one true

love, and the best piece of tail this side of heaven—would reach the hideaway in time to watch the sunrise while they enjoyed the breakfast of sweet cakes, boiled eggs, fruit, and coffee in his backpack. It was one of the most peaceful and surreal places on earth to Massimo, and he wanted to share it with the most important person in the world to him—alone.

For that reason, he'd left the campsite where they'd spent the night, long before the other campers awoke. The Masai guides who were facilitating the walking safari knew of its existence, but Massimo had asked them not to veer their party off the path toward it—at least not for a few hours. Massimo had plans for his wife in that isolated haven and in the plunge pool at its base.

The escarpment was close to the spot where his *nono* had found Jabari about twenty-six years ago. According to *nono*, the malnourished, six-month-old cub had been lying near the slaughtered bodies of his mother and twin sister who'd apparently been attacked by an unknown enemy. How he'd survived was anyone's guess.

He and Jabari had suffered the same fate, losing their mothers—the most important person in their lives—at too early an age, and ironically each also lost a sibling as well. Jabari had understood Massimo's pain like no one else who knew him could. Jabari had comforted him and given him a reason to wake up in the morning.

While most children were falling asleep with teddy bears and other inanimate items of comfort, Massimo had fallen asleep, cocooned in the security and warmth of Jabari's body and the steady beating of his heart against him, until it seemed they'd morphed into one entity. And each morning he'd wake up with a reason to face the day. Feeding Jabari, bathing, grooming, and exercising him through long walks and play, had eased Massimo's pain of losing his mother.

Their bond had been stronger than any others Massimo had formed in his lifetime—well, up until he'd met Shaina. And it was that extraordinary, mystical connection that had sent Jabari following him the day the rhino had attacked him. Jabari had saved him twice, and he hadn't been there for him when he drew his last breath.

"I'm sorry old friend, but my baby girl needed me." He patted the gold ceramic urn.

"He understands," Shaina said softly behind him, alerting Mass to the fact that he'd voiced his thoughts.

He stopped and turned around to smile down at her. They'd hardly spoken during the hour they'd been walking. Shaina had considerately kept silent to allow him time to reflect on his life with Jabari, to absorb the reality of his death and meditate on the fact that he was taking him to his final resting place. "Thank you for coming along with me, pussycat. Even though we aren't talking, I know you have my back."

She wound her arms around his waist, and gazed up at him with her captivating brown eyes, the eyes that had kept him alive eight years ago when he'd been attacked by that rhino. "I'll always have your back, Mass. I'll try to be as protective a pussycat as Jabari was."

Massimo tucked the urn under his arm and hugged her. "You already are," he said, his mind wandering back briefly to three days ago when Shaina had defended him against Galen, and then soothed him afterward. She had the uncanny ability to calm him and take his mind off his troubles, even when she wasn't trying. "Jabari liked you, you know, from the first day he met you."

"I liked him, too. He was special." She gasped softly. "Mass, look," she whispered, pointing into the bushes. "It's a giraffe. Two—a mother and baby."

Mass followed her gaze, and sure enough giraffes were grazing on the leaves of an acacia tree. "I think it's a tower, darling. I see… three, four, five heads. There may be more."

"I don't see…" She pushed out of his embrace and moved up the path toward a clearing in the trees. "Oh yeah, you're right. I see about eight, including two more calves. They're so quiet, you'd never know they were there if you didn't look hard enough."

Mass stood behind her, just barely touching her, but trembling from the smell and heat of her body as he remembered making love to her in the small dark hut last night. His usually vocal wife had taken him in almost complete silence, sinking her sharp teeth into his chest and his arms as she climaxed several times throughout the night. During their last session, he'd turned her onto her stomach on the narrow cot and taken her from behind, forcing her to bite herself when she came. She got a taste of her own medicine and some of his for a change.

"They're making sounds, I assure you. It's just too low for the human ear to detect. If we were giraffes, my chest and biceps wouldn't be aching this morning, and neither would your arm." He rolled up the sleeves of her cotton shirt and kissed the dark area on her arm where she'd bitten herself in her throes of passion.

She rolled her sleeve back down. "Our neighbors were just feet away, Mass. I had to stifle my screams. But I think the proximity of the huts, along with the cramped space and the pitch-black darkness intensified the ecstasy for both of us."

"I can't argue with that, my love. Mating with you is always intense, no matter where or under what circumstances, but last night was definitely one of the most passionate rides of my life. Perhaps it's because we were so close to nature—no soft beds, silk sheets, or fluffy pillows to distract us. Just a man and a woman with a fierce desire for each other." He snaked his hand around to her front and spread his palm over her belly. "I hope I didn't hurt our baby."

She chuckled softly and placed her hand over his. "If he likes to watch like his father, I'm sure he enjoyed it."

Massimo bit back his ripple of mirth. "I almost forgot about the foul language that comes flying out of that sweet mouth of yours—one of the many things I love about you." He dropped a quick kiss on her lips. "So you think it's a boy, huh?"

"I hope so. We've already broken the curse." She sighed and folded her arms around her stomach, trapping his to her body. "I miss Aria."

He nuzzled his nose against her neck. "Me too, but if she were here with us, we wouldn't have had last night, and we wouldn't be enjoying this predawn hike. You see how excited she gets on driving safaris. She's not old enough for walking. Her excitement would have scared away the giraffes, and the baboons," he said, pointing to his right at a troop of baboons swinging from the branches of a strangler fig tree. "You never want to sneak up on, nor piss off a baboon."

She snickered softly. "I know, but I still miss my baby." She paused and cocked her ears. "The jungle is coming to life."

"It never sleeps, love." Despite the painful event that had brought him back to Kenya so soon, Mass felt a bottomless peace as birds chirped out their morning greetings to their neighbors, and the rumble of the waterfalls from the Mara River, just up ahead, impregnated the air. A lion's roar in the distance heralded his reigning status as king of the jungle. Years from now, each time he saw a male lion or heard one roar, Mass would always wonder if that was the king that had attacked Jabari.

Kill or be killed, survival of the fittest, was the nature of the jungle. Jabari had encroached on the lion's territory. He couldn't blame the lion for defending his home and his family from intruders. *He* would have done the same thing.

He'd defended his mother's memory by attacking his half-brother. Mass knew he would have hurt Galen badly, perhaps put him in the hospital or the grave, if Shaina hadn't placed herself between them. His body tensed spontaneously.

"Will you see him when we get home?" Shaina asked.

Mass closed his eyes briefly. How was it that she could read his thoughts, understand his moods so easily without him uttering a word or her seeing his expression? They were indeed one. "I don't know."

"He said he was sorry and wanted to talk."

"Which could be interpreted in any number of ways. I've been in this business long enough to know that what people say and what they mean are often two different things. His text was as cryptic as he is. I don't trust him, especially because he sent it just hours after we fought. Nobody cools down that quickly. He wants something, and I bet I know what it is."

"You don't think he—"

"Let's not talk about him anymore. Come on." He untangled himself from her. "I'm getting hungry. I know you must be, too, with a little Andretti growing inside you. It's an hour and a half before sunrise, which gives us just enough time to get to the escarpment and enjoy our breakfast, without hurrying. I don't want you to miss it." He took one last glance at her before taking the lead again. "You sure you don't want anything to eat before we continue?"

"I'm fine, baby. I'll let you know if I get hungry." She placed her hand in his and fell into step beside him.

They hiked silently again, following elephant and buffalo trails—waiting patiently as they grazed—then moving on to observe zebras and elands playing on the lush green meadow along the way, and leopards on mounds, scouting for food that was in high supply because of the great migration season. At the summit of a small hill, they pulled out their binoculars and looked out along the flat plains at a pride of lions enjoying the prey they'd probably killed during the night.

"It looks like a wildebeest," Mass said.

"Poor bastard had no idea that when he crossed the Mara River from Tanzania, he'd never leave Kenya."

"The circle of life, my dear. The circle of life." No time was it more true for Massimo than at the present with the remains of his beloved Jabari clutched against his chest as he carried him to his final resting place, and his wife walking beside him, carrying their unborn child deep in the secret safety of her womb.

"Oh my gosh! Mass. I've never seen anything so indescribably beautiful."

He had. Shaina was the most indescribably beautiful creature he'd ever seen.

Massimo set his coffee mug down on the flat surface of the

plateau, picked up the urn and the folded blanket he'd brought with him, and went to stand behind Shaina who was leaning against the narrow trunk of an acacia tree. He set the urn at her feet and wrapped his arms about her as they gazed off into the woodlands that extended to the banks of the Mara River, separating the borders of Tanzania and Kenya. A herd of buffalos and zebras picked their way carefully through the crocodile-infested water—hoping to reach Kenya, while hippos just floated lazily in the cool comfort of the water, and pearly clouds like bales of silk hovered overhead.

Even though nature was putting on a spectacular parade for human viewing pleasure, Mass knew that the phenomenon that had triggered Shaina's outburst was the vast array of colors, ranging from soft pink to the deepest cerise—with orange, yellow, purple and blue in between—splattered across the horizon, blending sky and earth and water together. The sun was about to make its initial appearance above the horizon—the moment Mass had been waiting for.

"He snaked his hands up under Shaina's shirt and undershirt, and hooked his thumbs into the elastic waistline of her safari pants.

She stiffened and turned her head. "What are you—?"

"Shh. Don't take your eyes off the sunrise, or you'll miss it."

She shivered as he pulled her pants and her panties down to her ankles. He bent down and, lifting one of her legs, he freed her foot from the restrictions of the garment. On his way up, he used one hand to position the folded blanket against the tree trunk and the other to rid himself of his pants. He'd come commando, and his erection gave him a hearty *good morning* slap on the stomach.

"Mass," Shaina called in a broken whisper as he pushed her chest against the trunk cushioned by the blanket, and spread her legs apart.

God, she was so damned desirable. "Keep your eyes on the horizon," he told her again as she looked back at him, her eyes wide with disbelief, passion, and apprehension. "Hold this." He placed the urn in the crook of her arm and pressed his chest into her back, trapping her between him and the tree. He didn't want her coming before him, so giving her something to think about other than the fiery sensations surging through her body should do the trick. He spread her cheeks with one hand and with the other, positioned the tip of his hard shaft to the slick hot opening to her body.

She quivered and moaned at the delicate contact and the soft morning breeze kissing their hungry sexes.

Massimo pulled his shirt off and dropped it on the ground. "You can make as much noise as you want, pussycat. There's no one around to hear you. But whatever you do, do not drop this urn." Before she could respond, Massimo held her hips and sliced up into her body.

She screamed long and hard as he pushed his way to the core of her. When he could go no deeper, he wrapped his hands around her waist and began to ride her, slow and carefully at first, and then more forcefully as the juices began to flow from within her and her body began to thrash and buck as she tried to race to an orgasm.

Massimo wasn't having that. He eased off and took a long shuddering breath as he glanced down to see his shaft, coated with her slick juices, buried halfway inside her, and the twin hills of her backside begging to be plundered again. His gaze

212

shifted to the scar on his right side, and the memories sent fire and ice rushing through his system.

"Watch the sunrise. Tell me when it's about to come up," he murmured in a hoarse voice as he began to slide in and out of her again.

Her moans and groans of ecstasy, her calling out his name, mingled with the melody of birds singing in the treetops, and the distant roar of lions was a bubbling cauldron of natural aphrodisiac for pleasure, and the best remedy for sorrow Massimo had ever experienced.

"It's coming. It's coming," Shaina screamed.

"Don't you drop that urn," Mass commanded. She was quivering so hard, he had to hold her tight to keep her from collapsing to the hard rock they were standing on. Without missing a stroke, he shifted his gaze from the sweet spot where their bodies were intimately joined, and gazed over her shoulders at the rising sun.

Sure enough, it was coming. They were all coming together. The sun, Shaina, and him.

The next second, the sky erupted with a burst of light so pure and white it blinded him for an instant. He continued to thrust deeply into his wife as iota by iota, the majestic ball of white fire emerged in a blast of heat, melting all his sadness, his pain, his cares into oblivion. At that moment, Massimo sank his teeth into the back of his wife's neck and flooded her womb with his essence while the glorious sunrise of a new day, a new beginning bathed them in light.

His groans of passions, mingled with the piercing cries of his wife, echoed across the Masai Mara Lands as Mass and Shaina collapsed into the trunk of the acacia tree.

The urn fell to the ground and cracked open at their feet.

The wind danced around the ashes for a few seconds as if whispering "Welcome Home, Son" to Jabari's remains, before scooping the tiny atoms and whisking them across the Serengeti-Mara Plains.

Jabari was home where he belonged.

Overcome with emotions, Massimo buried his face into Shaina's back and wept.

CHAPTER FOURTEEN

The Summers Residence, Granite Falls – Friday afternoon...

B ryce inhaled sharply and pushed the doorbell of the New England style house in the upscale suburban neighborhood of Granite Falls. It wasn't Mount Reservoir, but it was nice. He held his breath as the sound reverberated inside.

Less than a minute later, the door opened and he was staring into the faces of Gerald and Ruth Summers—the parents of the woman who'd murdered his first wife, almost ten years ago.

Kaya, bless her sweet heart, squeezed his fingers and pulled him out of his trance.

"Come in. Come in." Ruth Summers swung the door wider and beckoned to them while her husband stood behind her with his jaws clenched and his eyes slightly narrowed as if warning Bryce that this was his turf and he was prepared to defend it if needs be.

With Kaya beside him, Bryce stepped through the door and into a living room furnished with a black leather sofa and two matching chairs, glass-topped lamp and coffee tables, knock-off oriental vases, a stereo set, an old jukebox, a grand piano, and a host of other trinkets the family had apparently collected over the years. It reminded him of his grandmother's house—warm and cozy. Yet Bryce felt anything but. As a matter of fact, it was a bit chilly. The AC was set too low.

Family pictures hung on either side of a fifty-inch TV screen mounted on one wall. One quick scope of the eye and Bryce noticed that there were no photos of Victoria among them. He wondered mildly if they'd removed them because he was visiting, or if they'd just axed her from the family tree.

"I'm Kaya."

At the sound of his wife's voice, Bryce let out the breath he'd been holding. The smell of freshly baked chocolate-chip cookies and fresh brewed coffee wafted from the next room where a dog let out an occasional bark and whine. He turned to see the Summerses shaking his wife's hand. Only then did it dawn on him that they'd never met Kaya—the wife who'd replaced the one their daughter had killed. It felt very strange to him, because if Pilar hadn't died...

"It's nice to meet you, Mr. and Mrs. Summers."

Kaya's voice sounded foreign to Bryce, and he wondered if they'd ever met Pilar. Had Victoria spoken about her to them? Did she tell them that she'd had an affair with him? Did they believe her? Is that why Mr. Summers was now watching him with contempt in his eyes?

"Please, sit." Ruth Summers indicated the sofa, and once he and Kaya were seated—still hand-in-hand—she and her husband both settled into the chairs on the other side of the coffee table.

As Bryce took in their wary expressions, he got a feeling of déjà vu from when he and Pilar had gone to her parents' home in Chicago to inform them that they'd gotten married. They hadn't known what to expect from him as a man, or as a husband for their daughter. Later, they blamed him for their daughter's death, for not protecting her from crazy Victoria.

"I baked cookies and made coffee," Ruth said, drawing Bryce's attention back to the room and the unbearable task at hand. "Would you like to have some?"

He declined, but Kaya accepted, out of propriety he supposed.

"I'll bring them in."

A snarl curved Bryce's lips as Gerald jumped up and practically ran out of the room. He was a medium-height, medium-built man in his late fifties, with balding salt and pepper hair, and a labyrinth of crow's-feet around the corners of his eyes, even when he was expressionless. He'd been the mayor of Granite Falls when Bryce first moved to town, and he'd resigned from that post shortly after his daughter committed her ghastly crime. If Bryce had to sum up Gerald Summers in one word, it would be *sad*. He wondered if he'd always been like that or if the tragedy had saddened him over the years.

His wife was a slender, attractive woman who wore her short natural curls in a twisty style he thought was very becoming. She was amiable and didn't seem to carry any of the animosity her husband was portraying toward him— perhaps because Victoria was her stepdaughter. The tragedy may not have affected her as deeply as it had her husband.

After a long awkward silence, Ruth said, "So Desire tells me she has taken over the planning of your wedding. She's so excited to get the opportunity to plan a wedding of this scope and magnitude."

"Yes," Kaya said when she apparently realized that he wasn't going to respond. "Don't tell Fae that I said this, but Desire is the best wedding planner around. We wanted to hire her at first, but didn't for obvious reason." She paused as Gerald came back into the room carrying a wooden tray with a plate of cookies, four mugs, a carafe of coffee, and cream and sugar. He placed the tray on the coffee table, motioned for his wife to remain seated, and began filling the mugs with coffee and handing them out.

Even though Bryce had declined the treat, he nevertheless took the mug Gerald handed him. He wanted to ask him if he had any Scotch or tequila. *What am I doing here? I don't want to be here.*

"She told me about her idea for the four aisles," Ruth continued in a jovial voice.

Bryce glanced at his wife. *Four aisles? What the heck was she talking about?*

Kaya smiled at him over the rim of her coffee mug. "We, the wives, couldn't decide what kind of flowers to use for the aisle, and Desire came up with the brilliant solution to give us each our own aisle, and the flowers of our choice, and ultimately our own spotlight. Each husband can focus on his wife as she walks toward him."

Not a bad idea, Bryce thought.

While Ruth and Kaya exchanged small talk about the wedding plans, Bryce met Gerald's gaze. Neither one of them had said anything since he'd arrived. Well, *he* hadn't. And all that had come out of Gerald's mouth was, "It's very nice to meet you, Kaya" and "I'll bring them in."

They were like two dogs sizing up each other. Bryce set his full mug of coffee down on the tray with a thud, causing some of the black liquid to spill on the surface of the wood, like Pilar's blood had spilled onto the floor that horrific night.

It grew deadly quiet and all eyes focused on him. "I appreciate the cookies and the coffee and the small talk between my wife and you, Mrs. Summers, but this—" He flared his hands. "This isn't the reason I'm here."

"We know, but we're trying to make everyone feel at ease," Ruth said.

"There's nothing easy about what happened with my wi— with Pilar nine years ago. Your daughter murdered her." He felt Kaya's hand on his back, rubbing gently as she tried to calm him down.

"I'm truly sorry about your loss, Mr. Fontaine. No man should have to go through what you went through. I can't imagine watching someone shoot my wife in front of me and then have her bleed to death in my arms. The thought gives me chills." Gerald set his mug down on a nearby lamp table and sat forward. "I'm in no way condoning what Victoria did, but," he added after a short pause, "you're not blameless in this tragedy."

The accusations, and condescension in his voice and eyes cleared it up for Bryce. So Victoria had told them lies about him. "Do you care to explain?" He sent Gerald a stone cold stare.

"Well, you were having relations with my daughter, weren't you? And then you tossed her aside to marry Pilar. Then you slept with her after you were married. She was hurt and confused. You pushed her over the edge when you fired her after she threatened to file a sexual harassment suit against you."

The anger Bryce had been trying to suppress sprang sharply to life. He balled his fists on his thighs. "The only relation I had with your daughter was professional, Mr. Summers. At no time did I enter into any form of sexual liaison with her. I fired her after she slid some naked photos of herself into a pile of letters she'd given me to sign. You got one thing right, sir. I do blame myself for the tragedy, for not realizing what a nutcase your daughter was."

Gerald jumped to his feet, shaking his fists at Bryce. "I will not sit here and allow you to insult my daughter's memory. Not in my house! The door is right there!" He pointed at it. "Use it!"

"Gerald!" his wife scolded him, and rushed to stop his forward advance toward Bryce.

"Good point—" Bryce was about to get up and head for the door when Kaya placed her hand on his arm. "Bryce, we knew it wasn't going to be easy. Please. You need to let this go."

Is this the kind of legacy you want to pass on to your children, son? Do you want to teach them to hold on to grudges and not to forgive those who hurt them?

Bryce took a deep breath and turned to look at Kaya. The plea in her beautiful brown eyes tugged at his heart. *It's not just about you. It's about the future of your children, of the Fontaine family. It'll make me very happy, Bryce. Even if it kills me.*

As the words reverberated inside his head, Bryce stared at Gerald, who was now back in his chair and eyeing him with barely contained fury. Ruth stood behind him, her hands on his shoulders.

"Bryce, be the man who you are. The man I love," Kaya whispered in his ear. "Take the high road, darling."

Bryce straightened his shoulders, drawing calm from Kaya's warm touch. "I apologize for insulting your daughter's memory, Mr. Summers. I didn't come here to fight. I came here to say that I— I— I—want to put this anger and animosity for your family behind me. I can't forget what your daughter did, but I can try to start forgiving her. I have to, for my sake and for the sake of my family." He placed his hand over Kaya's.

Gerald gave him a dubious look. "You really never had an affair with Victoria? Because you did have a reputation with women. You and your friends."

"Never. She tried to start something between us, but I never mix business and pleasure. Even when I had my *reputation*," he added, making quotations marks in the air, "I never juggled women. I never cheated on my wife. I never made advances toward your daughter. I never touched her." He felt as if he needed to say it all for emphasis.

"Victoria pulled the wool over your eyes, Gerry," Ruth said, squeezing her husband's shoulders.

Gerald stared out of a window for a long moment before bringing his attention back to his company. "Her mother was a flight attendant. She loved to travel the world and didn't want kids keeping her down, so she signed Victoria over to me when she was an infant, and she never looked back. To protect her, I told Victoria that her mother died when she was born." He shook his head in obvious sorrow and regret. "I did everything I could to make her feel wanted, but she always felt starved for attention."

"I understand how she must have felt," Kaya said. "I was abandoned by both my parents when I was a child. It's not something you get over easily." She shrugged. "If ever."

But you didn't turn into a nutcase and kill anyone, Bryce thought.

Gerald gave her a faint smile. "Thank you for sharing that." He placed his hands over Ruth's. "Vicki felt even less loved after Desire was born, even though I tried hard to show her that I didn't love her any less because I had another daughter."

Bryce's thoughts wandered off to Jason, Alyssa, and Anastasia. He hoped that they never felt less loved than Eli and Elyse. Yes, he shared a special bond with his biological children that he couldn't share with anyone else, not even his wife. It was natural. He wasn't making any apologies for it. The important thing is that all his children were equally loved, and they equally loved each other. He would charge into a burning building to rescue Jason and his sisters, just as quickly and easily as he would for Eli and Elyse. He knew that Jason felt the same way about the twins as he felt about his siblings, and that he would protect them as ferociously, but Jason shared a special bond with his sisters that he didn't share with Eli and Elyse.

Listening to Gerald speak of his daughter, Bryce put himself in the man's shoes, and soon Victoria Summers didn't seem like a monster to him anymore. She was a troubled soul. Lost.

"I'm sorry, Mr. Fontaine. You were… still are a respected man in Granite Falls." Gerald's voice penetrated Bryce's thoughts. "I should have looked into the matter before accusing you of wrongdoing, and blaming you for pushing my daughter over the edge." His voice faltered. "I didn't want her to think that I didn't believe her, that I didn't love her. I didn't want to make her feel any less important than she already felt. I realize now that was my mistake. You shouldn't love your children to the point where you're afraid to hurt their feelings by calling them out. If I had not taken Victoria at her word, she and your first wife would still be alive. I'm sorry. Truly sorry." Tears rolled down his cheeks as his wife wrapped her arms about him.

As Bryce watched him, the tension inside his chest loosened. He took a deep breath and realized that it didn't hurt. He was sitting in the Summerses' home, talking to them about their daughter, the woman who'd murdered his first wife, and he wasn't angry or tense anymore. *It hadn't killed him.*

Bryce turned to his wife and wrapped her in his arms. "I can breathe. Thank you. Thank you. I love you. I love you so very much."

"You're free, Bryce. You're free." She held on to him, crying softly in relief.

"Would you like a fresh cup of coffee, Mr. Fontaine?" Ruth asked after they'd all regained their composure.

"Yes, please, Mrs. Summers. That would be awesome. And you can call me Bryce."

❧

Big Boy's Pizza Shop – Sunday morning...

It had been one crazy week, and when it rained, it really poured. Literally and figuratively, Massimo thought, as huge raindrops pelted his windshield. His wipers were going at full speed yet it was hard for him to see as he carefully made his way down Union Street toward Big Boy's Pizza Shop.

He should be in church with his family and his friends and their families—especially the LaCrosses who'd laid Sarah to rest yesterday. He hadn't even been aware that the dear old woman had died until his return from Kenya early yesterday morning. Among other news, he'd learned that Desire Summers had taken over the planning of their wedding, with Bryce's blessings to boot, and that their wedding was now a community affair. Michelle's brilliant idea, that everyone thought was the therapy the town needed to heal old wounds, had gone public on Friday while he and Shaina were still in Kenya.

As he pulled his Lamborghini into a parking space in front of the pizza shop, Massimo wondered if Michelle's idea was the reason he'd received the letter from the mystery person waiting for him inside. The letter had been hand delivered to Andretti Industries, late Friday, and had been among the pile of mail he'd had sent from his office to the estate.

Massimo's hands shook as he pulled the note from his suit pocket, and his stomach tightened as he read it for the millionth time: *Dear Mr. Andretti, Your mother got a phone call the day she died. If you want to know who called her, meet me at Big Boy's Pizza on Union Street Sunday morning at 11.*

Massimo replaced the note and checked the time on his dashboard. It was five minutes before eleven. Shaina had offered to accompany him, but he'd declined. He had no idea if the note was from a man or a woman, a shady character or a respectable person. He didn't know if the person was local or foreign. And for those reasons, he'd declined Shaina's offer.

Yes, he was dying to know who called his mother that fateful day, and he would have loved to have Shaina's support, but he had to protect her, and his family, from the unknown. For all he knew, it could be a hoax and he could be walking into some kind of trap.

Massimo pulled up the hood of his raincoat, slid out of his Lamborghini and made a wild dash for the entrance to the pizza shop. The delicious smell of pizza, along with some old memories assailed him. He took a quick glance around to find it almost deserted, except for a woman and a small child at a table in the front dining room, watching the television mounted over the bar area.

As the proverbial bell on the door jingled, the woman glanced up, and stared at him before dropping her gaze to the slice of pizza on her plate. *So she wasn't his mystery meeting.*

Mass was amused as he watched her cheeks turn crimson red. She found him attractive. And he had to admit that she was attractive too. A few years ago, if he were between lovers, he would have gone over and introduced himself, and if she were available, he would have paid for a babysitter for the day, and then taken her to his lakeside villa. She wasn't the kind he'd tote around in public on his arm, just the kind he'd have under him in the privacy of his bed for a few hours.

Thank God those days were behind him. Shaina, his sexy pussycat, his passionate wildcat, was all the woman Massimo needed, wanted, desired, could handle… He shrugged out of his raincoat and hung it on one of the wooden hooks near the door.

"Massimo Andretti?"

Mass turned toward the voice and grinned at the man behind the bar, an old acquaintance from high school. He would know that Roman nose and those hooded eyes anywhere. Big Boy's Pizza was owned and operated by the Carboni family. Unlike the Andrettis and Andreases, old man Salvatore Carboni wasn't steeped in Italian traditions. The only things Italian about the Carboni family were their name and their pizza shop—that didn't even have an Italian name. And neither did any of his children, Mass thought as he walked over to the bar.

It was a wonder Salvatore hadn't dropped the 'i' from the family name and Americanized it to simply Carbon, but then his children would be nicknamed *Carbon Copies*, Massimo thought, recalling his nicknames as a little boy: *Mass Production*, *Mass Destruction*, *Sunday Mass*, and a host of other unpleasant *Masses*. Kids could be so cruel. "David," Massimo said, giving his old friend a solid handshake. "It's good to see you."

"You too, man. It's been a while."

"You disappeared right after graduation. Where the heck have you been?"

David rubbed the craggy beard on his chin and adjusted the collar of his plaid shirt peeking out from the top of his white apron. "I joined the navy, did a few tours in Afghanistan and Iraq. Got married, settled down in Rhode Island, got a couple kids."

"Good for you. I'm sure you heard I got married. I have a little girl, Aria. She's seventeen months old, and the cutest, smartest kid on the planet."

David shook his head and grinned. "I'd just gotten back when the news broke about your engagement to Nia Sylk, only weeks after you broke up with that Gabrielle woman. I thought for sure Judgment Day was approaching. Massimo

Andretti married? Now, after reading that article in the *People's* magazine, I understand why you were in such a hurry."

"Well, I did love Shaina when I married her. My father's will was the catalyst that drove me, so it all worked out in my favor. Shaina is the best thing that ever happened to me. So what brought you back to Granite Falls?" He perched on a barstool.

"My old man asked me to come home and take over the joint. He's getting on in years and couldn't handle the stress anymore." David shrugged. "How could I say no? This pizza shop paid for that expensive prep school my sister and I attended. Business is still good. It's taking care of my family, and maybe I'll send my kids to Granite Falls Prep. It's a good school."

Massimo folded his arms on the counter. "I remember you bribing your way through it. You had a reputation for promising the girls free pies for their all-night study sessions if they'd just flash their boobs for you, and sometimes even let you squeeze them."

David chuckled. "Well, I didn't have Andretti money, nor your good looks and charm, Mass. I had to work with what I had. Memories of those boobs kept me warm and sane many a cold lonely night in the desert."

"You should send the women 'Thank You' notes, then, let them know they should be proud to have kept one soldier safe, and brought him back home alive."

They laughed, then David said, "I know you didn't leave the dry comfort of your mansion on the hill to come down here on this miserable morning to chat about old times. And it's too early for drinking." He opened a bottle of mineral water, grabbed two glasses from beneath the counter, and filled them. "So what's your agenda?" he asked, pushing one in front of Mass.

The tension in Massimo's belly returned with the question. "I'm meeting someone."

David narrowed his eyes and leaned in. "Business or pleasure? You know I have a dining room out back. I can give you some privacy if you want to mess around."

Massimo jumped back with his hand up. "Oh no. Those days are behind me, David. I told you, I'm very happily married. There's only one woman in the world for me now."

"Hey, if that's your story, you stick to it." David picked up his glass and motioned for Mass to follow suit. "To old times, new habits, and business."

The men emptied their glasses, just as the bells of the door chimed, indicating the arrival of another customer.

Mass looked up to see a woman, who looked to be in her early to mid sixties, shaking out an umbrella. She placed it in a bucket near the door and looked at him, before walking hesitantly toward him, a look of apprehension on her face. Her gray, thinning hair, damp from the rain, was pulled back into a ponytail. She wore a black dress with a red and yellow flowery print, and clutched a black purse under her arm. She looked as if she'd just left Mass.

"Mrs. Marshall, what in heaven's name are you doing out in this rainstorm?" David asked, as he came from behind the counter to hug the woman. "Aren't there any pizza joints in Evergreen?"

"I have business, David," she said in a voice that was slightly tremulous.

David's eyebrow arched. He pointed from the woman to Mass. "This is your business?"

"I—I—" Mass had no idea.

The woman offered him her hand. "I'm the one who sent you the note. I'm Pamela Marshall."

Mass shook her hand. "I'm Massimo Andretti."

She pulled back her hand and gave him a *Duh* stare.

David scratched his head. "About that room in the back. Follow me."

Mass indicated for Mrs. Marshall to walk ahead of him as they followed David to the back room, where about ten tables were set for the afternoon rush. From what he could remember, Big Boy's Pizza was where many folks who lived on this side of town came for lunch after church on Sundays, while those on the other side headed to Ristorante Andreas. That was where he'd be meeting his friends after he was finished with Mrs. Marshall. The service at Granite Falls Community Church was broadcast live every Sunday, so he could watch it later.

"This should do." David stopped at the furthest table in the back of the room. "I'll make sure I fill up the front before I send folks back here," he said. "They'll start piling in in about an hour so." He glanced out a window. "By then the rain should have stopped."

"Would you like something to eat?" Mass asked Mrs. Marshall.

"No," she replied shortly, and sat down in the chair David held for her.

"I'll send in a bottle of water," David offered.

Mass pulled a pen from one pocket and a card from another and wrote his cell phone number on the back of it. He pressed it into David's hand. "Call me sometime. It'll be nice to have that drink and catch up. Oh, and you have an open invitation to the wedding, like all Granite Falls residents do now."

"Sure thing. I'll dust off my tux," David said on his way out.

Massimo's chest felt extremely tight as he took off his jacket and hung it over the back of the chair across from Mrs. Marshall. *So this was the mystery woman behind the note.* He eased his weight into the chair and watched her clasp and unclasp her hands on the table. "You don't need to be nervous," he told her.

"I can't help it. I knew I should have contacted you a long time ago, years ago, maybe after your father died, but I was afraid."

"Afraid of what, Mrs. Marshall?"

"Your father was a powerful man. I've witnessed firsthand how he dealt with people who crossed him."

"I'm not my father." Massimo placed his hand over hers, and soon she stopped her fidgeting. "I'm not going to hurt you. No one will hurt you. How do you know my father?"

She took a long time responding. "I used to work at Andretti Industries when he was still alive. You were just a little boy then. You were so cute and pleasant. I liked your grandfather, too. He was nice."

As a waiter brought in a bottle of water and two glasses, and proceeded to fill them, Mass reveled in memories of his grandfather. "What was your role at A.I. Mrs. Marshall?" he asked when the waiter left.

"I worked in the cafeteria in the daytime and as a cleaner at nights. I was a single mother with a young child to support. His name is Billy. I have two children now. Mindy came along much later."

Massimo nodded, trying to maintain his patience as Mrs. Marshall gave him her family history. He cleared his throat. "Not to rush you along, but David said we only have an hour before customers start piling in. You said you know who called my mother the day she died."

She leaned back into her chair and took a sip of her water. "Yes. Like I said, I kept quiet all these years because I was afraid. I've lived with this information for the last twenty-five years and each time July comes around, I get sick to my stomach."

Massimo was out of patience. "Who called my mother, Mrs. Marshall?"

"It was Judith Carmichael. Your father's secretary."

CHAPTER FIFTEEN

Massimo's nails bit into his palms. He closed his eyes and swallowed back the bile that rushed upward to his throat. All these years he'd known it. He just couldn't prove it. The voice of his father's whore might have been the last his sweet mother had heard. He could only imagine what horrible things that woman must have said to her—horrible things that had caused her to faint, to fall to the floor and hit her head so hard she'd slipped into unconsciousness.

He pressed his lips together to stifle the cry of despair as his chest rose and fell with his labored breathing. When he felt that he could speak without cracking, he opened his eyes. "How do I know that what you just told me is the truth?" he asked the bearer of the news.

She pulled her handbag from the back of the chair and fumbled through it. "I never liked that woman," she said, pulling out a small tape recorder and holding it in her hand as if it were a piece of gold. "She was an evil bitch. Excuse my French," she added in an acerbic tone.

Massimo was taken aback at her vehemence. "Oh, I know

French," he said. "That's not French. *Elle était une chienne mal.* That's French." What had Judith Carmichael done to this woman?

"She wanted your father and his money. She wanted your mother gone so she could move into her house, and she was prepared to do anything to get her way. The one thing she didn't bank on was that your father loved your mother and you, and that for him, she was just a cheap piece of ass."

Once again, Massimo was taken aback at the woman's bitterness toward Judith Carmichael.

"I know what you saw that day you came to visit your father." She paused to take a sip of water. "Judith knew you were coming, and she set the stage. She wanted you to run home and tell your mother what you saw, but you didn't, did you?"

"I couldn't hurt her, or embarrass her by letting her know that her little boy knew what his father was doing."

"You were a good son, a sensible son. But she knew. We women know, and for one reason or the other, we keep quiet, accept it, hope it'll go away. Sometimes it does and sometimes it doesn't."

Massimo eyed the recorder in her hand. "What's that?"

She set it on the table, but kept her hand over it. "I taped the phone call. I don't know if your mother responded to her, but—"

"She didn't. I was there when the call came. She didn't utter a word. She just went white as a ghost and then collapsed." He stated the facts and forced himself not to revisit that moment, not here, not now.

Mrs. Marshall pushed the recorder across the table. "She

was in shock. Once you hear what she said, you'll understand why. I have to warn you, it's nasty and filled with expletives."

Massimo glanced at the little black device for a long time. Did he really want to know? Did he want that woman's voice in his head? Did he want to remember the ugliness of the last words his mother heard? "What did she say to my mother?"

She tilted her head to one side and her brows furrowed. "You don't want to listen to it?"

"No. Tell me what she said and how and why you came to record her." He sat back and folded his arms across his constricting chest.

Mrs. Marshall shifted uneasily. "See, this is the part that always scared me. The reason I never told anyone. Because if your father knew I was eavesdropping on his private conversations—but only with her," she added hastily. "He would have fired me, or worse, and like I said, I had a child to support."

Massimo nodded.

"When she first moved here from England, Judith lived in my apartment complex in Evergreen with an American student who'd done a semester abroad in London. She'd followed him back here, and after they broke up, she stayed. She didn't have any money or friends, and she asked me where she could find work. She seemed nice, so I spoke to my cousin who owned a cleaning company. She didn't have any papers so he paid her under the table. Soon she asked to be on my crew at A.I. My cousin refused because anyone who worked at A.I had to be fully investigated with background checks. She slept with him to get her way." She swung her head from side to side. "I should have known she was up to something. Anyway, the next thing I know, your father's personal assistant retired and Judith took her place. I later found out that she'd slept with somebody else to falsify working papers for her."

"So she had her eyes on my father all along."

"She wanted to live in one of the three biggest mansions on Mount Reservoir. Mr. LaCrosse and Mr. Andreas were faithful to their wives, so she went after your father."

The notorious man-whore.

"I wanted to rat her out, but I was afraid my cousin would get in trouble for allowing her in the building in the first place. I could have lost my job, too. Judith held that over my head. Like I said, I'd seen how your father handled people who crossed him. I had to find some other way to get rid of her. So I started bugging her office. She was so stupid, thinking she was better than me because she was the personal assistant to the CEO of one of the biggest companies in the world, while I was still cleaning toilets—her toilet."

"That's how you found out about the false papers."

She nodded. "Among other things. She told your father she was on the pill all the while she was trying to get pregnant. The day she told him she was carrying his child, your father told her that he loved his wife and son and would never leave them, that her child was a bastard he would never acknowledge. He told her that you and his wife's unborn child were his true heirs and he would never force them to share their inheritance. He demanded a paternity test and if it was his child, he would arrange for a flat in London for her, a car and a sizable income. He would have his attorney draw up a contract that she would never tell the child about his paternity, ever, and she would never return to the U.S. or he would stop all financial support and put her child into foster care in a foreign country and she would never see it again. He told her that he was going home to spend some time with his family and see his attorney about the contract. He would return later that day and she would sign it, pack her things, and leave."

Massimo groaned as he remembered his father coming home unexpectedly, playing a Star Wars game with him on his Nintendo, before joining his mother in *Il Nido d'Amore* where they'd stayed for hours. His father must have been making up for hurting his mother. *Why couldn't he have come to his senses much sooner?*

Mrs. Marshall finished her water and eyed Mass' that he still hadn't touched. "Go ahead." Anything he put into his stomach would come right back up.

She drank half of it. "After your father left. Judith went crazy, ranting and raging and tossing things around."

"Is all that on this tape?" he asked, pointing to the menacing black box.

"Well, not on this one. I have others. This one just has the call to your mother. You want me to go on or you want to listen for yourself?"

He shook his head negatively.

"I'll leave out the expletives. They're even too repulsive for me to repeat." She inhaled deeply. "Judith decided that since your father wouldn't leave your mother, she would make her want to leave him, so she called her. She told her that her husband didn't love her, that he'd only married her to secure an heir for his estate. He had his heir and now had found true love with her, Judith. She told her that she was pregnant with his child, and that he was only waiting until your mother's baby was born before he divorced her and put her out of the mansion. She said that she and your father would raise you and your sister alongside the one she was carrying. She told her to save herself embarrassment and leave quietly, because whatever she just shared with him was a goodbye—" She paused and averted her gaze. "I'm sure you know what four-letter-word she used."

Massimo dropped his elbows on the table and his head in his hands as tears stung his eyes. *His poor, darling mother.* It was easy for her to believe those lies since Luciano was such a dog to her, and according to Aunt Bella, had only told her that he loved her three times: when he proposed to her, when he married her, and when Massimo was born. She was insecure, unsure of her place in his life. She should not have died with those lies in her head.

He pounded his fist on the table. *Damn his father! Damn Judith Carmichael! Damn them both to hell!*

"I'm sorry you had to hear the truth, Mr. Andretti."

He wished he hadn't. He lifted his head and stared at her. He was aware that his cheeks were wet with his tears but he didn't care. "Why after all these years are you telling me now? You said you didn't speak up before because you were afraid of my father. He's been dead for eight years. Why even bother telling me now?"

"Just in case you'd happened upon this information some other way, I don't want my daughter, Mindy, to get caught in the middle of this feud with you and your—with Judith's son."

Massimo frowned. "How is your daughter involved? *Please don't tell me that old bastard fathered your daughter as well.*

"Mindy is friends with your cousin's wife, Tashi. They used to be neighbors on Temple Street. Mr. Andreas gave Mindy a job working in a boutique at Hotel Andreas. That's where she met your—Galen. She told me you and Galen had a fight about his share of your father's company or something like that. The apple doesn't fall far from the tree."

No they don't, but once some apples fall to the ground, they roll for yards to get away from the tree that had borne them. Massimo stared out the window. The storm had passed. The sun was trying to peek out from behind gray clouds.

"I don't want that boy anywhere near my daughter," Mrs. Marshall said. "I figured if you knew the truth you'd do something about it."

Massimo shifted his gaze to her. His lips twisted into a cynical smile. Everybody wanted something. *Always.* She'd just given him the answer to a question that had been burning a hole in his heart and mind for the past twenty-five years—an answer he now wished he didn't have. All because she wanted him to do something to keep Galen away from her daughter.

Mass curled his fingers around the tape recorder. "Thank you for telling me, Mrs. Marshall. Is there any way I can get my hands on the other tapes you spoke about?"

"Sure. Sure. I can bring them by your office tomorrow."

That would work. He'd have time to listen to them before he took his family to Como for the week. "Say around nine in the morning?"

She nodded. "Nine."

"Does anyone else know you have them, or about what you just told me?"

"No, sir. You're the only person I've ever told. And they are the only copies I have."

There was no need not to believe her. "I'd like this to stay between us," he said in a quiet voice, yet edged with an ominous quality.

Her eyes widening with fear as she stared into his.

Satisfied that Mrs. Pamela Marshall would take her dirt on Judith Carmichael to her grave, Massimo glanced at his watch. "I have another appointment, so if you don't mind, we can bring this meeting to a close." He stood and walked around to her chair and helped her to her feet. "Now that you've gotten this burden off your chest, you can sleep in peace."

He, on the other hand, would probably lie awake for many nights with the vision of his mother standing in the music room with Judith Carmichael's obnoxious voice and ugly words in her ears.

Mass swept into the foyer when Galen opened the door. He'd called when he left Big Boy's to let him know he was paying him a visit. He stood near the door and swept his gaze around. The villa was just the way he'd left it when he'd given it up for Shaina—taupe leather sofas and chairs, marble tables, Persian rugs, crystal chandeliers, and expensive paintings on the walls.

"It's good to see you, Massimo," Galen said, holding out his hand for a shake.

Ignoring it, Mass took in the black and blue areas around his eyes and the scab on his lower lip. At least Galen was healing, physically, while the scars on the wounds of Mass' heart had just been ripped wide open. Mass wanted to crack Galen's lip open again and watch him bleed.

Mass, you can't blame Galen if it was his mother who'd called your mother. Promise me you won't take your anger out on him. Shaina's warning rang in his ears. And his devious wife had made him promise while they'd made love to Beyonce's "Drunk in

Love" last night, and then this morning in the shower to Case's "Shook Up." Both times her voluptuous body had bounced and undulated on his shaft like he'd never seen it done before. It was mind-blowing. He was still shook up. For her sake and in anticipation of being shaken up again soon, Massimo kept the promise he'd made to his wife and unclenched his fists.

"Would you care for some coffee?" Galen's voice broke into his reverie. "I just made a fresh pot."

"In your text, five days ago, you said you wanted to talk. What do you want to talk about?"

Galen ran his fingers through his dark curly hair and leaned against one of the columns that separated the small foyer from the open concept spaces of the kitchen, dining and living rooms. "I just want to say I'm sorry, in person. I'm sorry, Mass."

Massimo looked him up and down. He was a handsome young man, which was no surprise since he was an Andretti. He had their father's chin—the same chin Mass had inherited. "What are you sorry about?"

"For saying those things about your mother. I shouldn't have. I didn't know that room was special to you and I didn't realize that it was the anniversary of her death, and that Jabari had just died. If I'd known, I would have been more sensitive."

Meaning, you would have waited to ask for half of Andretti Industries. Caught me when I was in a better mood, and much more receptive. "You don't know a lot of things, Galen. You also insulted my wife by telling her that I forced her into marriage for money, the money would have gotten if she hadn't married me. So I'll ask you again. What do you want?"

Massimo just wanted to hear him say it out loud, so he, Galen, could hear how absurd it was.

Galen crossed his arms and looked Massimo straight in the face. "I deserve half of Andretti Industries. I'm Luciano's son, too. I was neglected and denied my birthright through no fault of my own. I deserve half of his estate, and I deserve a seat on the board."

Massimo laughed so hard, he had to brace his hand against the wall to keep from falling to the floor.

"So this is a joke to you?" Galen demanded in a vociferous voice. "You think it's funny?"

Mass sobered up and cleared the frog from his throat. "I'm not giving you half of A.I., Galen, nor will you ever sit on the board. Andretti Industries belongs to me as the rightful legitimate heir of the Andretti bloodline. It's the heritage of my children, and *their* children, for generations to come. My kids won't be fighting yours for power, decades from now. I won't leave them such an unstable legacy." And just in case Andretti Industries went under for some unfortunate reason, there was *La Banca di Bianchi*, the second largest bank in Europe. In a few years, it would be the largest. Massimo couldn't wait to groom Aria and her future siblings to take over the two empires he was safeguarding for them.

"You expect me to just walk away empty-handed like I came?" Galen asked.

"You can go out and start your own company. Carve out your own place in the world. I started *La Banca di Bianchi* all on my own."

"You had Andretti money for a startup."

"Wrong. I borrowed every penny of that startup, and paid it back with interest. You can do the same. Make your company whatever you want and wherever you want. You can stay here in the States, here in Granite Falls, or you can return to Europe. I don't care. Once you figure it out, I will give you the initial financial backing. Just tell me how much you need and I will write you a check up to a certain amount."

Galen's hazel eyes glowed with anger. "That's not fair, Massimo. You know it."

"Life's not fair, Galen."

"I didn't have my father in my life to groom me, to make me into the kind of man you've become."

Massimo chuckled softly. The man he'd become had nothing to do with his father, but everything to do with the sweet love of the remarkable woman he'd been lucky enough to find. She'd changed him from the bitter man-whore his father had turned him into. "You received an education equal to mine. It's much more than most bastards get. Use it. And if it's grooming you need, when you're ready, I'll groom you like our father groomed me. We make the most of what we get and play the hand we've been dealt. This is your hand. Play it. It's the best offer you'll ever get in your lifetime, so I suggest you take it. If you decide to accept my offer, you will sign an irrefutable contract that neither you nor your progeny will ever interfere in Andretti Industries business from here to eternity, and beyond."

"And what if I don't agree? What if I refuse to sign your contract?"

"You get nothing."

Mass could almost hear Galen's teeth grinding inside his jaws, and his knuckles cracking as he clenched his fists.

"I'm not making it that easy for you, Massimo. I hired an attorney. He thinks I have a good case, especially because you waited so long to fulfill the requirements of your inheritance in our father's will. My parents were in love, and it would have been mine if your mother hadn't chased mine out of the country."

Rage bubbled inside Massimo. He needed to bring this charade of a relationship to an end and get on with his life. Galen was his half-brother, and despite Mass' feelings about him, he wanted to see him succeed. Andretti's weren't failures. He understood Galen's anger and frustrations, because he'd been misinformed about his mother's relationship with their father, and blind to the fact that their father would not have sent Judith away and neglected her son if he'd truly loved her. Luciano was an Andretti. They were never manipulated, especially not by women they had no feelings for.

Shaina could make Mass do anything she wanted. *Anything.* Luciano's problem was that the *anything* he was willing to do for his wife had come too late. And he'd spent the rest of his life regretting it.

Mass would so love to throw the tape of Judith's ugliness into Galen's face, but every boy needed to think that his mother was a kindhearted goddess even if she were a conniving, gold-digging bitch. He was done listening to his shit and his whining. When Galen was ready to be a man, Mass would be a brother to him. But in the meantime…

Mass got into Galen's face, forcing him to look into his eyes. "Galen, you don't deserve any part of Andretti Industries because you've never contributed anything to it. It's that simple. I've been contributing to the success of that company since I was two feet high, and when it teetered on the brink of destruction eight years ago, I brought it back to life, singlehandedly. If you want to be pissed at someone for not having a role in Andretti Industries, be pissed at our father and your mother. *He* broke his vows to my mother and to me. *She* wrecked my mother's home, and killed her and my unborn sister—your sister. They robbed me of the chance of growing up with them in my life. You're not the only victim here. I suffered, too. Luciano and Judith are the only guilty parties in this entire affair."

Massimo took a breather—a deep slow one. He was tired. He was done. "One more thing," he added as he turned and walked to the door, "if you plan to remain in Granite Falls, find another place to live. I'm selling this villa." He didn't ever again wish to darken the door of this pleasure house his father had bought him on his eighteenth birthday.

Massimo stepped out onto the porch and headed for his car. He didn't flinch a muscle as Galen slammed the door behind him, so hard that the glass shattered.

Watch where you step, brother or you might get hurt.

Mass smiled as the engine of his Lamborghini roared to life. He supposed he'd have to ask Steven to be his Best Man now.

CHAPTER SIXTEEN

Ristorante Andreas – Sunday Afternoon...

The first to return from a bathroom break, and from switching from suits into casual attire, Massimo made himself busy at the cappuccino machine. His spirits were up in spite of the morning he'd had. He could credit his good mood to the fact that he and his best friends had been held up in a private barroom in Ristorante Andreas all afternoon. They'd indulged in a never ending supply of sweets and post-lunch delicacies and had played pool and darts, and enjoyed a college baseball game on the mounted TV screen in between reminiscing on old times, sharing recent events—some unpleasant, some celebratory—like his and Shaina's pregnancy, the trials and triumphs in each of their lives, and the wedding and honeymoon.

Each of their families had had to let go of something or someone in their lives this past week. The LaCrosses said goodbye to Sarah. The Fontaines faced past hurts and moved beyond anger. The Andreases dealt with the horrors of Tashi's mother's death, and saw justice prevail. Mass said goodbye to his beloved Jabari, the oldest and most valuable friend he'd ever had, and he'd solved the mystery of the person who'd called his mother.

The rain had stopped hours ago; the clouds had rolled back, and the sun had appeared, bringing hope that the worst was behind them.

After leaving Galen, he'd walked into the private dining room across the hall to find three generations of LaCrosses, Fontaines, Andreases, and two generations of Andrettis bumping and rocking to R. Kelly's "Joyful People." Even Alex and Fiona—the youngest ones in the family—had been rocking in their walkers. It had been the boost Mass needed after the morning he'd had—the week he'd had. He'd never been more confident about his future, more content with his life as when he'd picked up his daughter from the floor and danced with her and her mother.

Today was the first day of a new chapter in all their lives, and they'd started it off with an eight-course lunch with their entire families, including the grandparents, Steven, Libby, and their daughter, Jenna, and Pastor Kelly and his family. The guests, the grandmothers, the wives, and the kids had left shortly after lunch to give the men some time together since their bachelors' party had been canceled yesterday, due to Sarah's funeral and Mass' absence. The grandfathers had left after the game, giving their sons time alone before the wives rejoined them for a sunset dinner cruise on the Andreas yacht around Crystal Lake. They'd also hired a live band for some dancing.

Their hectic schedules, and travels abroad, made it impossible for them to get together often as a whole group, so they cherished moments like these—Sunday afternoons when they were all home and could just kick back and relax after church. These Sunday dinners were for their children as much as they were for the adults. It was important that their children saw them socializing as one big extended family. They wanted them to love and trust each other, to never feel that they were alone in the world.

Bryce and Kaya stepping in to take care of Michael and Lauren's children had made them all realize how imperative it was that they remain in close contact with each other, so that their children could grow up together, and hopefully love and care for each other like their parents did. They'd pledged to be there for each other's children if, God forbid, any became orphans.

Mass placed the four mugs on a tray and took it over to where they'd been sitting near a window overlooking the lake. And not a moment too soon, he thought as his friends returned, poking and wrestling each other, and racing like little boys to grab the chair nearest the wall.

Anyone watching them cavort would think they were drunk, but they weren't—well, not from alcohol. They'd made a rule never to drink on Sundays since it was the families' get-together day. They were high on love and happiness.

"So what's this I hear about Jason and Precious kissing?" Mass set the cups on the serving tables near each chair and took his seat among his friends. "Shaina gave me a snapshot version, but I'd love to hear more."

Erik's humor dwindled at Mass' question. They'd discussed every topic but that all afternoon. He wasn't thrilled about revisiting that subject, but it was only fair that Mass was brought up to date. They shared everything, and besides, he should know in case Precious and Jason tried to pull one over on him during a visit to Andretti estate. "Apparently my daughter and Jason shared their first kiss," he said, picking up his cup of cappuccino, and raising the scalding liquid to his lips.

"A real kiss?" Massimo asked with raised eyebrows.

Bryce sent Erik a rueful glance. He gave him a lot of credit, because if it were his daughter, he would have demanded Jason stay away from her until she was older. He figured that Erik's experience of no premarital sex with Cassie played a big role in his decision to let Precious date. *His daughter. His decision.*

He, Erik, Michelle, and Kaya had sat down with Jason and Precious after the funeral yesterday and set some ground rules for them to follow. They hadn't been happy, since all they were allowed to do was hold hands and kiss on the cheeks for no more than five seconds, tops. They were not to fondle each other nor swap any kind of bodily fluids, or else... "As real as a kiss can get," he told Massimo when he realized that Erik had deliberately tuned out.

Massimo whistled. "Wow. Jason is starting early. Those hormones have kicked in, huh?"

"No earlier than you," Adam reminded his cousin. "You had your first French kiss at twelve, and God knows what else you had at that age." Adam had his suspicions about Massimo and Dafne, but Mass would never deny or admit to having sex with her. If Paul and Dafne ever became a couple, Massimo would have to come clean. Paul would have a right to know. "The rest of us were much older," he added. "Even Bryce, the second runner-up in the group, didn't have his first real kiss until he was sixteen."

"More power to Jason, then." Mass raised his cup in toast.

"Hey!" Erik sent Mass a warning flash of his eyes. "It's my daughter you're talking about. Be a little sensitive."

Mass set his cup on the table and leaned forward in his chair. "I'm sorry, Erik, but you knew that day was coming. They're just growing. Discovering their sexuality. It's harmless. They're both good, sensible kids. I doubt they'll do anything they shouldn't. They were raised well. They have stellar role models as fathers." He nodded perfunctorily at both Erik and Bryce. "And mothers."

"Well, thanks for the flattery," Erik said with a hint of sarcasm. "Let's see if you're still singing the same tune, in say…ten and a half years when some horny fourteen-year-old sticks his tongue down your twelve-year-old daughter's throat."

"That will never happen. As soon as Aria starts showing signs of puberty, I'm confining her to the estate and hiring a governess. She will have no interactions with boys until she's twenty-five."

"Yep. Spoken like a reformed man-whore turned Daddy. You'll hide her because you know boys that age think of one thing, and one thing only." Bryce gloated with satisfaction.

"Precisely!" Mass slapped his hands against his thighs.

"Good luck with that," Bryce said, as they all burst into laughter.

When they settled into their chairs again, Bryce turned to Erik. "By the way what did you say to Jason when you took him aside yesterday? The poor kid looked so petrified when he rejoined us. He wouldn't even look at Precious. When we got home, he went straight to his room."

The amber specks in Erik's gray eyes flickered. "I told him

that if he laid a hand on my daughter, I would break all his fingers and reset them crookedly, then castrate him so he'd never be able to obtain pleasure from another girl ever again."

"Aww, Erik." Adam's hand flew protectively to his crotch. He was certain that when he had daughters, he'd also lock them up when they reached Precious' age. Tashi had been sheltered, and she'd turned out fine—real fine, he thought with a grin.

"Oh man." Bryce wiped his hand across his forehead. "You probably turned my son off sex for life. I threatened to send him off to boarding school if he violated the rules we set for them, but promising bodily harm—"

"I love Jason, Bryce, but I love my daughter more. Of course I won't physically hurt him, but I had to put the fear of Dr. Erik in him, nonetheless. He can have all the sex his young body can handle, just not with my daughter."

"I'll remember that if and when Little Erik—JP—" he rolled his eyes at the name change, "ever becomes interested in Anastasia or Elyse."

"Not Alyssa?" Adam asked.

"Brrr," Bryce snickered. "JP wouldn't be able to handle Alyssa. *I* can't handle Alyssa. I feel sorry for any boy who's brave enough to show an interest in that girl when she reaches the appropriate age. He would be on his hands and knees and crawling on his stomach for the rest of his life."

"That's not a bad place to be," Erik drawled. "We've all been on our knees and crawling on our stomachs since we met our wives, sometimes with our hands tied together, like in my case."

They rocked with the laughter of revelers, then Bryce asked, "Anyone else have been making love to love songs lately, or is it just me? Since I got back from my conference, every time we get into the groove, Kaya stops to put on some sultry song."

"So does Michelle. It started Thursday morning when I returned from South America."

"Shaina, too. She was adamant about making love to songs last night and this morning."

"I guess my wife didn't get the memo," Adam said. "We've been making love without songs."

"She's been preoccupied with her mother's trial and the verdict. But I'm sure she's in with them. You might get your songs tonight, Adam, and you will enjoy every moment," Erik assured him with a secretive smile bubbling in his heart. "Something's going on with our women. And whatever it is, I'm not complaining."

"Hear, hear." They raised their cappuccino cups in another toast.

"Who would have guessed twenty plus years ago when we were fighting pimples and body odor, hiding the evidence of wet dreams from the maids, and learning how to put on a condom, that we'd still be together, still best friends and all married to sexy, intelligent women?" Massimo asked.

"Don't forget kickass," Adam said with a proud lilt in his voice. Tashi had been practicing martial arts at a second-rate school during the year and a half she'd been hiding out in Granite Falls. Once they were married, she'd enrolled in Granite Falls Studio of Self Defense—the best martial arts school in the area. She had continued her training, with limitation, up until the middle of her second trimester when she was forced to take a break until after Alex was born. She was back at it and practicing hard for the regional Karate

ANA E ROSS

Purple Belt tournament next month. Even though she was under the protection of the Andreas name and her FBI Special agent father, Tashi was determined never to become a victim ever again, and had even coerced Paul to teach her how to shoot a gun with precision. Not that Paul needed any coercion. He was as determined as Tashi that she learned how to defend herself.

"Yes, cousin. Definitely kickass women, who love and care for each other as we did back then, and still do today."

"God has really blessed us. We've all worked hard, and are now some of the most prosperous men in the world. We have wonderful legacies to pass on to our children," Adam said.

"Well, I worked hard," Bryce remarked smugly. "The rest of you were born coated in dough."

"Sure, rub it in, Fontaine." Erik chuckled. "Seriously though, we have a lot to be thankful for. We've come a long way."

"Especially you and Bryce, Erik," Mass pointed out. "You lost your first loves along the way. And neither of you thought you'd find love again, but here you are. Here we all are, blissfully happy beyond our wildest imaginations."

As if reading each other's minds, the men stood to their feet, lifted their almost empty cappuccino cups and recited their special toast: "To God, Life, Love, Family, Friends, Prosperity."

"So this is what you do when we're not around."

The men turned at Michelle's voice, their faces breaking into big grins as their wives piled into the room in single file. They'd traded their fashionable Sunday clothes for casual cotton and linen dresses and sandals—moonlight sailing attire. None of them were toting handbags, which suggested that they'd been chauffeured here, most probably together. They walked up to each of their respective husbands, who automatically pulled them close and kissed them as if they hadn't seen them for ages.

"We do a lot of things when you're not around." Erik came up for air.

"I can make some more *cappuccini* if you like," Mass offered the women.

"Nah." Shaina took his cup. "I'll just finish yours."

"So that's why you lost weight when she was pregnant with Aria," Bryce said, even as his wife took his cup from him.

"That, and twice as much sex as I've ever had in my life. I hardly got any sleep for eight straight months."

"None of us do when they're pregnant," Adam said. "A few times I stayed at the office until I knew for sure Tashi had gone to bed. I was that worn out." He chuckled.

Tashi slapped him in the gut, then pulled his hair making him yelp. "You'll be begging for it next time, Mister."

"That'll be the day. You know you can't keep your hands off me or my hair." He picked up a handful of strands and brushed it lightly across her neck, making her shiver. "Mmm."

"You all complaining?" Shaina gave each man an indifferent look. "Because we can decide not to give you any when we're big with child." She poked Mass in the chest. "Seeing that I'm pregnant, what you got this morning might be *it* for you, Buster."

Mass pulled her up against him. "Let's head into the next room and see if you can put your money where your mouth is."

"I don't think it's her money she'll be putting anywhere, seeing she ain't got none," Kaya said on a giggle.

"And you know that how?" Bryce stared down at her. "You used to be so pure and innocent-minded. What happened to you?"

"I married you, you big sweet hunk." She tightened her arms around his waist, rested her chin on his chest and battered her eyelashes at him. "And the next thing I know, you were ordering me to take of my panties. That's what happened to me."

"And you take them off so quickly and ardently every time, my darling." He rubbed his hands across her back. "Are you wearing any now?"

"Maybe. Maybe not. Should I check your pockets for a pair?"

"You are nasty, Fontaine." Erik said. "I will never stick my hands in your pockets."

"Neither me," everyone, but Kaya acquiesced.

A chorus of laughter erupted as the men fell into their chairs, and pulled their respective wives down on their laps.

"It's a shame you had to cancel your bachelors' party. We had a surprise planned for you." Michelle kissed Erik's cheek.

'What kind of surprise?" he asked.

"We were planning on crashing it, and dancing for you," Shaina answered.

"You could have danced when the entire family was together earlier. We were all having such a good time anyway." Bryce said.

"Ha. The kind of dancing we have in mind cannot be performed in front of our parents and in-laws, and definitely not in front of our kids and Pastor Kelly," Kaya informed them.

Four square jaws dropped, and four mouths hung open. The ladies quite graciously pushed them closed.

"Since we were denied the chance to crash your party, we have one request," Tashi said.

"Yes," the men said in unison, their eyes riveted on their wives' faces.

Shaina cleared her throat. "Wherever you're taking us on our honeymoon, just make sure there's a private room, or a secluded patio or lawn or some place with a stage and poles. And—"

"Wh…what… Poles? What kind of poles?"

"Shh." Mass gave Erik a backhand slap on his arm.

"And make sure you have four comfy chairs where you'll be seated, dressed in loose clothing, preferably a robe with nothing under it, and facing the stage," Tashi added.

All the men automatically swallowed.

"You can add one pole to each bedroom too, if you want. You don't have to if you don't feel like it," Tashi laid on the temptation as she combed her fingers through Adam's long thick hair.

"Oh yeah, and if you want, you can bring along some leather straps, handcuffs, blindfolds," Michelle winked at Erik. "Feathers."

"Games." Tashi licked Adam on the cheek.

"Whips." Kaya smiled at Bryce. "We've never tried that, but I'm game."

"Just let your imaginations run wild. We're up to trying new stuff." Shaina glued her lips to Massimo's, making him moan.

"Get your man on the line, Bryce. Now!" Adam barked.

"You realize it's 3 a.m. in Astana. He's probably sleeping."

"For what we're paying him," Mass declared, "I don't care if he's dead. You tell St. Peter to wake him up."

All of a sudden, the women found themselves alone on the chairs in unceremonious heaps. They looked up to see Bryce pull his phone from his pocket as the other men followed him out of the room, adjusting their crotches.

The women high-fived each other and rolled in hysterics. They had them right where they wanted them. Putty in their hands.

§.

Fontaine Estate – Jason's bedroom – Sunday evening…

Jason didn't take his eyes off the TV screen, or his hands off the controls of his Xbox when his phone sounded the warning that he'd gotten a text. Another one. He'd been getting texts all afternoon, but he hadn't responded to any of them.

He liked Precious. He liked her a lot better than he liked any other girl he'd ever met, but her dad scared the crap out of him. He was glad she was his first French kiss, though, and he was kind of looking forward to more from her. He still remembered the taste of pepperoni and mushroom on her breath. He'd probably remember her every time he had pepperoni and mushrooms on his pizza.

But copping kisses from her wasn't worth getting his fingers broken or his nuts cut off. He liked his fingers and his nuts more than he liked Precious. And he knew if he didn't stay away from her, he would probably lose them both. She was hot, the hottest eight-grader in her school. She'd skipped a grade because she was so smart. He liked smart girls, especially hot smart girls like Precious. He was a freshman in high school and a lot of older, more mature girls were already letting him know that they would let him French kiss them—if he wanted to. He'd turned them down because his eyes had been on Precious.

But with his own dad threatening to send him off to an all-boys' boarding school in Europe, and Uncle Erik promising to hurt him, Jason figured that the only way for him to remain in Granite Falls, with his fingers attached to his hands the way God made them, and his nuts intact, was to fight the temptation of Precious LaCrosse...

His cell phone rang this time. He glanced down at it. Precious' picture—the one he'd taken of her in a blue bikini at his pool before he went away to Karate camp—flashed on the screen. Yeah, he would have to delete that pic, too.

His phone kept ringing until it went to voice mail. After a brief pause, it began ringing again. Jason paused his game and picked up his phone. "Hi, Precious."

"Why aren't you answering my texts and my calls?"

She sounded worried, sad, and he knew it was because of him, and because of her grandma dying. He'd wanted to hug her yesterday when they'd gone to her house after the funeral, and then this morning after church at Uncle Adam's restaurant. He'd wanted to dance with her like they used to before that kiss changed everything, but he was afraid to touch her. "I'm answering now."

"Don't you like me anymore? Are you like all those other guys, when they get what they want, they dump a girl?"

What other guys? Jason's heart missed a beat and he stood up and walked to his window overlooking the playground where his sisters and the nanny were riding on the merry-go-round. Eli had gone mini-golfing with Grandpa. He perched on his windowsill. "You been kissing other guys, Precious?"

"No, you know you're the first boy I ever kissed, Jason. So are you dumping me?"

Jason tightened his lips. He didn't know how to answer that. He didn't want to hurt her. "I like kissing you, but we can't do it again. We can't do anything but hold hands. That's stupid."

"What do you want to do? You want sex?"

"No!" Even he wasn't ready for that, and he was a guy.

"Why, 'cause you don't think I'm hot?"

"You're the hottest girl I know." He could almost feel and hear her smiling. "And that's why I have to stay away from you. I'm scared of your dad."

"We can kiss in secret."

"We promised, Presh. My dad would ship me off to a boys' school in Europe and we won't see each other for years. Is one stolen kiss worth it?"

They were quiet for a long time, then Precious said, "Jase?"

"Yeah."

"Are you gonna start kissing other girls 'cause you can't kiss me again?"

Skye Harrison's red, juicy lips danced into Jason's mind. She was in his science class and was always trying to get his attention. She had a reputation for letting boys feel her up— something else he couldn't do with Precious. Skye had gone as far as to rub her big jugs up against his arm a few times in passing, and once, she'd sneaked up on him and blown in his ear when he was standing at his locker. His body had come alive and he'd even felt hotter than when he'd kissed Precious. And that night he'd dreamed about Skye, and woken up with a...

"Jason? Are you going to kiss other girls?"

Precious sounded as if she was about to cry. "No, Precious. I'm not gonna kiss any other girls. You're my only girl." Jason told his first lie to Precious, and he felt like a scumbag for making a promise he knew he would break.

He'd known what sex was since he was eight. He hadn't really thought about it until he started high school last year, and now it was all he could think about. His dad was right; sex was complicated. Shoot, thinking about it was complicated, but he couldn't stop himself.

He knew he should treat all girls with respect, the kind of respect he wanted for his sisters, like he and Dad had talked about. But what if the girl didn't want to be respected? What if she asked him to do stuff with her? The kind of stuff he couldn't do with Precious. Should he do it?

His dad had said he could go to him with any question he had about sex and girls. He would ask his dad.

CHAPTER SEVENTEEN

Crystal Lake - Inside the master cabin of Andreas yacht. Late Sunday night...

A dam moved his mouth over Tashi's, devouring its softness as he pumped in and out of his wife to the tune of The Weeknd's "Earned It." She'd earned it, he thought, as she rose to meet him, their bodies moving together, and edged on by the melody and tempo in a continuous wave of fiery passion.

It was his turn to experience the thrill of making love to his wife by song. His buddies had compared notes, and had learned that their wives had been using the same list of songs between them. From that discovery, they'd surmised that those were the songs they were planning to pole dance to on their honeymoon. They'd agreed that it was a good thing the bachelors' party had been canceled because they sure were going to enjoy watching their sultry wives dance for them on the private island for their viewing pleasures only.

As soon as their friends and the band left, he and Tashi

had begun making love—starting on the upper deck to the tune of "Temperature's Rising," and when another yacht anchored too closely, they'd brought it down to the lower deck, where she'd sat him on the sofa in the lounge and straddled him, backwards, and bounced up and down on him while "Feel the Fire" streamed from the yacht's built-in stereo.

That fire had rained down on Adam in a continuous maelstrom as he'd held on to his wife's hips and pounded her sweet delicate buns while they watched their reflections bumping and grinding together in a mirrored wall. And just when he thought it was over for the night, his insatiable nymph of a wife had pulled him into the bedroom, thrown him down onto the bed, straddled him, facing forward this time, and rode him to the melody of "Behind Closed Doors."

So now here they were on the bed still with her silky legs wrapped around his waist, her arms locked around his neck, the moans of ecstasy slipping from her lips and the uncontrollable shaking of her thighs indicating that she was on the verge of another orgasm.

She was hot. Wet. Tight. The walls of her celestial palace gripped him pulling the essence out of him.

"Have I earned it, Adam?" she panted, "Have I earned your hot juice, love?"

"Yes, baby, yes. You've earned it, *cara*. You've earned it. Every single drop."

"Then give it to me. I want to feel you explode inside me. Fill up my womb, baby. Fill me up. Oh God, yes, yes…*Scopami, Adamo…*"

Adam hooked his arms under her thighs and pressed them into her stomach, leaving her open and vulnerable as his final desperate, erratic thrusts took him to the deepest depth of her woman's sex. The lyrics, the beat, the lapping of the waves against the sides of the yacht, her dirty talk, all worked together to pitch them toward that ever-spinning vortex of ecstasy. He rode her hard as their bodies danced to the beat of their own song—a song that only lovers knew.

When the fire spread through him and the electricity short-circuited his body, Adam collapsed on top of Tashi. His jade stalk exploded inside her, filling her with his juices. Their piercing cries of pleasure whipped across the dark surface of the lake.

As he drifted off to sleep, Adam realized that Tashi was probably making up for her lag behind the other wives, and storing up for the time he and she will be spending away from each other next week. His mother, Tashi, Alex, and Paul were leaving for Santorini tomorrow. He and his father were leaving for Tokyo the following day, and they wouldn't be seeing each other for four days until they reunited in Positano on Friday. Adam toyed with the idea of sending his father to Tokyo alone.

Sometime during the night, Adam was awakened by his ringing cell phone. With a tired groan, he untangled his arms from around Tashi and reached toward the nightstand. Squinting through one eye, he checked the screen. It was from Massimo. He was relieved that it wasn't a call about Alex, but annoyed that his cousin was calling him at one o'clock in the morning?

He slapped the phone to his ear. "Yes, Mass. What is it?"

"Hey, Adam. Is Tashi with you?"

"Duh."

"You guys still on the yacht?"

Adam turned as Tashi moaned and snuggled up to him,

the smell of passion rising from her soft warm body causing a tingle in his groin. "Yes, Massimo. She's snuggled up naked next to me in bed, which is where you should be with your wife."

"Then you might want to step away from her, because you probably don't want her to hear what I'm about to tell you. No need to scare her unnecessarily."

Adam felt like a torrent of sharp spikes had been dumped over his naked body. Only one thing would scare Tashi—trouble from New York City. But they'd taken care of all that last year. Boris and most of his gang were dead, and the others were in jail—or were they? "Okay, hold on."

Adam eased off the bed and pulled the sheet up over Tashi's moonlit body. He grabbed a robe from a closet and shrugged into it as he stepped into the lounge and closed the door to the bedroom. He glanced out the portholes into pitch-black darkness. "Okay, Mass. I'm listening. What's going on?"

"You remember David Carboni from high school. His family owns Big Boy's Pizza on Union Street."

"Yes, I remember David. You called me at one in the morning to talk about David Carboni?"

"I just received a call from him. He's over at the Jagged Edge Bar on the Esplanade."

Adam ran his fingers through his hair. He didn't see where this was going. "Okay?"

"He struck up a conversation with a man who claimed he's from New York, but David said he had a heavy Russian accent. Adam, he was asking questions about Tashi."

Adam collapsed onto the sofa where he'd made loved to his wife a few hours ago. "What kind of questions?"

"He told David that he knew Tashi when she was living in

New York. His daughter went to college with her. They're taking a family road trip to Montreal and thought they'd overnight in Granite Falls since they know Tashi married some local billionaire and now lives here. According to David, his daughter wants to get in touch with Tashi to catch up."

Adam pressed his fist into his stomach, closed his eyes and breathed in deeply and slowly.

"Adam? Are you there?"

"Yes, Mass. I'm here. Do you know if the man is still at the bar?"

"I'm not sure, but David said they're staying at the Motor Lodge over on Evergreen Drive. Now, I don't know how you want to handle this, but you know the boys and I are here to help in any way you need us."

Adam pushed off the sofa. "Thanks, Mass. I appreciate the offer, but this is something I need to take care of on my own."

"I understand, but the offer is open."

"I know. Go back to bed, Mass. We'll talk later."

Adam returned to the bedroom, stood over Tashi, and watched her sleep. He loved to watch her sleep. He loved knowing that she felt safe with him, that her world was safe because of him. She'd been through enough in her young life —from almost being sold into sexual slavery, to having to kill to stay alive, and then living for fifteen months in filth and fear, and now just recently, she had to watch her own mother's horrifying murder.

Abbastanza! Non più!

He'd killed for her once and he would do it again in a heartbeat.

I have nothing to lose. I have no wife or children for you to threaten.

The one good thing about prison is that you have a lot of time to think, to plan your revenge. Not you, you meditating sissy, and not this FBI double-crossing son-of-a-bitch can watch her twenty-four, seven. The only way to keep her out of my hands is to lock her up on that Fort Knox you call your home and never let her out. And I might even find a way inside your guarded gates. One way or the other, she will end up in a whore—

Bang!

Adam jumped at the memory of the blast. Reaching out with trembling fingers, he brushed his knuckles gently against his wife's cheeks. If his next heartbeat was the one in which he proved his love again, then so be it. He would put aside the yogi tonight and be an Andreas, his father's son.

Shrouded in the darkness of night, Adam walked stealthily across the parking lot from the main office of the motel, and toward the end of the building on the other side.

As soon as he'd hung up with Massimo, Adam had brought the yacht into the marina and called Paul. Paul had wanted to accompany him on his midnight rendezvous, but Adam was adamant that he watch over his daughter, instead, and had promised him that he'd be back before sunrise.

He'd made two other calls on his way into town: one to Ben Herbert the owner of Highway Motor Lodge. Ben's sister worked in housekeeping at Hotel Andreas so Adam was well acquainted with the family, and had no problem obtaining critical information about the guest in room 51, and a spare key to said room. His other call had been to Moscow for more pertinent information and also to set a chain of events into motion. How they played out was up to the occupant of room 51.

Adam stopped outside the room and listened for sounds from within. All he could hear was the whizzing of a window fan and heavy snoring that thankfully drowned out the rattling of the key turning inside the rusty lock. He turned the knob, slipped into the room, and closed the door quietly behind him. The room smelled like old farts and cheap whiskey.

The moonlight streaming through the bare window on the opposite side of the building bounced off the steel barrel of a revolver on the nightstand. Good, he wouldn't have to sully his, tucked in the waistband of his jeans. The moon provided adequate lighting for him to make out the form of the man sprawled on the bed, wearing nothing but a pair of white boxers. Adam took a moment to assess Yuri Golub. He was heavy set, about five feet nine, and weighing in at around two hundred pounds. Yuri was a Russian *kot*, his wife a *bandersha*, and between them they operated six brothels in the district of Tverskoye in Moscow.

When Adam had told Paul about Mass's call, Paul had finally revealed the plan Boris had for Tashi last year when he'd sent "Jake" to Granite Falls to kidnap her. Adam remembered asking Paul what Boris wanted with his wife and Paul responding that it was too disturbing for a father to think about, much less repeat. Tonight, Adam had understood Paul's revulsion. Boris' plan was for him and his top guards to rape Tashi—break her in—and then ship her off to the worst whorehouse in Moscow. Since he'd intended to kill "Jake" after he delivered Tashi to him, Boris saw no harm in revealing his plan to the then undercover FBI agent. Adam wished he'd been privy to that information before he put the bullet into Boris' neck.

On his way to the motel, Adam's Russian associates had reported that Yuri had paid Boris a sizable amount of money for Tashi in advance. To Yuri, a woman as beautiful as she would bring in thousands of rubles as a classy *kot* instead of the meager kopecks he would earn off her in a common whorehouse. Yuri was here to collect his goods and avenge his friend's death. *Worst mistake of his life*.

Adam's stomach churned at the thought of what this piece of garbage could have done to his wife if he'd gotten his hands on her. At no time was Adam's faith in a higher power stronger than it was tonight. There had to be a God to have sent Massimo to Big Boy's Pizza yesterday, and then for Mass to leave his number with David Carboni, and then to lead David to that bar to run into this worm sprawled on his back in front of him.

Adam tiptoed to the head of the bed, grateful that the room was on the first floor and the floor apparently made of concrete. He would hate for a squeaking floorboard to tip off Yuri of his presence. He sucked foul air into his lungs as he noticed a four-day old newspaper clipping with a photo of him and Tashi at the courthouse in Cleveland lying under the double action revolver. It must have been the international publicity of the recent trial and the upcoming wedding that had brought Yuri out of the woodwork. He probably thought Tashi would be an easy target because everyone would be preoccupied with wedding plans. *Worst calculation of his life*.

With methodical dexterity, Adam picked up the revolver, opened the trap door, rotated the cylinder, ejected all but one of the six rounds into his left palm, closed it, pulled back the hammer, placed his finger next to the trigger—not on it—sat on the side of the bed, and jammed the barrel into Yuri's gaping mouth.

Yuri snorted and jerked around before his eyes flew open. His right hand reached toward the nightstand.

"*Именно в ваш рот*," Adam said, as he switched on the bedside lamp with his left hand. He'd decided to have this conversation in Russian so Yuri understood every word, perfectly.

Yuri gurgled something unintelligible and his eyes widened in terror as he became fully awake and aware of his situation. He raised his hands in a defensive move.

"I wouldn't do that if I were you," Adam said, as slowly and calmly as if he was speaking to a little child. "I'm kind of pissed right now. Pissed that I had to drag myself from the warm comfort of my bed and my wife's arms to see you. My finger is itching to press this trigger, so I suggest you settle down and relax for this interview." He opened his palm and dropped the five rounds onto Yuri's big gut. Four bounced off to the mattress, and one rolled south to nest in the opening in his boxers.

"We're going to play a little Russian Roulette. I assume you're familiar with this game since you're, you know —*Russian*. So just take a deep breath before we begin."

Yuri's hairy chest rose and fell a couple times and Adam almost gagged from the decaying odor issuing from his mouth.

"Now, I have a few questions for you, Mr. Golub—just *Yes* or *No* responses. With your right hand, raise one finger for *Yes*, two for *No*." He demonstrated with his fingers. "If I don't like your responses, if I think you're lying to me, or if you refuse to respond, I *will* pull the trigger. *Capisci*?"

Yuri nodded.

"No, no, Yuri. Don't shake your head. The slightest movement could send my finger against the trigger. You have four chances of walking out of this room instead of being carried out in a body bag. You don't want to waste any of them. So I ask again, do you understand?"

Yuri raised one finger.

"*Bravo*! Now, do you know who I am?"

Yuri raised one finger.

"Did you come to Granite Falls to kidnap my wife and smuggle her back to Russia?"

Again, one finger went up.

Adam pulled his smart phone from his shirt pocket and turned it on. He held it up so both he and Yuri could watch the live streaming video of Yuri's wife and four young children —two sons, two daughters, ages twelve to two—having brunch at Café Pushkin on Tverskoy Boulevard in Moscow. Adam could feel Yuri struggling to swallow the excess saliva that had probably backed up into his throat. He eased back the barrel to give him room. He didn't want him choking to death on his own saliva. If Yuri was going to die today, it would be at Adam's hands—deliberate, not accidental. He had a message to send to every *kot* in Russia, and every other place on the planet.

When Yuri emitted a whimper, Adam said, "You have a beautiful family, Yuri. They seem to be having a good time, aren't they?" It was a rhetorical question, so he didn't expect him to respond. He returned his gaze to Yuri's face. "I'm sure you're smart enough to realize that I have them under surveillance, so my next question is, "do you love your family?"

Yuri stared at him, then at the video, apparently unsure of how to answer. He probably thought that if he admitted to loving them, Adam would have them killed in front of him as punishment.

If he were in Yuri's position, he'd be thinking along those lines, too. And that was the difference between Yuri and Boris. Boris had nothing to lose so he had no chance of living, but Yuri—well, his life hinged on his response. To help him decide, Adam pulled the trigger, and felt absolutely nothing when Yuri squealed like a pig, tears rolling from the corners of his eyes. "You have three more chances to walk out of here, Yuri. So I will ask you again, "Do you love your family?"

Again Yuri kept his eyes glued on the cell phone screen and refused to answer.

Adam pulled the trigger again. "Do you fucking love them?" he barked, leaning closer to Yuri's ashen face, his finger at the ready to pull the third time.

One finger on each hand went up. Yuri began trembling and whimpering like a baby, and low and behold he pissed his boxers.

Adam let out a deep breath, sat back, and returned his cell phone to his pocket. "It seems we have something in common, Mr. Golub. Perhaps we can work together. You think we can?"

Yuri responded positively.

"Wonderful. Now, listen well, because this is the only conversation you and I will ever have. Like you, I love my wife. I absolutely adore her. I love my son, and I already love all the other sons and daughters we will have in the future. I think your friend and business associate, Boris, understood the lengths I would go to in order to protect my family, moments before he choked to death on his own blood. The thing is, I have no intention of living in fear of you or anyone else. I will not spend the rest of my life looking over my shoulders. So from this day on, you will forget that my wife exists in your world. I don't even want you breathing the same air she breathes."

He picked up the newspaper clipping and held it in front of Yuri's face. "You know what she looks like, so if you're in a certain country and you see her, or even hear she's there, pack your bags and leave, or I will view your decision to stay as a breach of our agreement. You will also forget this meeting, and go on living as if you never met me. However, you and your family will be under constant surveillance until the day they put you all six feet under. If anything suspicious happens to my wife, to my son, or to any Andreas for that matter— even if you had nothing to do with it—I might be inclined to think differently. Consequently, your mother and father, your two uncles, your aunt, your three sisters, your brother, and all your in-laws will be removed from this world. And then I'll mutilate you.

"I'm not into harming children, but I will take your two sons, your two daughters, and your seven nieces and eight nephews and ship them to different orphanages around the globe. They will never see each other again. They will never know their true identities, and you will spend the rest of your miserable life wondering where they are, whether they're happy or sad, dead or alive. I won't kill you, Yuri, but when I'm done with you, you *will* wish you were dead.

"This is not *Taken*, and I'm not Liam Neeson. So don't for a moment think that taking me out will solve your problem. The wheels of your family's demise are already set in motion. *You* put a mark on your loved ones' heads the moment you set foot in Granite Falls with intentions to destroy mine. Whether or not your children grow up in their seemingly happy home with you and your wife is all up to you. You hold the cards to their fate in your hands. Do we have an understanding?"

Yuri raised one finger.

Adam slapped him lightly on the cheek. "Now, since you're prohibited from breathing the same air my wife breathes, I suggest you make a hasty departure from this town and from this country. My advice is that you never return to the United States, ever again." He pasted the clipping to Yuri's sweaty forehead, pulled the revolver from his mouth, dripping with drool, and slammed it on his chest.

"I promised my wife a sunrise breakfast on the lake with our son. I don't want to be late. Oh, and they're leaving for Santorini later today, so if you have plans to visit Greece or Italy within the next week, cancel them."

Adam got up and walked to the door. With his hand on the knob, he looked back to see Yuri curled up on the bed in the fetal position, cradling his gun and bawling as a brown stain slowly appeared in the seat of his boxers.

Adam could almost hear his father's proud voice and see the sparks of admiration in his eyes. "*Ora, il figlio mio, che è il modo un Andreas si occupa di minacce alla sua famiglia.*" Yes indeed, that was the way to deal with a threat to his family. After all, he *was* an Andreas.

Adam opened the door to the musky motel room and stepped out into the light of dawn. With a smile on his lips, he looked up at the blue sky and inhaled the fresh crisp air of his beautiful hometown of Granite Falls.

La vita era incredibilmente bella!

CHAPTER EIGHTEEN

*Channel 9 News - Granite Falls People News Segment.
Saturday Night...*

"Okay Lester, you're on in five, four, three..."
Lester Cobbs adjusted his earpiece, straightened his shoulders, cleared his throat, and focused his eyes on the teleprompter.

"Good Evening. I'm Lester Cobbs, and welcome to tonight's segment of *Granite Falls People News*. Tonight we'll be focusing on the exciting local highlights of the day. As many of you know, I've been reporting news for seventeen years—locally, nationally, and internationally. I've been fortunate to cover celebrity and other high profile weddings, political and charitable campaigns, et al. But never have I witnessed anything as grandiose as the wedding that took place today in my little hometown of Granite Falls, New Hampshire. Before I run the uncut video of the events, I think you will appreciate it even more if you knew some of the history of the church where the ceremony was performed, and of the families involved.

"Granite Falls Community Church, now a historical landmark, was the first church to be built when the town was chartered in 1788." Lester waited for the picture to appear behind him. "As you can see, back then, it was just a small wooden chapel on the corners of Main Street and Highland Avenue, but it was the only place of service for the town's residents. From street cleaners to wealthy magnates— including but not limited to the LaCrosse, Andretti, Andreas, and Forsythe families—worshipped there together." A series of photos of the church at various stages flashed as he continued.

"Over the years, the building underwent several major overhauls, increasing in size to accommodate the growing membership each time. Its biggest and most recent transformation occurred a few years ago, when business mogul Bryce Fontaine bought the adjacent block and expanding the church property three and a half acres in size." He paused as a photo of the church in its present state was posted. "In addition to remodeling the building into a magnificent two-story structure from locally queried granite, imported marble, stained-glass windows, Renaissance style doomed and skylight ceilings, he also built a playground, a free church-run daycare, and a preschool on the grounds.

"The Fontaines weren't among the founding families of this beautiful, mountain mecca that I and many of you who're watching call home, but the Fontaine name is now as revered, and carries as much weight in the area as other prominent families.

"Many of you know the history of the LaCrosses,

Andrettis, and Andreases—the current leading families of our town. But what you may or may not know is that Bryce Fontaine first arrived in Granite Falls as a freshman at Granite Falls Preparatory School. It was there that he met and formed a bond of brotherhood with billionaire heirs, Erik LaCrosse, Massimo Andretti, and Adamo Andreas, who were all born and raised in Granite Falls." School photos of the young friends in various grades were posted. "Even though, Bryce was not yet a billionaire or even a millionaire, together, the friends formed their exclusive Billionaire Bachelors' Club and made a blood oath to always be there for each other.

"It is reported that upon graduating from Harvard University, Bryce inherited a small fortune from his grandmother. He then placed himself under the tutelage of business tycoons Alessandro Andreas, and the now deceased Luciano Andretti, and within a decade, he turned his small fortune into a multi-billion-dollar corporation. Fontaine Enterprises, along with Andretti Industries, Andreas International, and recently incorporated Erik LaCrosse Doctors Abroad Foundation, and the Michelle LaCrosse Children of the Future Foundation, is now among the leading corporations in the world. The rest, we can say, is mogul history.

"Today, during a group wedding in the beautiful Granite Falls Community Church, Erik, Bryce, Massimo, and Adamo —the Fabulous Four as they've been fondly nicknamed— renewed their vows of love and devotion to each their wives: Michelle, Kaya, Shaina, and Tashi, and their commitment of friendship to each other, and each other's families."

ANA E ROSS

The Wedding – Saturday Morning 10. A.M...

From his vantage point on the second floor balcony—and in an area that was quartered off for the crew from *Granite Falls Times* newspaper, and WFCN, one of the television stations owned by Fontaine Communications Network—Lester looked down on the arriving guests as they were escorted to their seats by teams of ushers dressed in black and white tuxedos.

People from every walk of life and every corner of the globe, including several Hollywood and Broadway celebrities, renowned artists, politicians, Heads of States, and CEOs and representatives from many of the world's leading corporations, were among the honored guests. Lester had heard that the First Family had been invited, but they'd canceled at the last minute due to a family emergency of their own.

Just the thought of the President of the United States rubbing elbows with the humble citizens of Granite Falls made Lester smile with pride to be one of them. He was also grateful that of all the reporters on the planet, many far more seasoned and respected, he had been the one chosen to report on this grandiose wedding of the decade.

Things weren't always amicable between Lester Cobbs and the billionaires, who'd provided a lot of juicy gossip for him to feed on over the years. But since the Fabulous Four had settled down into marital bliss and stopped generating infamous fodder, he and they had arrived at a tacit respectful understanding. That mutual respect had crystalized when they'd allowed him to interview them a few months ago, at which time they'd relayed the stories of meeting the loves of each their lives and talked about the upcoming wedding ceremony that was presently unfolding before his eyes.

276

Everything concerning this wedding was local: the designers for the bridal, bridesmaids, and flower-girls' dresses, the tailors who made the morning wedding suits for the grooms and the other male members of the wedding party, the jeweler who'd designed the four duplicate diamond and precious stones rings, the wedding planner, and the eighty-member Granite Falls Symphony Orchestra that was currently rendering *Pachelbel's Cannon in D* as everyone awaited the arrival of the four couples—Granite Falls' own homegrown, and much loved celebrities.

The only thing not local about the wedding was the honeymoon venue. It was rumored that not even the wives knew where their husbands were taking them for a week of love and romance. It could be anywhere in the world, and since the location was highly secretive, Lester was certain it would be private and paparazzi-free. Just as highly secretive were the bridal gowns and the four rings. No one, but the designers had seen them.

The husbands had given Lester an inside scoop about the designs of the platinum diamond rings they would place on their wives' fingers. The platinum shank was split into three lanes—representing their Past, Present, and Future—and studded with diamonds that extended into the gallery and shoulders. The head was designed with two layers of platinum and white gold, asymmetrically placed to form eight V-shaped, leaf-like halos, all randomly studded with the birthstones of the four couples and their children, with room for future offspring. One of the halos had been damaged during the design, and instead of fixing it, the couples had requested that all the rings contain a broken halo to show that none of them were perfect.

Wow! Talk about humble.

The center stones on each ring—a twenty-five-carat Princess cut blue diamond—were equal parts of a one-hundred-carat diamond. Side stones, representing the birthstones of the husbands, nested in the prongs that secured the center stone. The rings were engraved with the couples' motto: *To God, Life, Love, Family, Friends, Prosperity*. The motto said it all.

Lester sighed, completely overwhelmed. If the honeymoon haven possessed any of the aura of the romantic Cinderella theme that the church and the ballroom at Hotel Andreas where the reception would take place, then Lester knew it would be a place of pure exotic splendor. The walls of the church were draped with red, pink, purple and gold lace, threaded with strings of illuminated pearls. They were replicas of the drapes that were hanging on each side of the back entrance to the sanctuary.

Colorful garlands, wrapped around each of the numerous Corinthian columns, were held in place with satin ribbons of the same colors as the drapes. Crystal candelabras hung from the ceiling and crystal vases hosting long-stemmed roses of varying colors were situated in different locations around the church. Lester had heard that there were enough vases and strings of pearls for each guest to take one home. Just below the first of seven steps that led up to the podium at the front of the church, a black and white rug made from bales of silk stretched the width of the church from one side door to the next.

Awed by the enchanting, fragranced atmosphere, the murmur of the guests as they waited with baited breaths, and the soothing melodies from the orchestra, Lester turned his attention to the four aisles where the brides would be making their trips toward their husbands. Flamboyant, elegantly fashioned arched floral trellises with silk and satin ribbons were stationed at the beginning of each aisle. Five-foot gold pillars, topped with mauve burning tapers and decorated with colorful bouquets, decked the entrance of each row of white, satin-cushioned chairs, the backs of which were draped with yards and yards of white ribbons and lace. Silk runners, bordered by a polychromatic parade of petals extended from the back to the front of each aisle. The only differences between the aisles were the individual flowers and the colors of the silk runners.

The first, Michelle LaCrosse's, was lined with a red covering and adorned with a variety of lilies—pink Peruvian, red and white calla, and white and yellow valley. Next to her, Kaya Fontaine's aisle was aglow with a sheet of gold, embellished with pink, white, and yellow orchids. Third in line, Shaina Andretti went all out with a stunning purple throw beautified by red, pink, and white tulips, while Tashi Andreas, snatcher of the last remaining Granite Falls billionaire, would take her walk on a baby pink layer, garnished with red, white, and pink peonies.

One would think mixing that many varieties of flowers and colors would be overkill, but quite contrarily, they were so esoterically blended together, the scene could only be described as exquisitely magical.

Lester leaned forward in his seat and looked toward the front of the church as pastor Kelly dressed in a black and white Minister's gown with gold sashes and four gold crosses on the front, and his wife, Samantha, along with three other clergymen emerged from the side doors, walked along the satin path, and made their way up the steps to the podium. Pastor Kelly took his place behind the pulpit. The ushers closed the drapes at the back of the church and Pastor Kelly raised his hands, indicating that the ceremony was about to begin.

The chatter waned to a stop and heads turned to the back of the church in anticipation of the grooms' parents' entrance —as explained in the wedding playbill. The orchestra switched tunes to Boyz II Men's "A Song for Mama." Everyone stood in honor as the grooms' mothers—Felicia LaCrosse carrying baby Fiona, Lillian Fontaine, Arabella Andreas carrying baby Alessandro, and Aziza Shomari (Azi) —distant cousin of Massimo Andretti, who'd stepped in as a mother figure after his mother died—appeared under the trellises. The Matriarchs, dressed in beautiful, floor-sweeping lace and silk gowns, the color of their individual daughter-in-law's runner, were slowly escorted up the aisles by their husbands: Philippe, Henry, and Alessandro, while Galen Carmichael, Massimo's half-brother, accompanied Ms. Shomari.

Once the grandparents were seated in their respective family section, a litany of *Ohhs* and *Ahhs* penetrated the air as the grooms appeared under the trellises. They looked unequivocally debonair and handsome in white morning coats with diamond-studded lapels over charcoal embroidered vests. Ascots, matching the color of their individual wife's aisle runner were held in place around their necks by silver stickpins jeweled with white pearl and onyx stones, and a white rose nestled in each their pockets. The conductor signaled the orchestra, and as a collection of photos of the four couples and their children at play were displayed on the church's teleprompters, the grooms began marching down the aisle to the orchestra's rendition of Snow Patrol's "Chasing Cars."

At the front of the church, they faced the audience and began singing the lyrics to the song—substituting the words *"If I lay here, will you lay with me?* to *"If I stand here, will you stand with me?"*

Lester choked up at the elation on those men's faces and the melodious sounds of their voices as they sang from the bottom of their hearts, expressing the burning passions that could not be contained. Except for Bryce, Lester had no idea the Fabulous Four could sing so beautifully and convincingly. He scanned the now seated and totally captivated crowd. Women gazed at the husbands, mesmerized and perhaps a bit envious that they weren't the ones who'd captured their hearts and souls. The men looked on with a *so that's what women like* expression on their faces. The children were just excited to be part of something so memorable, even though they didn't quite understand what was happening around them.

When the men concluded their serenade, their Best Men: Philippe, Henry, Galen, and Alessandro—who were dressed identically—joined them at the front of the church, amidst an uproar of clapping and cheers until Pastor Kelly raised his hands to silence the room. There was a slight commotion at the back of the church and everyone turned as the most beautiful little Flower Girls appeared under the trellises: Tiffany LaCrosse, Alyssa and Anastasia Rogers, Elyse Fontaine, Aria Andretti, and Brittany Marshall for the Andreases. They looked astonishingly adorable in white satin and silk tulle dresses with sashes the color of the runners garnishing their waistlines and hanging like mini trains to the

ANA E ROSS

floor behind them. They wore white satin shoes on their feet, and colorful garlands of flowers on their heads. In their white-gloved hands, they carried round silk baskets, fashioned from the flower of their individual aisle and that matched the color of their sashes.

Lester placed his hands over his mouth to stop his scream of adoration as the pretty little girls began their march, dropping petals on the way to the tune of "Beautiful as You" by Jim Brickman, while the grooms and their Best Men sang the lyrics to their darling daughters, granddaughters, and daughters of their dearest friends. Undeniably apropos, Lester thought, dabbing at a tear in the corner of his eye.

With three-year-old Tiffany and an almost three Elyse occasionally stopping to admire the flowers, and say "Hi" to the first person in each row, it took a while for the Flower Girls to reach the front, but no one seemed to mind. In fact, they found them endearing, especially when little Aria dropped her basket halfway up the aisle and ran to her father yelling, "I don't want to, Daddy. I don't want to." Amidst the laughter, Massimo walked her back to the aisle and helped her scatter her petals before placing her on the lap of her adopted grandmother, Azi. *What else can one expect from a seventeen-month-old?* Lester thought with affection.

The Bridesmaids: Precious LaCrosse, Liberty Lynd, Monica Hamilton, and Mindy Marshall were next to emerge from behind the drapes, wearing black and white bridesmaids dresses with flower tiaras on their heads and colorful bouquets in their hands. Behind them, the Pageboys: Erik LaCrosse III, Eli Fontaine, Marc Castle Jr. for the Andrettis, and Kyle Marshall for the Andreases, dressed in smaller replicas of the grooms' attire, carried white satin pillows with red velvet heart-shaped boxes fastened in the center, and red, gold, purple, and pink ribbons hanging down the sides. They marched to the orchestra's rendition of Billy Ocean's "Color of Love," and once they took their places on the black and white carpet, the drapes were closed once more.

Finally, the magical moment everyone had been waiting for, since the wedding announcement eight months ago, had arrived. Pastor Kelly directed the guests to stand. Four ushers entered through the side doors, walked to the front of each aisle, and blew golden trumpets as was customary in Fairytales to announce the arrival of the Princesses.

CHAPTER NINETEEN

The curtains parted and a plethora of sighs of admiration simultaneously reverberated through the congregation, then all mouths seemed to freeze open. Lester swore he could hear the heartbeat of every single guest present drumming in his ears. They held their breaths as if afraid that if they let them out the brides, embraced in layer upon layer of luxurious elegance, would disappear into obscurity.

To say the brides were beautiful would be a gross understatement. They were quintessentially heart-stopping specimens of supreme regal sophistication, and aptly wearing tiaras studded with diamonds and other shimmering jewels. As they stood smiling under their trellises giving everyone a chance to admire their bridal gowns, their husbands, accompanied by the church's harpist, began singing Elvis Presley's "Can't help Falling in Love."

Those four ethereal creations were white, strapless, dramatically cut, and featured sweetheart necklines and glamorous bodices dripping with teardrop diamonds and pearls. Yet, each was intricately and uniquely designed from an assortment of premium satin, silk, organza, taffeta, tulle, embellished lace, and jeweled embroidery, to the finest details. The gracefully fashioned and jeweled waistlines were comprised of two dropped, one empire, and one natural, but all subtly hugged the delicate figures of the brides, giving each a sweet and feminine, yet timeless and extravagant touch. Nothing less would have been accepted for this glamorous affair.

No one could help falling in love with them, indeed.

Lester was out of words to describe the surreal scene, and not a moment too soon as the Giver of the Brides appeared, dressed like the grooms, and carrying the bridal bouquets held together with ribbons, of the day's four dominant colors. Robert Carter stood next to his sister, Michelle, and handed her a bouquet of red and white calla lilies; Jason Rogers joined his Aunt Kaya with a bouquet of white orchids; Cameron Norwood stepped beside his sister, Shaina, and handed her an arrangement of white and purple tulips, and Paul Dawson hugged his daughter, Tashi, before giving her a bouquet of pink and white peonies.

As the husbands' song faded out, and the orchestra began to play Deniece Williams' "Black Butterfly," the brides began their dazzling walk under their motorized trellises, toward their husbands, whose eyes were fastened on them with tears streaming down their faces. They were obviously mesmerized as they watched the stunningly exquisite loves of their lives, their prides and joy, the mothers of their children, their soul mates with whom they would grow old, walk toward them to freely and willingly offer themselves to them once more.

Lester looked around. There wasn't one dry eye in the

church as those four amazing women made their way to the front, shimmering in an aura of opulent beauty and class.

Finally, the wives stood in front of their husbands, gazing up at them through teary eyes.

"Who give these women to these men?" Pastor Kelly asked.

"We do," the brides said in unison as they handed their bouquets to their Bridesmaids.

"And so, let it be duly noted," Pastor Kelly responded, to which everyone chuckled as the Father Givers placed the wives' hands into those of their husbands', before joining the families in the front rows.

Pastor Kelly indicated for the audience to sit, and then for the next few minutes, Felicia, Lillian, Azi, and Arabella, took turns reading short scriptures from the Holy Bible, short passages from Kahlil Gibran's *The Prophet*, and from *Love Poems of Rumi*, after which Pastor Kelly asked the couples to face the pulpit.

"Dearly Beloved," he began. "We're gathered here today before God, family, friends, and acquaintances to witness the reaffirmation of the wedding vows of Erik and Michelle LaCrosse, Bryce and Kaya Fontaine, Massimo and Shaina Andretti, and Adamo and Tashi Andreas…"

Twenty minutes, later the Pageboys stood in front of the couples and the husbands opened the velvet boxes. Another series of *Ohhs* and *Ahhs* filled the room as the multitude of diamonds from the duplicate platinum rings coruscated in the light from the skylight ceiling. Lester couldn't see them up close but he was certain that the identical intricately designed platinum rings were elegant, and rightly portrayed the purity, strength, and durability of the couples' love and commitment to each other, just as the inherent qualities of platinum itself signified.

The orchestra softly played "Give me Forever" in the background. The husbands held their wives right hands and while slipping the rings on their ring fingers, they said in unison, "With these four rings, we thee wed." They embraced, gazed into each other's eyes, and sang the words of the song. It was angelic and melodious. During the final chorus, they all walked to the center of the front, and exchanged hugs and kisses on the cheeks while they finished singing their vows.

The aura of passion, love, devotion, and commitment was so thick between them, one couldn't cut through it with a machete. Nothing, nothing in this world would ever separate these men from their wives, or these friends from each other— not even death itself.

They tuned to the audience and said, "As we've just pledged ourselves to each other, we also pledge our commitment to each and every citizen of Granite Falls. We are devoted to make this town safer, friendlier, more prosperous, and the most coveted little town on the planet. As God is our witness."

Pride and joy bubbled in Lester's heart as the guests— most of whom were Granite Falls residents who'd won a lottery that placed them on the list of invitees—came alive with shouts of cheers and well wishes, and "We Love you Fabulous Four."

Eventually, Pastor Kelly raised his hand to silence the audience. "Husbands, you may kiss your wives," he said, grinning from ear to ear.

With excited shouts, the men picked their grinning wives up off the floor, gathered them into their arms and kissed them deeply and passionately, and as Ed Sheeran "Thinking Out Loud" spilled from the built-in surround sound system, they placed them back on the floor and the couples enjoyed their first dance together, right there under the sacred pulpit of Granite Falls Community Church.

Okay, it was official, Lester Cobbs was jealous. He, like everyone else watching the couples waltz to that beautiful song of everlasting love wanted that kind of love, romance, and Happily Ever After.

When Ed Sheeran's voice faded out, the couples motioned for their eleven children to join them. They hugged and kissed them relentlessly, and as the orchestra began playing Sugarland's "Stuck Like Glue," they danced down their respective aisle with their children, and with their parents and other immediate family members in tow, and out the door to four white limousines that would take them to Hotel Andreas.

There they would enjoy some food, more dancing, and good old down-to-earth fun with their family, friends and guests, before leaving for Granite Falls Regional Airport, where they would kiss their children goodbye before boarding their jets to their honeymoon locations.

Where they were headed? Well, only the husbands and the pilots knew.

Baia degli Amanti – A Private Island – Saturday P.M...

"Can we take off our blindfolds?" Kaya asked as the eight-seater, twin-engine plane took off from somewhere. She turned and batted her eyelashes at Bryce, then sighed when she remembered he couldn't see them.

"Yeah, can we?" Michelle added from the opposite front row. She squeezed Erik's hand. "We've been blindfolded since we left the Fontaine jet. I mean what's the point of having the window seat if I can't enjoy the view." She tapped annoyingly on the windowpane.

"Amen, sister," Shaina said directly behind her. "We're supposed to be going on our honeymoon, not to some Italian Don's secret hiding place." She elbowed Massimo in the gut. "We have a right to know where we're going."

"Soon, ladies." Across the aisle, Adam came up for air from kissing Tashi who seemed to be quite content in her present situation. She was used to it from the myriad of games they'd been playing. "Perhaps if you blindfolded your wives once in a while, they wouldn't be complaining now," Adam said with a depth of authority.

"Yeah," Tashi said, backing up her husband. "Live and learn."

"Well, lookey here who's talkin'," Massimo drawled as he turned sideways to stare at his cousin and his wife. "The couple among us who've been married for the shortest period, and except for Erik, the man who've had the least amount of sexual conquests."

"You, of all people should know that when it comes to sex, it's quality not quantity that counts, cousin."

"Oh, you want to go there, huh?"

"*Ragazzi. Ragazzi.* No need to get into a competition." Bryce turned and eyed them.

"One of these days, we should put gloves on them, toss them into a ring, and let them duke it out. The one left standing is the infinite champion. Then we won't have to listen to their squabbles ever again," Erik said.

"Blindfolded," Adam declared as everyone laughed at the childish rivalry the Italian cousins just couldn't seem to shake.

"We did it." Kaya hugged Bryce. "We pulled off the wedding of the decade."

"Despite the odds."

"Desire is a real mistress of her art." Michelle smiled. "Everyone was talking about those motorized trellises. Now every bride wants one at her wedding. She was taking orders left and right at the reception."

"It was nice of Galen to come through for you, Mass," Shaina said, toying with the duplicate copy of the ring that her three dearest friends in the world also wore on their right ring fingers.

"That was a surprise after what went down between you two," Bryce added.

"A surprise, indeed," Massimo said sarcastically. "But I know a con when I see one."

"What do you mean?" Erik asked.

"Come on guys. He wasn't there for me. He's an Andretti," he said, almost with a level of respect. "He knows how to manipulate a situation. Before we left the church, and all during the reception, he was busy introducing himself as Luciano's son to the board members and executives of Andretti Industries who were present." Galen had done his homework in the two weeks since he and Mass had last spoken. Mass hadn't even seen him until he walked into the dressing room at the church and asked if he could honor him by being his best man. "He's laying his ground work."

"For what?" Bryce turned to look at him.

Massimo stared past Shaina's head out the window to the blue ocean below them. He hadn't told anyone about Galen's threats yet. They weren't significant enough to discuss. "He thinks he can take me to court and win half of my company."

"If you knew what he was up to, why didn't you ask him to leave? It not as if you didn't have a Best Man. Steven was already dressed." Adam pointed out.

"Because I love a challenge, especially one I know I will win. It's always good to know your opponent's moves, know what cards he holds. Galen was exposing himself in every which way today, and I was watching." He squeezed Shaina's hand. "I will give my little brother all the rope he needs to hang himself."

"Just like he did to me." Shaina chuckled with the two-year-old memories.

"Okay, this is supposed to be a happy time for us. No more morbid talk, no work-related talk, just good-vibes talk for the next week," Michelle stated. "I didn't begin drinking liquor today for this. I just want to have fun."

"I agree, Michelle." Bryce smiled across the aisle at her even though she couldn't see him. "Can we talk about that pole dancing show you ladies are putting on for us?"

"Nope." Kaya waved his question away. "That you'll have to wait for, just as we have to wait to see where we'll be honeymooning."

To cool their anticipation, the men changed the subject and they spent the next half hour of the flight reminiscing events of the wedding ceremony and the reception, especially Paul's show-stopping request to dance with Tashi to his and her mother's favorite song: Sting's, "They Dance Alone."

"I never knew my dad was so romantic," Tashi said from the back row. During their dance, pictures of her mother and her as a child were displayed on the ballroom walls. Everyone just stood back and watched as father and daughter honored her mother and the one true love of his life. "I felt her presence. It was as if she was watching me being happy and fulfilled."

"That was a beautiful tribute," Adam murmured.

The Andreas pilot announced their descent and then they were on the ground and taxiing.

"Remember, only our parents and the guardians of our children are to know where we are. And be sure you're back here in two days for my son's meals," Adam said to the pilot when he took off his headset.

"Yes, Mr. Andreas. I will be here Monday afternoon at three, sharp."

"So, LaCrosse will be pumping, huh?"

"Shut up, Erik!" Adam glared at him.

"I'm just saying…" Erik said amidst the chuckles as the plane came to a complete stop and they were plunged into quiet.

The men unfastened their seatbelts and then undid their wives'.

"Now can we get these stupid things off?" Michelle asked when the door was opened and a fresh blast of air entered the cabin.

"I smell the ocean," Kaya said. "Are we on one of our islands?"

"We weren't in the air long enough. So I'm guessing from experience that we're on a Caribbean island." Shaina turned her face toward Massimo. "Are we on Dulcina?"

"Patience, my dear. Patience. And no peeking."

The ladies were lifted from the plane, carried for a short distance, placed into an open jeep and driven along a paved path. After a few minutes, they were lifted from the jeep and placed on the ground under a tree with instruction to stay put. They listened to the roar of the ocean and breathed in the salty refreshing air as the men unloaded the luggage. They didn't have many bags since they were told that everything they needed had been provided. They'd only brought along the necessities they couldn't do without.

Finally the plane engine started up and the aircraft taxied away, until all they could hear was the low hum as the pilot retraced his sky route. The ladies waited, biting their lips and wringing their hands. They couldn't do anything else.

Shaina frowned when a few minutes went by and they still heard nothing from their husbands. "Hey, guys," she called.

No answer.

"Where do you think they are?" Tashi asked.

"Why are you asking us? We're just as blind as you." Michelle's irritation had returned.

"This is ridiculous," Kaya said. "They're playing with us. Maybe they're making us wait because we made them go for a whole week and a half without sex."

"That's it. I've had enough of this bull." Shaina ripped her blindfold off. Her mouth dropped open when her eyes encountered the four men standing on a circular granite platform with their arms folded and gazing at the women speculatively. The platform was under a wooden thatched roof, supported by eight square yellow columns. An outdoor kitchen was situated in the center and wicker lounges and chairs of varying styles, sizes, and heights were placed strategically about.

Taking her eyes off the men for a moment, she took in the natural sights around her. Two cobbled stone walkways extended from the center platform and into her direction—one leading to an infinity pool and the other to a humongous hot tub. Four paths led away from her and curved behind a cluster of fruit trees. From her visits to Dulcina and other islands, she recognized avocado, mango, papaya, golden apple, and passion fruit, along with a few banana trees. About fifty feet above the thatched roof of the cabana, a flamboyant tree blossomed with deep red and orange flowers. In the background, a coral sea completed the romantic atmosphere of this island paradise. The scent of varying flowers planted along the garden paths filled the air.

"Damn!" Shaina whispered as her gaze returned to the men just in time to see Massimo hand the fob to his Lamborghini to Erik.

"What?" Tashi asked beside her.

The men silenced her with their fingers to their lips and motioned for her to join them.

"Shaina, where're you going?" Michelle yelled, flapping her hands in front of her. "You can bump into something and hurt yourself, girl."

"Shaina," Tashi called.

"She's gone. You think the bogeyman got her?" Tashi asked with a chuckle.

"Well, I gotta pee." Kaya removed her blindfold. "Owe!" she screamed when Bryce tossed a wad of cash at Adam. She glanced at Michelle and Tashi. "You can take off your blindfolds. It's over." She stood rooted to the ground as she took in the splendid natural beauty around her.

"What's over?" Tashi asked.

Michelle sucked her teeth and pulled hers off. "They were

making bets on us. "Oh, my God," she added, pressing her hands against her heart, "this place is breathtaking."

"We won. We won." Tashi ripped off her blindfold and raced toward the bungalow.

"Give her a chance. She's new," Michelle said, exchanging a wry look with Kaya.

"Hmm. In a few months, she'll be tired of their silly games, too."

"What did we win?" Tashi asked, jumping into Adam's arms.

"A couple million," he said, spinning her around. She still had no idea about Yuri's visit to Granite Falls. There was no need to worry her since they will never again encounter any trouble from him or anyone else. He and his father had seen to that. His friends knew though, and they'd congratulated him for going psycho on the man who'd threatened his family. They'd been shocked that he'd lost his cool, but they'd been proud, nonetheless. A man had every right to protect his family in every and any way necessary. "You know we have to donate the money to charity, right?" Adam asked Tashi as he set her back on her feet.

"I know. I'm just glad I don't have to do whatever the losers have to do."

"We don't have to cook tonight. But we're very lucky that Bryce and Kaya lost."

"We have to cook our own meals?" Michelle asked, her voice edged with anxiety.

"Yep," Adam responded. "The pantry and refrigerator are packed with all the food we need for the week. There are a variety of fruit trees on the island, and an herb and vegetable garden. The only thing we don't have is the catch of the day. That will arrive every afternoon in time for dinner. For today, we have mahi mahi. At least with Kaya's expertise in the kitchen, we'll be having something tasty tonight." He thumped his nose at the Andrettis and the LaCrosses, the two couples who knew nothing about cooking.

"Yeah, you better hope we never lose at the same time," Erik told him. "And Mass. I don't want your car." He tossed Mass' fob to him. "We'll work something out."

"Oh thank God." Mass kissed his fob. "If you knew what Shaina and I have done inside it, you wouldn't want it anyway."

"Eweee." Erik made a disgusted face, the exact face Precious made when she was grossed out.

"So this is what you've been hiding from us?" Kaya walked to the edge of the platform and looked out over the spread of white sand and the beautiful emerald ocean where flocks of brown pelicans dove gracefully below the surface to catch their evening meals. There was nothing else in sight but sky and water for as far as she could see. "I can't even find the words to describe it. Where are we?"

"In the Caribbean, my love." Bryce wrapped his arms around her from behind. While on vacation, they'd come to a decision about extending their family. She wanted to give him another son, and upon returning home, they'd gone to see Dr. Walsh who'd given them the okay to make their wish come true. With any luck, they might conceive on this very island, this very week. He couldn't wait to make love to her, to place their next child securely inside her.

"Not just any island," Mass said. "It's our own private island—all eight of us together. We bought it, ripped down the dilapidated building that was on it and had Bryce's architect build this." He waved his hand around.

"It's so lovely," Michelle murmured, as she and Erik, and the other two couples joined Bryce and Kaya at the yellow wooden railing.

"We named it, but you're free to change it if you want," Adam said.

Tashi gazed at the beds of oleander shrubs sporting pink petals, and the blue and purple wreath-like clusters on the petrea vines running along the sides of the veranda, and the sprawling shrubs of sea grape vines extending toward the ocean, some with clusters of purple grapes hanging from the branches. "What did you name it?" she asked in a voice trembling with emotion.

"Baia degli Amanti," Massimo answered.

"Lovers' Bay," Michelle translated. "I like it."

"Yes, darling. You each have your own island halfway across the world. We wanted something closer to home where we can escape to for a day or two without spending most of the time traveling back and forth." Especially since they'll be adopting soon. Adopting was something they'd discussed a while ago, but since he'd given Michelle the good news about his staying home, she'd decided that they go ahead and begin with a son, a little boy close to JP's age. During his travels around the globe, Erik had met so many little boys and girls who needed loving homes. He was thankful to have the means to provide that happy home for some of them.

"We can come here together," Kaya said.

"Or alone."

"Bring the kids."

"Or not."

"Whatever. It's conveniently close to home. But we plan to build a twelve-bedroom compound on the other side of the island for when our families visit. That way, we can all be together," Bryce said.

"And when we want some privacy at night or in the middle of the day, we have our own little niche on this side," Adam added.

"Where will we sleep?" Shaina asked.

"I don't think we'll be doing much sleeping, pussycat, but since you asked, those four garden paths," he said, pointing with his finger, "each lead to a private one-bedroom bungalow complete with an en suite, a mini kitchen, and a lounge."

"They all have ocean views in the front and natural rainforest in the rear."

"There are no other islands in sight." Kaya scanned the horizons.

"It's as if we're alone in the world," Bryce said.

"So we can be as wild as we want and no one will see us or hear us. We can go back to the mainland with our dignities intact."

"We tried to build the sleeping quarters as far apart as possible and still afford each an equal view of the ocean. But depending on how loud we are, we might hear each other." Mass splayed his hand across Shaina's stomach, as he recalled their hot night in the hut in Kenya a couple weeks ago. Soon, her little belly would be swollen with their second child. He hoped it was a son this time. He would so love to have a son.

"Well, it's not like we don't know what we do with each other." Michelle flipped her wrist. "We talk. We're all adults here. By the way," she added, smiling seductively up at her husband, "I hope you don't mind me wearing a wig with long black tresses when I dance—kind of like Shaina's hair. I just want to fit in with the girls and their long hair."

"We're pole dancing together, in a group," Kaya explained at Erik's confused frown.

The men exchanged quick glances over their wives' heads.

"Well, about that, ladies, we talked and as much as we love each other and share a lot of our personal lives with each other, watching each other's wife pole dance is…"

"We don't want to be that close," Adam finished when Erik seemed to be searching for the right words.

"So we're not pole dancing?" Tashi asked.

"Oh you're pole dancing, just not as a group. We'll have private sessions on the front terrace of each bungalow. You can pole dance for us every night if that's your desire."

"And we brought your whips, and cuffs, and the blindfolds you've been complaining about all afternoon."

"Ladies, your poles await you."

They laughed at the double entendre.

After some fun in the warm Caribbean sea and frolicking like children on the beach, the couples sat on the patio and enjoyed a delicious dinner of mahi mahi grilled on the open fire pit, a tossed green salad with papaya seed dressing, breadfruit fritters, baked red peppers stuffed with conchs, some tasty Australian wine and local passion fruit drink, followed by a variety of deserts they'd brought from the wedding reception. Then they'd bid each other good night, and walked hand in hand down the moonlit garden paths to their individual sleeping quarters.

Now, wearing nothing but white silk robes, each husband

made himself comfortable on a loveseat on the private patio overlooking the ocean, and waited anxiously for his sexy bride to emerge from the bungalow unto the dimly lit stage where her pole was stationed. The men had been sexually starved for almost two weeks and although they wished for nothing more than to take their wives to bed, watching them slither, scantily clothed, up and down a pole, wasn't something they wanted to pass up.

At a specific previously discussed time, the women simultaneously hit their stereo buttons and Janet Jackson's "Nasty" flooded the air. The brides strutted unto the stages and up to their poles, wearing nothing but red high heel stilettos and the white lace garter belts they'd each worn under their wedding gowns. With their long tresses brushing the swelling mounds of their breasts and flowing freely down to their stomachs, they leaned back against their poles, and stood poised with their legs apart and their hips thrust forward for a few breathtaking moments before they sprang to life and danced across the stage, swaying their hips and rocking their naked bodies to the music.

Each of the men's hearts stopped, their eyes bulged, and huge tents immediately appeared in their robes. Each watched, hypnotized, and open-mouthed as his wife danced back to her pole. She leaned her back against it and, leisurely reaching above her head, she wrapped her hands around it. Smiling at him enticingly, she began caressing the shiny metal. Up and down around and around. Short quick whacks followed by long slow strokes—gripping, squeezing, releasing, jerking, pumping in the exact same way she gave her husband a tantalizing hand job.

Nasty thoughts crept into each husband's mind. Deep

groans of carnal need, and wanton sighs of anticipation echoed like thunder beneath the starry night.

Grasping the pole, each wife gracefully turned around, giving her husband a tasty view of her long hair cascading like a dark silky cloud across her delicate back and tapering off at the delicious crest of her tight round buttocks. Enthused by the music, she spread her legs, dropped her shoulders forward, and arched her back, deliberately exposing the inviting slick folds between her thighs to her lecherous audience.

At the sound of a harsh moan, she began to gyrate her hips—back and forth, side to side, her slender body moving like a weightless cloud of flesh against the warm air, her buttocks and breasts jingling and glittering like globes of gel in the moonlight.

Her husband wiped at the drool dripping from the corner of his mouth and, easing his robe aside, he began to stroke himself as his wife continued to tease him by thrusting her hips at the pole, rubbing into it, up against as if it had morphed into an impassioned lover, daring her to get closer.

As Janet gave way to the slow seductive ballad of "Behind Closed Doors," each husband began to understand why his wife had insisted on making love by song lately. He squeezed his shaft as she scaled the pole like a barroom dancer, heaving her body against it on the way up, to finally wrap her arms and legs around it like a lover's body.

Locking her thighs and legs in place, she curved her body backward and, swinging upside down, she spread her arms wide and rotated her head from side to side in time with the music. The locks of her hair flowed from her crown like silken threads and swept the mat beneath her.

Her husband moaned as visions of that lustrous mane

brushing his naked flesh sent tingling sensations rushing up and down his spine.

When "Earned It," began, she effortlessly brought her body upward, unwrapped her limps from around her inanimate lover and fluttered sensuously down to the floor. With a titillating smile, she sashayed to the front of the stage, working her hips to the music, shaking her breast and her buttocks to her husbands delight. Turning her back to him, she widened her stance, bent forward, and picked up a white satin scarf from the floor.

She passed the satiny material between her legs and holding it in place with one hand behind and one in front, she began to ride it as she twirled in circles on her toes as if she was seated atop a bucking bronco, twisting her body and undulating her hips, the muscles in her stomach churning like a skilled belly dancer's as she worked the strip of cloth, making it earn her love, her passion, the feminine essence of her delectable damp body.

Her husband began to pump his rock-hard cock as his heart beat against his chest like a jungle drum. He swore his wife was trying to give him a heart attack. Not a bad way to go.

Facing forward, she met and held his gaze, her eyes dreamy and bewitching in the low light. She rolled the tip of her tongue across her lips in time with the music and her gyrating hips, and when the material was soaked with her juices she tossed it into the air and watched it float like a butterfly satiated with sweet nectar to land on her husband's awestricken face.

He curled his fingers around the warm damp scarf, inhaling her intoxicating fragrance, as he remembered pumping his cock deep inside her to the tune of the song to which she now danced. It was going to be a long perfect night. *Oh yes, she would be punished for teasing him.*

Once "Temperature's Rising" began, she slithered to the mat and stretched her sexy body like a lazy cat, before crawling on her hands and knees from one end of the stage to the next, stopping occasional to grind her hips into the mat, humping it the way she humped her husband in the woman-on-top position.

"Oh God, baby. Yes. Just like that," he groaned in a husky voice.

Smiling, she fluttered onto her back, raised her feet high in the air, and gently caressed her smooth toned legs with her fingertip, moving along her shapely thighs, over her garter belt and up to her Venus mound. She planted her feet flat on the mat, raised her hips, and started to thrust upward against her middle fingers nestled just below the surface of her slick folds, as if her body was indeed yearning for love, for fulfillment.

Sensual! Hot! Sultry! Erotic!

Her husband groaned again as her fingers, now wet with her juices, slithered across her undulating stomach and over her temptingly swelling breasts. She molded her soft firm flesh and tweaked her pebbled nipples, and then her hands were caressing her cheeks, her eyes, her nose, her lips, just like her lover had done countless times, and then to his wanton amazement, her crimson lips parted and her middle finger disappeared inside her mouth. She began to suck her digit, spreading her beautiful lips around it, making little slurping sounds as she simulated sucking her lover's shaft.

OK. He could not take anymore of this naked nymph, this beguiling strumpet teasing him with her lasciviously sinful wares. It was time to feast. Burning up with raging lust, her husband pushed his robe off his damp shoulders and rose from his seat.

He kept his eyes on the tantalizing body of his wickedly sexy wife, and eased down on the mat beside her. He ran his fingers down the length of her damp soft body as she continued to heave beneath him like an exotic danseuse.

His hot lips followed in the wake of his fingers, and when he reached her toes, he held her legs and spread her thighs wide. He settled himself between them and, gazing into the enchanting wonder of her lovely hypnotic eyes, he guided the tip of his shaft to the slick tight hot entrance of her body, and just as TLC began to sing "This is How it Works," he took her deeply.

They held each other tightly and cried out together as the fiery hunger gripped them, melding them into one ball of sweltering rippling flesh. The ocean waves, lapping upon the white sands of the beach below them welcomed their passionate groans of ecstasy, and collecting the varying symphonies of pure delight, ferried them across the Caribbean Sea.

Oh yes. This was precisely how love worked.

THE END

TRANSLATION PAGE

Italian	English
Abbastanza! Non più	Enough! No more
Aria ama Papa	Aria loves Daddy
Ehi, dolcezza di là, e papà ama il suo piccolo angela	Hey there sweetness, and Daddy loves his little angel
Papà sei mancato tanto	Daddy missed you so much
Come è chiedere una banana correttamente?	How do you ask for a banana correctly?
Per favore, può Aria hanno una banana, Mamma?	Please, can Aria have a banana, Mama?
Certamente, la mia bambina	Certainly, baby
Ti amo, Mamma	I love you, Mommy
Mamma ama anche tu, Aria. Moltissima Cosa dice l'elefante?	Mommy loves you too Aria. Very much What does the elephant say?
L'elfante dice…	The elephant says…
Brava, la mia ragazza	Great, baby
È dolce, e io sarò essere chiamandola al dovere più tardi stasera, probabilmente da dietro	It is sweet, and I'll be calling it to duty later tonight, probably from behind
Vuoi guardare tua lingua, per favore?	Would you watch your language?
C'è un bambino in camera	There's a child in the room

Hai intenzione di avere un fratellino.	You're going to have a little brother.
O una sorella	Or a sister
La vita era incredibilmente bella	Life was amazingly beautiful
Mio figlia. Mio figlia bella, dolce	My beautiful sweet daughter
Papà ti amo. Papà ti amo così tanto, Aria	Papa loves you so much, Aria
Non hai una banana fino a quando si chiede correttamente	You won't get a banana until you ask correctly
Ok, Aria. Di mamma essendo estremamente. Vediamo qui fuori.	Okay, Aria. Mommy's being extremely persistent. Let's hear her out
Ora, il figlio, che è il modo un Andreas si occupa di minacce alla suo famiglia	Now, son, that's the way an Andreas deals with threats to his family
Troppo	Too/Also

French	English
Ma petite biche	My little doe
Mon chéri	My darling

Russian	English
Именно в ваш рот.	It's in your mouth

NOTE FROM THE AUTHOR

Dear Reader,

I hope you enjoyed catching up with the Billionaire Couples of Granite Falls, and following them as they continue their journeys to love and *Happily Ever After* in With These Four Rings.

I enjoyed revisiting them and watching them grow, learn, and teach from each of their individual experiences. I am deeply saddened that their journeys have come to an end, but we will catch glimpses of them in my *Beyond Granite Falls* series.

ABOUT THE AUTHOR

Inspired by the strong heroines and flawed alpha heroes in the stories she read as a young girl, *New York Times* and *USA Today* Bestselling Author, Ana E Ross writes steamy and sophisticated, multicultural contemporary romance novels. Her drama-filled stories feature charming, powerful, larger-than-life billionaires and strong, independent women who fight and love with equal passion.

Born and raised in Nevis, Ana now lives in the Northeast, U.S., and loves traveling, tennis, yoga, meditation, everything Italian, and spending time with her daughter.

www.anaeross.com
ana@anaeross.com